#4

TOXIC TOFFEE

Center Point
Large Print

Also by Amanda Flower and available from Center Point Large Print:

Assaulted Caramel
Lethal Licorice
Premeditated Peppermint

TOXIC
Toffee

An Amish Candy Shop Mystery

Amanda Flower

CENTER POINT LARGE PRINT
THORNDIKE, MAINE

My Dear Readers

Acknowledgments

Thank you to all the readers who have fallen in love with the Amish Candy Shop mystery series. I love hearing from you about how much you enjoy it. Without you, I wouldn't be where I am today.

Thanks to my amazing publisher, Kensington, which has been so supportive of this series and me. Special thanks to my editor, Alicia Condon, and everyone on the incredible marketing team.

Thank you as always to my super agent, Nicole Resciniti, who always knows what our next move should be. You are a dream maker, Nic!

A special thank you to Gwen Mayer, who is an expert on rabbit care and lent me the name Puff from one of her prized bunnies. Thank you.

Always thanks to my friends David and Mariellyn for their support, and to Delia for testing recipes with me. Love to my family, Andy, Nicole, Isabella, and Andrew, for their constant support.

Finally, thanks to my Father in Heaven for letting me tell so many stories.

Chapter 1

Charlotte Weaver stood in the middle of Times Square with her mouth hanging open and the ties of her black bonnet flapping on the hot air pushing its way through the subway grate, as the trains rumbled below.

"Charlotte!" I took hold of her arm. "Close your mouth. Your Amish is showing."

She snapped her mouth shut.

The truth was Charlotte's Amish had been "showing" the entire time that we had been in NYC. In Holmes County, Ohio, no one would blink an eye at the pretty redheaded girl in the plain dress, sensible black tennis shoes, and black bonnet, but in New York, she stuck out like a gorilla on the subway. We had been in the city for the last six weeks shooting six episodes for my candy maker television show, *Bailey's Amish Sweets*, to appear on Gourmet Television in the summer season.

Charlotte was in Manhattan as my kitchen assistant and would also appear on the show giving it that extra "Amish oomph," as producer Linc Baggins liked to say. Yes, "Baggins" like the Hobbit. It was best not to mention that when he was around since his resemblance to the hairy-footed character was uncanny.

Typically, an Amish person would never appear on television. It was against the rules they lived by, but Charlotte was able to appear on the show with me because as of yet she hadn't been baptized in the Amish church and could do more English things while on her *rumspringa*. Her church elders were not thrilled with the idea of her being on TV, but until she was officially baptized, there wasn't much they could do about it. I didn't want Charlotte to get in trouble with her church, but I'd invited her along anyway. Her heart was so set on going with me to New York that I couldn't bring myself to disappoint her.

"I—I've never seen anything like this!" Charlotte said in awe.

I glanced around and tried to take everything in through Charlotte's eyes. Thousands of people of every race, ethnicity, and language milled around; the bright lights and signs glittered on the towering buildings; the smell of bodies, hot dogs, car exhaust, and street vendor flowers mingled together. It was sensory overload for anyone, and for a girl who had lived most of her life in a very conservative Amish community, it must have been like the dark side of the moon.

I wrapped my arms around her shoulders. "Since you've been working so hard on the show, and since we haven't been able to get out much with the shooting schedule, I'm glad that we had time for me to show you some of the city."

"Is all the city this loud and bright and . . . ?" She trailed off, searching for the right word.

"Maybe not this loud and bright," I said with a smile. "We are in the thick of it now, but every city has life to it. That's not any different from Holmes County."

She looked at me with wonder in her large blue eyes. "How can you say that? This place is nothing like back home."

"Holmes County has as much life and color as New York does; it's just shown in a different way."

My best friend Cass Calbera ran up the side-walk, maneuvering expertly through the crowd like someone who had lived in New York her entire life, which she had. "There you are! I've been circling the square for the last ten minutes looking for you two." She glanced at Charlotte. "I thought it would be easy, considering, but I got fooled by a nun in full habit walking down the street. I swore it was Charlotte."

I rolled my eyes. "Charlotte doesn't look like a Catholic nun."

"From the back she might. Anyway, why weren't you answering your phone? I tried to call too!"

I pulled my phone out of my pocket; I had put it on silent during our last shooting session and forgotten to turn the sound back on. Whoops.

"Seriously, Bailey, you've lived in Amish

Country too long. I think being away from electronics has addled your brain. You don't know how to behave in normal society."

"What is normal society?" I asked.

She shook her finger at me and, as she did, her purple bangs fell into her eyes. "Don't you go and get philosophical on me, King!"

Before I could say anything, she retorted, "Now, Jean Pierre sent a car. I left it just up the street. It was the only place the driver could find to park. We have to go. No one keeps Jean Pierre waiting if they know what's good for them."

That much was true.

The ride through the city to JP Chocolates was slow, but by the looks of it, Charlotte didn't mind a bit. She had her nose pressed up against the tinted glass, taking everything in. I could just imagine the stories she would tell my grandmother and Emily Keim, our other shop assistant, when we got back to Swissmen Sweets.

When we finally walked through the front door of JP Chocolates, a wave of nostalgia hit me. This was where I had spent six years of my life working eighty to one hundred hours a week. Unlike Swissmen Sweets, my grandmother's Amish candy shop back in Ohio, with its hardwood floors and pine shelving, JP Chocolates was striking white and sleekly accented with chrome. It would have even been considered sterile or plain if it had not been for the chocolate itself. Elaborate chocolate creations sat under glass encasements. There was a replica of the Statue of Liberty that I had carved in white chocolate in one of the glass cases.

With Easter just a week away, JP Chocolates was dripping with Easter bunnies in every size and flavor of chocolate. I even saw Easter rabbits made from molded peanut butter, marshmallow, and red licorice

"I wish I could have spent more time with you in the last week, but you know what a nuthouse this place is around any holiday," Cass said as she walked through the showroom to the back of the shop where the chocolate happened. Cass was the head chocolatier at JP Chocolates, and it was obvious that she was the woman in charge as the apprentice chocolatiers backed away from her and avoided eye contact when she passed by. Cass didn't seem to notice the power she had over them.

I most certainly did. Before Cass got the position as head chocolatier at JP Chocolates, I had been next in line to receive the promotion as Jean Pierre's long-time protégée, but then my grandfather died, and I found myself giving up the position to live with my grandmother in Holmes County, Ohio, helping with the candy shop that had been in our family for generations. I left thinking that I would never return to the city for more than a short visit, but then Linc offered me my own show on his network. I hadn't thought much would come of it, but to my surprise, the network loved the screen test that we shot in Harvest, and the next thing I knew I was in NYC shooting my own candy-making show. Somehow fate had decreed that I would have the best of both worlds: Holmes County and New York, the two places on earth that had captured my heart. I called it fate, but my Amish grandmother called it providence.

"Ma chérie!" Jean Pierre floated into the giant kitchen. "You have come back to me. Please say that you plan to stay!" Jean Pierre Ruge was a tall, thin, silver-haired man with a Parisian nose who carried himself as erect as a dancer. He moved his arms in such a way that it seemed he might have been just that once upon a time.

I gave Jean Pierre a hug and he smelled of chocolate, which wasn't all that surprising considering what he did for a living. The only thing was that he wasn't supposed to be doing it for a living any longer. Months ago, he had retired from the business and Cass took over. From what Cass said he was there every day giving her advice. Cass said that she didn't mind it. As aggravating as Jean Pierre could be, you couldn't help but love his flamboyant personality.

"You know I can't stay, Jean Pierre. Charlotte and I leave tomorrow morning. We just dropped by to say our good-byes."

He clicked his tongue in disgust. "Oh, dear me, how are you getting home?"

"We have a flight going out of Newark."

"A commercial flight?" He shuddered. "You should take my plane. No protégée of mine should ever fly commercial."

I chuckled. "I appreciate the offer, Jean Pierre, but the network paid for the flight and Charlotte and I will be more than comfortable."

He sniffed. "What kind of television network would fly their star commercial? It is a disgrace!"

"Not to worry, Jean Pierre," Cass chimed in. "Hot Cop is picking them up from the airport."

I rolled my eyes. "Hot Cop" was the name Cass called my sheriff deputy boyfriend, Aiden Brody, back in Ohio. Her description was accurate on all counts, but it was also embarrassing. As of yet, Aiden hadn't heard the nickname, and I would do everything in my power to keep it that way.

Jean Pierre set a long finger against his cheek. "I do not know of this Hot Cop. How do I not know about Hot Cop?"

Cass patted his arm. "I gave him the once-over and Bailey has my support on this one. We both know what a bulldog I can be."

Jean Pierre sniffed. "This is very true. You make a judgment on a person's character and stick with it. I like decisiveness. This is a good skill to have in chocolate and in life. In chocolate, there are no second chances."

15

"In life there might be," I mused.

Jean Pierre smiled. "Perhaps. That is my wish for you, *ma chérie*." He clapped his hands. "Now if you want to help us weave some more chocolate Easter baskets, we won't turn you away."

I grinned. Making chocolate Easter baskets and weaving with chocolate was one of my favorite jobs at JP Chocolates. I planned to teach my grandmother the fine art when I got home. "I thought you would never ask!"

I was just settling in to weave chocolate when my cell phone rang. I had turned it back on after Cass's reprimand. I removed my gloves and pulled the phone from my pocket. When I checked the screen, I saw the name "Margot Rawlings" there. Margot was the village of Harvest instigator. Whatever she had to say to me, chances were high I wouldn't like it. Against my better judgment, I answered the call.

Without so much as a hello, she said, "I need to talk to you about a rabbit."

And a dark cloud of foreboding fell over me.

Chapter 2

Charlotte squeezed my hand when our flight descended for landing early the next day in the tiny Akron-Canton Airport. As the plane's tires bounced on the tarmac, I gave a huge sigh of relief. It was good to be home. The thought surprised me. When I had traveled to Ohio the previous summer, I would never have considered the state, let alone rural Amish country, as home, but that was how I felt now. The little village of Harvest, Ohio, felt more like home to me than New York ever had in all the time I had lived there.

We deplaned without incident and without causing a scene. The people of Ohio were used to seeing the Amish, and they didn't so much as blink an eye at Charlotte when she strolled through the airport in her plain dress and bonnet, rolling her little red suitcase behind her.

Sheriff Deputy Aiden Brody stood just on the other side of security in his Holmes County Sheriff's Department uniform. His blond hair was tousled as if he had just removed his hat, and his dark brown eyes scrutinized everyone who walked by him. Years of being a police officer had taught Aiden to always be on the lookout for trouble.

His face lit up and the adorable dimple in his right cheek appeared as Charlotte and I came into his line of sight. Charlotte waved at him with a big smile on her face, but I was much more reserved. I adjusted my carry-on bag on my shoulder and took a deep breath. It truly was good to be home.

Aiden gave me a smile that I knew was meant for me alone, and my stomach did a little flip. We had spoken on the phone every night while I was away, but it was so good to see him in the flesh. I didn't dare run up to him and give him a hug. That would have to wait. Public displays of affection embarrassed the Amish, and I had already put Charlotte through enough by taking her with me to New York. The poor girl could only take so much Englishness.

Aiden seemed to sense this, and he simply said, "It's good to have you home." His voice was deep and fuller of emotion than I had ever heard it.

"It's good to be home." I smiled back, feeling a little choked up myself.

He grabbed the handle of Charlotte's suitcase and took my bag from my arm. "Let's go pick up your luggage."

The drive back to Holmes County was made lively by Charlotte's Amish view of life in New York. "Do you know that you can buy hot dogs on the street there?" she asked Aiden. "Not for a festival either! Any day of the week. I ate so many hot dogs."

Aiden chuckled and looked at me in the rear-view mirror. "I'd say that was a great takeaway from life in the city: hot dogs on every corner."

Charlotte frowned. "Not every corner, but a lot of them."

Aiden smiled. Growing up in Holmes County he was used to the Amish literalness. The plain people say what they mean and mean what they say. "Many corners then?" he asked.

" 'Many corners' works," she said in all seriousness.

"The New York City tourist board would be pleased," I agreed. "I got a call from Margot just before we left the city. Something to do with rabbits."

"Oh." Aiden glanced at me from the corner of his eye. "I hoped to get you to Swissmen Sweets before that came up."

"That sounds ominous."

"It's Margot we're talking about here." He paused. "I think it would be better for you to see it before I try to explain. It's a little hard to describe."

"That doesn't sound terrifying or anything."

Aiden laughed. "You know Margot. Bigger is better. More, more, more. She wants Harvest on the tourist map and will do anything to get it there."

"Anything?" I raised my eyebrows.

He looked at me in the mirror again. "Just about anything, yes."

Main Street in our little village of Harvest, Ohio, was buzzing when Aiden turned his departmental SUV onto it. Buggies and cars were parked along the street and a whole cluster of people stood in front of the white gazebo in the middle of the square. Aiden illegally double-parked his car so that we could get out and see what all the commotion was about. Since Aiden was a police officer, I didn't think he was worried about getting a ticket for the parking violation.

"Oh my," Charlotte said when she climbed out of the front seat of the car. "Look at all those rabbits."

I was still struggling to yank my carry-on out of the backseat. "Rabbits?"

"Bunnies, so many bunnies. I've never seen so many rabbits." Her voice had a bit of awe in it.

Finally, the bag came loose, and I stumbled back and would have ended up on my rear end in the middle of Main Street if Aiden hadn't been there to catch me. He squeezed the back of my elbows before letting me go and taking the carry-on from my hand. "Bunnies?" I asked in a small voice.

"Oh yeah," Aiden said with sparkling milk chocolate eyes. "Take a look for yourself."

With more than a little bit of trepidation, I peeked over the roof of the car and saw the rabbits. Just to the right of the gazebo was a pen that held at least thirty white rabbits of all sizes. A large Amish man with a white beard and a round belly stood in the middle of the pen holding the biggest rabbit of all with a bright pink bow around its thick neck. He held the rabbit like she was a baby to be burped on his shoulder.

I glanced at Aiden. "Easter in Harvest?" I asked.

He grinned, and the dimple was out full force. "Margot's version of it at least."

As he said this, I spotted Margot Rawlings with her short curls, waving her arms in the middle of the square. She was clearly giving everyone there her marching orders. I knew it wouldn't be long until she heard I was home and ordered me about as well. I still didn't know exactly what she'd meant when she had said to me, "I need to talk to you about a rabbit." Was it one of these rabbits that she meant? Our conversation had been interrupted by Jean Pierre, who had plucked my phone from my hand and disconnected the call. He had said that the people of Harvest could have me back the next day, but as long as I was in New York, I should pay attention to him.

I loved Jean Pierre. He was a kind and generous man. He had never been anything but nice to me, but he did have an inflated opinion of himself. I supposed being told you were the best chocolatier in New York City for the last fifty years would

21

eventually go to a person's head. He was a bit of a prima donna when he wanted to be.

It soon became clear that I wouldn't be able to stay under Margot's radar for long. The town's super organizer spotted me from across the village square and waved frantically. It was clear that she wanted me to run to her side that instant.

I waved back as if I didn't understand what her "come here" gestures meant. "We had better duck into Swissmen Sweets," I told Aiden. "I don't want to be waylaid by Margot before I even say hello to my grandmother."

"Understood," Aiden said, and he guided Charlotte and me to the other side of the street where my family's candy shop stood directly opposite the white gazebo. As Aiden opened the door, I was welcomed home by the comforting smells of warm chocolate, sweet caramel, and fresh berries. The same scents mingled in the air at JP Chocolates, but in Holmes County it was different. The sweet smells mixed together with the scent of hay, horse, and the apple blossoms from the trees that lined Main Street. In that moment, I could see why so many people who have never been to Amish Country are fascinated and enchanted by this place. The Amish might not believe in magic in the literal sense, but they did have a little magic of their own making in this small corner of the world.

The bell on Swissmen Sweets' front door jingled

as we walked through. My grandmother was behind the glass-domed counter, putting a tray of molded chocolate Easter eggs out on display. Her wrinkled face and bright blue-green eyes, just like mine, lit up when she spotted us. "My girls are home!" She lifted the hinged piece of wood that separated the area behind the counter from the rest of the shop and came to us. She enveloped Charlotte and me in a hug, and then pulled Aiden in for good measure.

I was most definitely home.

Chapter 3

My grandmother finally released us from her crushing hug. For a small woman, she was very strong. "It is so *gut*, so *gut* to have you home. These last six weeks have been long. Emily has been a great help, of course, but I have missed you so!"

Emily Keim, formerly Emily Esh, had recently married. With her marriage over the winter to Christmas tree farmer Daniel Keim, she'd been able to give up her job working at Esh Family Pretzel, the shop just next to Swissmen Sweets. Emily had worked in the family business her whole life with her older brother and sister, but it had never been an easy job for her. Both her sister Esther and her brother Abel had been unkind to her ever since she'd made a few mistakes during her *rumspringa*. They had never forgiven her or forgotten those mistakes and continued to make her pay for them years later.

Daniel, a kind young man from a hardworking family, had given her a chance to start a new life, and with the windfall that I had earned from my cable television show, *Maami* and I had been able to hire Emily to provide extra help around the candy shop. I hoped that as the business grew I would have more work to give her or even hire her permanently as a member of our staff, which at the moment consisted of *Maami*, Charlotte, and me.

Emily had held down the fort at Swissmen Sweets the last six weeks while Charlotte and I had been away. I knew that Charlotte and I wouldn't have both been able to go without Emily's help, and my producer Linc Baggins had insisted he needed both of us. He said having a real Amish person on the show gave it that Amish flavor it needed.

"I feel whole again having my girls back." My grandmother hugged us once more. "It was too quiet here without you."

I buried my face in her shoulder, and her fresh lavender scent wafted around me. For the second time since I had returned to Ohio, I truly felt like I was coming home. "We missed you too," I said, and let her go.

Maami patted my cheek. "You came home at the perfect time. There is quite a to-do in the village about Easter. I'm sure that you have seen the commotion across the street." She eyed me. "And Bailey, Margot is very eager to speak to you. She has a project for you."

My orange cat Nutmeg ran out from under one of the shelves lining the front of the shop and purred. I bent over to pick him up. I had missed the little cat too.

"I know," I said. "She called me while I was

25

in New York, but I didn't have much time to talk other than to hear her say something about a rabbit." I paused. "And I saw the bunnies across the street when we were coming in. Another one of Margot's grand schemes, I gather."

"Oh yes, she has great plans for you when it comes to the rabbits."

I set Nutmeg back on the pine-planked floor. "Do you know what they are? I think it might be easier for me going into the conversation with Margot if I have a clue as to what she's talking about. That way it will be less likely she will talk me into something I don't want to do."

Charlotte laughed as if she thought I had no chance of *not* being talked into whatever scheme Margot was cooking up. Charlotte had a point. Margot had talked me into playing Mother Mary in the Christmas parade the previous year because the other four Mary contenders had taken themselves out of the running. As Cass had said at the time, I had been a fifth string Mary. It was one of the more ridiculous things I had done since moving to Ohio. Which was impressive because I had garnered quite a long list of ridiculous things.

"Margot wants you to carve a giant chocolate rabbit," *Maami* said. "You won't have to have anything to do with the live ones, I don't think."

I squinted. "That's it?" It was hard for me to believe. Because carving a giant rabbit out of

26

chocolate was not only something that I was capable of doing, it was something that I would actually enjoy. In fact as far as work went, carving elaborate showpieces from chocolate was the aspect of my old position at JP Chocolates that I missed most. Jean Pierre had displayed pieces like my Statue of Liberty in his showroom and at important events and trade shows.

There was no such thing as a chocolatier-carving trade show in Holmes County, Ohio, and even if there were, I didn't have the time to do anything about it. We had a busy shop with a small staff, and, around the big, sugar-heavy holidays like Easter, it had to be all hands on deck in the shop. I didn't know how I could take the hours upon hours that it would require for me to carve a large chocolate bunny away from the main part of Swissmen Sweets' business, and that was selling candy.

"If that's all she wants me to do, I don't see any issue with it except for lack of time."

"I knew you would say that, so I've asked Emily if she could work a little extra time for us through Easter, and she can."

"That's a relief," I said. "I promise to make it up to you."

She waved me away as if it was of no concern, but it was a concern for me. I wanted my grandmother to enjoy her life and not work all the time. Charlotte and I shared a look. We had discussed sending *Maami* on a trip to Pinecraft, the Amish community on the west coast of Florida, sometime in May. What Charlotte didn't know was that I planned to send her too. They both worked so hard. It wouldn't hurt me to stay behind and mind the shop.

Aiden shifted his weight. "Now that I have seen you both safely home, I should head back to the station. I'm sure the sheriff has an assignment or two for me." He frowned. Aiden and Sheriff Jackson Marshall were like oil and water. I was convinced the only reason Marshall kept Aiden on the force was he was well-liked by both the English and Amish communities in Holmes County, so Aiden was a good face for the department.

"*Danki* for bringing the girls home," *Maami* said, and she guided Charlotte into the kitchen. "Charlotte, I want to show you the cookies-and-cream fudge eggs that Emily and I made yesterday. I think they will be a top seller."

"Oh!" Charlotte said. "I love cookies and cream."

"I know, dear." My grandmother winked at me over her shoulder before she and Charlotte disappeared through the swinging door that separated the front of the shop from the industrial kitchen. I knew she was giving Aiden and me a moment of privacy.

After the kitchen door swung closed behind

them, Aiden spoke. "I'll drop your luggage at your house on my way out of town."

"You don't have to do that. I can roll it there after I leave the candy shop for the day."

He smiled. "Will you let me take your suitcase to your house? I'll just stick it inside the garage. I have to go that way to get back to the office."

I knew that wasn't true. There were more direct ways to reach the Holmes County Sheriff's Department than to go by my little rental house. "You may."

The dimple appeared in his cheek. "Good. It wasn't so hard to let me do something for you, was it?"

"I suppose not," I said.

Maami and Charlotte could be heard chatting in the kitchen, and there was no one else in the front of the shop. It seemed that everyone else in the village was across the street with the rabbits.

Aiden looked this way and that to make sure the coast was clear and then he leaned forward and kissed me on the lips. "I missed you. Welcome home. Are you glad to be back?" he asked in a whisper.

"Very glad," I whispered, meaning it.

"Good then, because I plan to take you on a proper date just as soon as I can."

I grinned. "What's a proper date in Holmes County?"

"You know, the typical thing—square dancing."

I put my hands on my hips. "What if I said I don't square dance?"

"Then I'll just have to take you to dinner and a movie."

"Dinner and a movie sound very nice." I blushed.

He shrugged. "It's your loss on the square dancing though." He do-si-doed to the door. "I'm a mighty fine dancer." He walked through the front door laughing.

"I'm sure you are," I whispered after he left.

Chapter 4

I remained in Swissmen Sweets, cowardly hiding from Margot, for another hour, going over supply lists and Easter orders with my grandmother. It seemed that Charlotte and I had come back home just in time. There was a long list of last-minute Easter orders that we had to make. We would have to create chocolate bunnies double time. I was glad Emily would be able to pitch in too, but I saw a lot of late nights at the candy shop ahead of me in these few days before the holiday. It was important that all the bunnies were tucked in the baskets for the waiting children Easter morning. I didn't want to be the one responsible for the Easter bunny being a no-show. This, of course, was a worry exclusively for the English homes in the area. The Amish didn't believe in the Easter bunny, and for them, Easter was a much more solemn and serious holiday.

After an hour of list making and logistics, I gathered up the courage to cross the street to learn more about the giant chocolate rabbit I was supposed to carve. I was sure I could do it. My only concern was the short and unrealistic time-table that Margot would assume I could meet. Part of me expected her to tell me that she wanted the rabbit done by the next morning, which would be impossible.

When I went through the front door of the candy shop, I found the village just as it had been an hour ago. Main Street full of buggies and cars, the square full of rabbits. A compact car was parked on Main Street and emerging from it was an English woman with waist-length black hair whom I had never seen before. Ruth Yoder, the steely-haired wife of the bishop in my grandmother's Amish district, spotted the woman at the same time I did and marched over to her. "You are not welcome here!" She shook her finger at the woman.

The woman wore cropped jeans and a T-shirt. She tugged on a lock of her long hair as if it was a piece of rope. "I'm just here to see a friend."

"I know what you do to your friends." Ruth set her hands on her ample hips. "You are not welcome in Harvest. Go back to Millersburg, or better yet, leave Holmes County altogether."

The woman said something that I couldn't hear.

Movement in the car caught my eye, and I spotted a man sitting in the passenger seat. I couldn't make out his features because he had his head bent staring at his lap. I guessed he was looking at a phone.

"You need to leave," Ruth said, bringing my attention back to her and the black-haired woman. "Right now."

I bit the inside of my lip. Usually, my curiosity would win out, but in this case, I decided that

I didn't want to know. Even my gentle grand-mother thought Ruth was insufferable, so I gave the pair a wide berth and focused on the task at hand, finding Margot.

Margot Rawlings stood with a large Amish man in front of the gazebo. She was facing me, but the man's back was to me. She held a bullhorn loosely in her right hand. I groaned. It would be a great public service if someone could hide that bullhorn from Margot. I would be willing to donate to the cause of getting rid of it. She was plenty loud enough without it. I wondered if Aiden could confiscate it in the name of public safety. I made a mental note to ask him.

As if she could sense my criticism of her bull-horn, she lifted it to her mouth. "Bailey King! I see you standing across the street there with your mouth hanging open. Get over here, girl! We need to talk!"

Everyone on the square, including the rabbits, turned and looked at me. I realized that I had two choices: I could go over to the gazebo as she demanded, or I could dash back into Swissmen Sweets, pretending that I hadn't heard her. The second option was risky at best. No one would believe that I hadn't heard the bullhorn com-mands, and she would just stomp into the candy shop after me now that she knew I was back in the village. Option one really was the only choice.

I straightened my shoulders and walked across the street.

As I drew closer to her, the man she was with turned, and I saw that it was the Amish man holding the big white bunny with the pink bow that I'd seen earlier in the bunny pen. The same rabbit was in his arms.

"Bailey, thank goodness you're back in the village," Margot said in a normal voice. I was grateful she didn't use the bullhorn at this point since I was close enough that hearing loss was a very real threat.

"We need your expertise for Easter," Margot continued in a rush. "As you can see, we have decided to expand the Easter celebration this year. After the success of the Christmas Market, I thought, why don't we do something big for Easter too? Isn't Jesus's resurrection as important as his birth?"

"Some would say it's more important," I said mildly. I smiled at the Amish man standing next to her. "I'm Bailey King from Swissmen Sweets." I held out my hand.

"I'm Stephen Raber." He smiled back, adjusted the rabbit on his arm, and shook my hand. "I know your grandmother. She's a fine woman."

Most people in Harvest, whether they were Amish or English, thought the same thing about my grandmother, but I smiled all the same.

"How rude of me," Margot said, smacking herself on the top of her short curls. Each curl on Margot's head was perfect. It made me think that she was one of the ladies who went to the village hair salon every week to get their hair set and to pick up on the latest gossip. Margot seemed to know more about what was happening in the village than anyone else. I wouldn't have been the least bit surprised if she knew the number of my return flight to Ohio.

"Stephen is from Raber's Rabbits," Margot said. "He's what made having all the white rabbits here this week possible. Aren't they darling? I wouldn't be the least bit surprised if a lot of little boys and girls got white bunnies for Easter."

"If they have a *gut* home, they just might," Stephen said around something he was chewing. "I won't sell my rabbits to just anyone. I have to know that they will be going to a *gut* home."

"That's admirable of you," I said, but I was a little surprised. The Amish had a very different view about animals than most modern English people did. To many Amish, animals were for work and work alone. Or for food. Even dogs and cats were kept for the practical purposes of herding animals or catching mice. If Stephen had a rabbit farm, selling rabbits must be his livelihood, which was why I was surprised that he would be picky about what homes the rabbits went to. That wasn't always a consideration for the Amish when it came to livestock.

Stephen smiled back at me. "In many ways, the bunnies are like my own children. I can't give them to just anyone."

"I can understand that," I said. "I'm sure I would feel the same way."

He nodded. With his round belly, white beard, and cheerful smile, he would do very well as Santa Claus, but the Amish didn't believe in jolly old Saint Nick, or his elves, and it was Easter not Christmas. The large white rabbit with the pink bow around her neck wiggled her nose.

I studied the rabbit in his arms. "I desperately wanted a rabbit when I was a kid. My neighbor across the street had a black and white one, and I loved to go over to her house and play with it. She even taught her rabbit to do a few tricks. I remember the bunny jumping through a hoop."

He smiled even more broadly. "Rabbits are much smarter than people give them credit for being. Puff knows all sorts of tricks."

"Puff?" I asked.

He patted the bunny's head. "Her name is Puff."

"Like the magic dragon?"

He looked confused for a moment. "I think like a cotton puff."

I inwardly shook my head at myself. Of course, because Stephen was Amish, he wouldn't get my reference to a children's movie.

He pivoted so I could look the large, white rabbit in the face. "She's my lead bunny, the one who shows all the others how to behave on the farm. My rabbit farm is not too far from here, perhaps five miles. So, it's a short buggy ride."

I nodded at the rabbit. "It's nice to meet you, Puff."

"Now that everyone has been formally introduced, can we discuss Easter Days?" Margot asked.

"Easter Days?" I asked.

Margot beamed. "That's what I'm calling this week! Isn't it clever?"

"Very," I said mildly. I wasn't the least bit surprised to hear that Margot had named the week. The woman had marketing down to a science. Honestly, I could learn a thing or two from her when it came to my own business.

"This week leading up to Easter, I thought it would be fun to sell Easter crafts, candies, and, of course, the children visiting could pet Stephen's rabbits. Perhaps he will even sell a few bunnies to good homes."

"Everyone in the village is okay with this?" From what I knew of the Amish, they didn't like to make much fuss over the holidays for fear of commercializing them. I would guess that Easter was the very last holiday that they would want to make commercial in any way.

"Everyone in the village thinks it is a wonderful idea. Whatever brings the tourists in, you know?" She clapped her hands. "Now, we should talk about your part. Swissmen Sweets will be providing the candy and sweets, but that is just the beginning of my plans for you."

I thought it would be best to cut to the chase. "My grandmother said that you want me to carve a giant chocolate bunny. That's easy enough for me to do. It will take a couple of days, but I should be able to make it. I probably can have it done the day after next."

She smiled. "Good, good, but I don't actually want a chocolate rabbit."

I inwardly groaned. I knew it was too good to be true. "Oh?"

"I want you to mold the largest toffee Easter rabbit in history!" She said this as if she was presenting me with a very prestigious award. Unforunately, this was an award that I didn't want to win.

"You want me to mold a rabbit out of toffee?"

She clapped her hands. "Yes!"

"Why toffee?" It seemed the most obvious question.

"Because I love it," she said, as if the answer was as simple as that. "My mother was English," she went on to say. "And I don't mean English in the way that the Amish use it to designate anyone who speaks English. I mean that she was born and raised in England. She came to the United States in the fifties and married my father. The rest is history. In any case, she never gave up her British sensibilities. She drank tea every day of her life and she loved a bit of English toffee with her evening nightcap. Even more important, if we have a toffee rabbit we would be different from every other town in the country with a giant chocolate rabbit in the middle of their town square. I'm trying to make Harvest distinctive, Bailey." She gave me a beady look. "I hope that you can appreciate that."

I opened and closed my mouth, trying to decide how best to argue my point on this one. Margot wasn't one to give up an idea easily. My argument for a simple chocolate rabbit would have to be well thought out. The truth was I wasn't sure how a toffee rabbit would work. Toffee was usually hard. It would have sharp bumps and edges. It most certainly wouldn't be a smooth Easter rabbit. I would have to use chocolate to bind it all together.

I was about to share these concerns with Margot when Stephen held the rabbit out to me. "Can you hold Puff?"

Before I could argue with him, he put the large rabbit in my arms. The rabbit farmer's breath came in rasps, and a trail of sweat ran down his cheek. Just a moment ago he had been fine. I settled the rabbit in my arms. "Stephen, you don't look well at all. Maybe you should sit down. We can get you some water."

Margot's eyes widened. "Yes, Stephen, it looks

to me as if you may have overdone it with all the preparations for Easter Days. Let's have a seat somewhere in the shade so you can collect yourself." She dropped her bullhorn on the ground and made a move as if she was going to help Stephen find a shady seat.

Before she could do that Stephen gasped and clutched his chest. He fell backward, toppling like a tree struck by lightning. He hit the ground and didn't move. His eyes stared blankly into the blue sky.

Margot and I stood there by the gazebo, dumbfounded.

The bunny farmer had dropped dead right before our eyes.

Chapter 5

I don't know how long I stared at Stephen Raber's body before my good sense kicked in and I fell to my knees on the ground. I set the rabbit next to me.

Without looking up, I cried, "Margot, call nine-one-one!"

She yelped, and I prayed that meant she would follow my order.

Two Amish men ran over to me and helped me with Stephen. "We have to try CPR," I said. I pointed at one man. "Chest compressions."

He placed his hands just under Stephen's rib cage and began compressions.

He stopped, and I blew in Stephen's mouth. There was nothing. We went back and forth like that for several minutes, but how long it was I couldn't exactly say. I stopped when an EMT pulled me away from Stephen's side and took over CPR. The Amish man who had been helping me was gone. I hadn't even noticed that he'd left until I stood up. I guessed he slipped away when the EMTs arrived. Many Amish had an aversion to English officials of any kind.

I stumbled to my feet. Out of the corner of my eye, I saw Puff-the-Bunny, pawing at Stephen's foot like she was trying to convince her friend to wake up. The sight was heartbreaking.

One EMT shook his head at the other, and I knew there would be no waking Stephen Raber up ever again. He was dead. I stared at his unseeing eyes. Another dead body. How was this even possible?

"Must have been a heart attack," someone in the crowd said. I didn't know who.

Another man nodded at the statement. "He is a large man. He's bound to have a bad heart."

Before I took another step back, I bent over and picked up the large rabbit. No one stopped me, but I couldn't stand there and watch her paw at her owner like that. As I stood up straight, I saw a young Amish man of about twenty with dark brown curls and gaps in his teeth standing off to the side. Tears ran down his face. No one else on the square was paying any attention to him. I walked over to him. "Are you all right?"

He looked at me with watery green eyes. "That's my *daed*," he said.

My heart ached for the boy. "I'm so sorry."

"Is he dead?" he asked, and rubbed his eyes. His face was red, but I suspect that was more from embarrassment over crying than from the crying itself. The Amish weren't ones to show their emotions. Especially not Amish men.

I glanced back at the EMTs and Stephen. The rabbit farmer was all but surrounded now except for his large feet. He giant black shoes poked out from the ring of emergency workers around him.

"Is he dead?" the teen repeated the question.

"Is there anyone I can take you to?" I glanced around the square. "Do you have other family here today? Anyone at all? Your bishop maybe?"

"Let me have Puff. My *daed* would want me to have her." He took the large white rabbit from my arms. When he had Puff firmly in his grasp, he turned and ran away as fast as a hare in a foot race. He left without so much as a backward glance. He left before I could ask his name.

"Bailey!" Aiden shouted from across the square. He was coming from the direction of the large white church where his mother, Juliet, who was in love with the church's pastor, Reverend Brook, spent most of her time.

I waved to him and hurried over.

"What happened?" Aiden wanted to know. "I came as soon as dispatch gave me the call. I was in the church when the call came in. I could have been here much sooner if you'd called me directly. I can't believe I was right there." He gestured at the church.

"I'm sorry. I was just shocked by what happened. I told Margot to call nine-one-one while an Amish man and I tried CPR on Stephen." Tears gathered in the corners of my eyes. "But I don't think there was any use to it. He was dead before he hit the ground."

Aiden gathered me in his arms and pulled me toward him. "I'm sorry. You did the right thing.

I should never have questioned you." He let me go. I knew he was aware of people watching. He couldn't show me any kind of special treatment when he was in uniform.

"Why were you in the church?" I wiped away a stray tear that had escaped from the corner of my eye.

"Reverend Brook called. There was a break-in. I was following up."

"*What?* Someone broke in to the church?"

"Shh, please keep your voice down about it." He squeezed my shoulder. "We can talk more later, but I need to get to the scene of where Stephen fell. I want you to tell me everything that you know, but hang tight for a minute. Can you do that for me?"

I nodded and watched as Aiden strode away from me.

Even though I'd agreed to "hang tight," it wasn't something I was very good at doing. My brain immediately went to wondering about the church. It was much easier to think about than dwelling on the demise of poor Stephen Raber or his son who'd run away from me. I bit my lip. I should have told Aiden about the young Amish man first thing. I took a step toward the scene and stopped myself. Aiden was surrounded by EMTs and sheriff's deputies. This wasn't the time to interrupt.

I glanced back in the direction of the church.

A break-in at the church? Who would want to do that? And this close to Easter too. Reverend Brook, who to me always looked like he was on the brink of tears, must be a mess over it, and I couldn't even guess how Juliet Brody, Aiden's mother and a constant fixture at the church, would take it. To say she was excitable was an understatement. I dearly hoped that she had her comfort pig Jethro with her to take the edge off.

Actually, I didn't need to hope that because I saw Juliet across the street from the church. She held her black-and-white polka-dotted pig Jethro under her arm like a football. She was running so fast, Jethro, who was typically treated like royalty by Juliet, looked as if he was wondering what on earth was happening. The little pig's ears bounced up and down as she ran.

Juliet wore a pink-and-white polka-dotted dress and a white cardigan. She loved polka dots almost as much as she loved her pig, and I don't think I had ever seen her not wear polka dots somewhere on her clothing. I could appreciate the fact that she had a look and committed to it.

"Bailey!" she cried, waving her free arm. "Bailey!"

I hurried over to her because I was afraid that the heel of one of her pink pumps would get stuck in the grass on the square and cause her to fall. That wouldn't end well for Juliet—or for Jethro.

She came to an abrupt stop as soon as I reached

her. She placed the back of her hand on her forehead. "Oh, my word," she said in her light Southern drawl. "I'm so glad you're home, my sweet girl. I'm so glad that you're home. We've had a terrible time while you were gone. We have just been completely at a loss without you. You can't imagine how hard it has been on my sweet Aiden. I don't know how the two of you are going to plan a wedding with you off in the big city so much of the time. You need to think about your future."

Jethro sneezed, and pig spit flew onto my bare arm. My return to Harvest was going famously.

I removed a tissue from the pocket of my jeans and wiped my arm.

"Jethro has a cold. It's the change of seasons. It's always so hard on him." She kissed the top of the pig's head between the ears. "Are you back in Harvest again for good? I've been talking to your grandmother about wedding plans. Clara is so sweet, but she refused to move ahead with any ideas until you returned. Are you ready to talk about the wedding? What about outdoors in June? It's a lovely time of year."

I shoved the tissue back into my pocket and gaped at her. June was less than two months away. She was relentless when it came to Aiden and my supposed wedding. Because Aiden's mother was so dead-set on Aiden and me getting married, it had taken us some time to actually come to the conclusion that we wanted to date each other. I think we both balked at the idea because his mother was so sure that we were, in her words, "a match made in heaven."

I had never been one for someone else planning my life. My parents had wanted me to go to an Ivy League college after high school and instead I moved to New York to work for Jean Pierre and worked my way through culinary school. To say that they hadn't been happy with my decision would be an understatement. It took two years for them to come and visit me in New York and to be willing to admit that I had landed on my own two feet following my own path.

It was time to change the subject. "Juliet, Aiden said that there was a break-in at the church. What happened?"

"Oh yes!" she cried. "It was terrible. Poor Reverend Brook has been a complete mess over it. I have never seen him so upset. He was even more upset than the time he tripped and fell in the middle of Christmas Eve services two years ago." She placed a perfectly manicured hand on her cheek. "It was so embarrassing for him."

I blinked. "Was he hurt?"

She shook her head. "Only his pride."

I closed my eyes for a moment. "I don't mean Christmas Eve two years ago. Was he hurt during the break-in at the church?"

She shook her head. "No, thank heavens. He

wasn't there at the time of the break-in. The church would be at a complete loss without the reverend."

I thought that Juliet would be at a complete loss without the reverend too, but I didn't say that. "How did Reverend Brook learn of the break-in?" I asked.

"When he came into the church today to work on the Easter sermon—you know that's the most important service of the year, so he spends a lot of extra time on it. The man works like a dog." She shook her head. "I really think members of the community should give him more credit for everything he does." She pursed her lips.

"Juliet, the break-in," I repeated. "How did Reverend Brook learn about it?"

She blinked. "The back door of the church was wide open when he came in this morning. He usually doesn't go that way into the church but wanted to make sure everything was okay because the church will be a focal point of Margot's Easter Days. We have to look our very best for the event!" She took a breath. "He took a lap around the building and saw the door. That's when he knew trouble was afoot."

I wrinkled my brow. Trouble was afoot? It seemed to me that Juliet had been reading too many Sherlock Holmes stories lately. "Was anything missing?"

"Not as far as Reverend Brook could see,

but there are a lot of nooks and crannies in that church. It will take some time to inventory everything that is there."

"Was anything disturbed?"

She nodded. "The kitchen. It was a mess! Someone cooked in there and didn't put a thing away, just left it. You would think if you were breaking in to a place, you would like to cover your tracks, but not this culprit."

I blinked. "So, you are saying someone just broke in to the church to cook?"

She hugged Jethro to her chest, and the little pig snuffled his displeasure. "That's what it looks like. It's horrid to think of someone messing up our nice clean kitchen that way."

"What did they make?"

She shook her head. "I don't know, but something sticky and sweet. It's all over the counters. It will take the whole day to clean the kitchen."

"Sticky and sweet." I shivered. "Like candy?"

She nodded. "Exactly like candy. I was cleaning the kitchen just now when a church member ran in and said that someone had died on the square. I wasn't the least bit surprised to see you here, Bailey. You have a knack for finding dead people." She placed a hand on my arm. "You do know you don't have to find dead people to get my son's attention. He likes you just the way you are."

I inwardly rolled my eyes. It wasn't like I went

out looking for dead people. Dead people found me.

"Who told you that someone was killed?"

"The church member ran into the church saying someone was dead on the square, and a second later Aiden, who was talking to dear Reverend Brook, got a call telling him to go to the square right away. What could we think other than it was someone who had been murdered? Murder is becoming a very common thing in the village."

I grimaced because Juliet was right. There had been *three* murders in Harvest within the last year. I prayed that Stephen Raber had died of an unfortunate heart attack just as the EMTs on the scene thought and his death wouldn't add to the murder total.

Juliet gasped and covered her mouth as if she'd just thought of something.

I put my hand on her arm. "Juliet, what is it? Are you all right?"

"Do you think the man's death and the break-in are related?"

I denied it, but part of me wondered if she was right.

Chapter 6

Juliet went on, "What if there is a madman on the loose breaking in to churches and killing Amish farmers? No one is safe! What has the world come to? What will we do?"

"Juliet," I said as calmly as I could while I took a quick glance over my shoulder. I gave a sigh of relief when I saw that Juliet hadn't gotten anyone's attention. An EMT was setting a stretcher on the ground next to Stephen. "Juliet, I don't know how these two things could be connected. The break-in at this church was last night, and this is a day later. Stephen was talking to Margot and me when he fell, and there was no one else around who might have wanted to hurt him. I think it was just a sad case of a heart attack." I took a deep breath. "There is no reason to think it has anything to do with the church at all," I said.

She shuddered. "The two crimes were too close together to be an accident."

Juliet had me there, but we still didn't know that Stephen's death was a crime. I prayed that Stephen had died of natural causes. Still a tragedy, but not a crime.

"When I heard what happened on the square, I had to come and see what I could do to help.

I didn't want to leave Reverend Brook in the church alone, but when I heard that someone had fallen, I knew I would do better to come here and offer my assistance."

Only Juliet would believe that she could offer any assistance under these circumstances. She was a sweet woman, but maybe a tad delusional about what she could do in a crisis situation.

"These two terrible things might be related," Juliet said. "They really might." She looked around. "Which means we must keep an eye out for the third. They say bad things always come in threes."

I shivered. I prayed that Juliet was wrong about this one.

"Bailey!" Aiden called my name as he walked toward us.

Juliet hurried to her son, hugging Jethro to her chest as she went. She gripped Aiden's forearm. "Aiden, do you think this death could be connected to the break-in at the church? Do you think someone is breaking in to churches and killing people?"

Gently, Aiden squeezed his mother's hand and removed it from his arm. "Mom, I don't see how at this point."

I frowned as I noted "at this point." That told me that Aiden wasn't ruling it out completely.

His eyes narrowed. "And why do you say Stephen Raber was killed? What do you know?"

She dropped her hand to her side. "I don't know anything, son, but you must admit that murder has become more and more common in the village."

Aiden closed his eyes for a moment as if he couldn't believe that he was having this conversation with his mother. He turned to me. "Bailey, I need to take your statement."

I nodded.

He said to his mother, "Why don't you go back to the church. Reverend Brook will need you. Deputy Little will be there within the hour, just to make sure the church is secure."

She patted her son's cheek. "All right, son. You're such a good boy." She turned to me. "I was just telling Bailey that we must start discussing the wedding, now that she's back in the village."

I grimaced.

Aiden and I watched as his mother and Jethro made their way back across the square.

Aiden glanced at me. "Wedding?"

"No wedding. You don't think I was behind any wedding talk, do you?"

A slight frown crossed his forehead. "I would never think that, Bailey."

Before I could spend much time wondering what that meant, he asked me to recap what had happened up to the moment Stephen fell and then immediately after. I did as I was asked, and this time I remembered to tell him about Stephen's son, who'd taken Puff from my arms.

"Did you get the son's name?" he asked.

I shook my head, feeling disappointed in myself.

He gave me a half smile, and the adorable dimple in his right cheek appeared. "Don't worry about it. It will be easy enough to find out if he's Raber's son."

"Thanks." I paused. "I just can't believe that there has been another sudden death in the village. I told your mom that it couldn't have been anything other than a heart attack, but I don't know."

He frowned. "I don't know either. The coroner will be the one to tell me." He ran his hand through his blond hair. It stuck up in all directions, and despite the solemnity of the situation, I couldn't help but notice how cute he looked like that.

"Bailey, Bailey!" Margot cried from across the square. "We still need to discuss the toffee rabbit when you're done with the police."

I sighed. "That woman has a one-track mind."

"Tell me about it," Aiden replied.

Chapter 7

After speaking with Aiden, I left the square. There wasn't much more I could do there, and if I stayed too long, I was afraid Juliet would return and start talking to me about china patterns. As I crossed the street to my candy shop, my head spun with rabbits, death, breaking and entering, and toffee. Even I knew that was a weird combination.

It seemed so strange to me that someone would break in to the church kitchen to cook. In all likelihood, the church would have let that person use the kitchen in a pinch. I had even used it last year when the one at Swissmen Sweets was closed. Why break in when all you had to do was ask permission? I thought that the incident at the church made me more uneasy than Stephen's death. Probably because like Juliet, in my heart, I suspected that the two incidents were related. The only reason to break in to the church to cook something would be to whip up something you shouldn't be cooking—or at least that was my working theory.

I knew that I should let Aiden get to the bottom of it all. He was the cop. He was the best cop. I should trust him to take care of this because I had more than enough to worry about on my own plate. I knew I should stay out of it. But past experience told me I wasn't sure that I could.

In an attempt to ignore my natural curiosity or what Aiden would call my natural nosiness, I spent the rest of the day working in the candy shop and making a plan for the giant toffee rabbit. The more I tried to talk Margot out of the toffee bunny, the more she dug her heels in. The woman really loved toffee. I settled on a six-foot-tall tan-and-white rabbit. The rabbit would be standing on his hind legs to provide the extra height. Margot wanted him tall. I decided that I would carve him out of Rice Krispies treats covered in chocolate, and then use toffee pieces as the top layer of his body to resemble fur. Hopefully, that would be enough toffee to satisfy Margot. The easiest way to make the rabbit would be to carve him in three pieces: the head, the torso, and the hindquarters, and then fuse those pieces together. I was excited to see how it would turn out. It would certainly be unlike any rabbit in any other Amish town. Charlotte and I worked on the rabbit throughout the rest of the day, and I had the hindquarters and head almost completely carved before I grew too tired to see straight.

It was seven in the evening, still early by all accounts, but it had been a long day traveling from New York, seeing a man die in front of me, and then working on the giant rabbit.

Across from me, Charlotte was drooping over

a tray of toffee. She was as tired as I was. My grandmother, who would be up at four the next morning to make fresh candies for that day, had retired over an hour ago.

I set my chocolate carving knife on the stainless-steel island in the middle of the kitchen. "Charlotte, you should quit for the evening."

She snapped to attention. "But I can't leave you here to do all the work yourself."

I smiled. "I appreciate that, but I'm going to call it quits for the night too. We can finish the rabbit tomorrow. We both have had a long day. We'll do better work after we've rested."

"If you're sure," she said, looking relieved.

"More than sure."

Charlotte and I made short work of cleaning the kitchen. I said good night to Charlotte and Nutmeg and left the shop for my new home.

The best part of my rental house was I could walk there. I went to the corner of Apple Street and Main, traveled two blocks down Apple, and turned onto Cherry Lane; the third house down was my little yellow house. The small, nine-hundred-square-foot home was the perfect size for me. After months of sharing the spare bedroom in my grandmother's apartment above Swissmen Sweets with Charlotte, the space felt giant.

Next to the little house, there was a one-car unattached garage, and just as Aiden had promised, my suitcase was just inside the side door.

I rolled the suitcase out of the garage and to the back door of my little house. With my hip, I held open the back screen door as I unlocked the wooden door. I stepped into the kitchen. After being gone for six weeks, I thought I would find the place very still and more than a little dusty. I couldn't have been more wrong. There wasn't a speck of dust in the kitchen and there was a vase of bright pink tulips on the kitchen counter. There wasn't a note as to who had cleaned the house or who had left me the flowers, but my grandmother's footprint was all over the place. It was just like her to do this without telling me and to do it even when she was swamped with Easter candy orders. I was so touched that tears sprang to my eyes. I really was tired. I had told Charlotte to go to bed, and I think I needed to follow my own advice.

I inhaled the vinegar-and-lavender scent of the kitchen, which was even more proof to me that my grandmother was the one who'd cleaned the house. Those two smells mingled together always reminded me of her.

My apartment back in New York had been in a newer building. Much like JP Chocolates, my small studio had been styled in white, clean lines, and chrome. My new home in Harvest was nothing like that, and I realized that's how I liked it. The kitchen was old with a porcelain farm sink and black-and-white checkered floor. The tile was chipped and worn from years of use, but a few strategically placed Amish-made rugs covered up the worst of it.

There was a large case opening that looked out through the kitchen into the combination dining and living room. A big picture window in the front of the house showed the tiny front yard that was dominated by a crabapple tree. The tree was in bloom with bright pink blossoms. I had only just moved into the house before I'd left for New York, so I still didn't have any blinds or curtains on the front window. Tulips and daffodils that the previous tenant had planted years before were in bloom around the base of the tree and on either side of the front door.

I should have put some type of window treatment up, but honestly, there wasn't much to see if someone decided to peek in the window.

The front of my house was bare. I had a small table with four chairs, a loveseat, and a low bookcase that held some of my many cookbooks and a small television. It was all I really needed. After living with my grandmother so many months in a half-Amish existence, I had learned that I could make do with a lot fewer possessions in my life. I never bothered to have most of my things shipped from New York. Cass sold them or gave them away for me. She really was the best friend a girl could ask for.

I turned on the fan in the overhead light fixture

in the main room. The fan made a *click, click, click* sound until it got started. When it spun at a certain speed, the clicking stopped. I thought I would have Aiden look at it the next time he visited, which I hoped would be soon. I hadn't realized until I saw him at the airport how much I had really missed him. I had been in a few relationships in the past. Some bad and some okay, but when I had been away from those men, I couldn't remember ever missing them. The fact that I missed Aiden was telling.

As I walked around the living room, out of the corner of my eye I saw a shadow move across the window. I jumped and then shook off my jumpiness. I knew that it must be from travel fatigue coupled with what had happened to Stephen Raber on the square. I still couldn't believe the man was dead. In the few minutes I had spoken to him, he seemed like such a nice person, and I couldn't help but wonder what would happen to all those rabbits. They would need to be taken care of by someone. Raber's mysterious son maybe?

I was convinced that I'd imagined the shadow at the window, but just to make sure, I walked over to it and looked out onto the yard. I didn't see anything amiss, and I was about to turn away when I caught a glimpse of a person at the front door. I nearly jumped out of my skin.

A knock came, and I told myself I was being ridiculous. It was probably just a neighbor stopping by to say hello. Folks did that in the country.

I looked through the peephole in the door, but I didn't see anyone there. I grabbed a throw pillow from the couch and slowly opened the door. I didn't know what I planned to do if there was some type of bandit—as Juliet would say—on the other side of the door. Challenge him to a pillow fight perhaps?

Finally, with the door all the way open and the pillow ready in my left hand, I saw who was on the other side. It was the young Amish man I had seen on the square that morning, and even if I hadn't recognized him, the white rabbit with the pink bow in his arms would have given his identity away.

"Why are you holding that pillow like that?" he asked.

I lowered the pillow. "I was fluffing," I said matter-of-factly. "You know how pillows can lose their shape when they are sat on too much."

He pressed his mouth into a line as if he were not sure about that at all, and as if he weren't sure about me either. "If you are busy with your pillow, I can come back later." He took a step back.

I smacked the pillow a few times. "The pillow is fine. What are you doing here?" I hated that the question came out so bluntly, but he had scared me half to death.

"I—I wanted to talk to you." He removed his

61

black felt hat and made a move as if he was going to enter the house with the rabbit.

I blocked him.

"Can I come inside? I need to talk to you."

"To me? What about?" I asked, not moving an inch.

"About my father."

He looked so heartbroken that I naturally stepped back, and it was just enough space for him and the rabbit to enter my home.

"I—I'm sorry for bothering you like this." His voice was hesitant.

I still had a firm hold on my pillow just in case. "Why did you want to talk to me?"

He opened and closed his mouth. It was as if the words were there, but he just couldn't get them all the way out.

"It's okay," I said, dropping the throw pillow back on the loveseat. "Why don't we start with an easier question?"

He nodded.

"What's your name?"

"Eli. Eli Raber."

"It's nice to meet you, Eli. I'm Bailey King."

"I know." He nodded again. "Everyone in the village knows who you are."

I wrinkled my brow. I wasn't sure if that was a good thing or a bad thing.

"Why don't we talk at the table?" I pointed at the small table in the corner of the room.

Eli nodded and sat in one of the chairs.

"Would you like something to drink? Water? Coffee? Tea? I'm sorry to say I don't have much else in here. I've been away from home for two months."

He nodded. "You were in New York on television."

I wasn't too surprised that he knew about my show since it had been announced in the local Millersburg paper and had been hot gossip in the village for a few weeks. "I guess. I haven't been on television yet. We were just filming my upcoming cooking show. Did you read about the show in the paper?"

He shook his head. "I know Emily Esh—I mean Emily Keim."

I smiled, feeling a little better that Eli was friends with Emily, whom I trusted. "I'm getting used to the idea of Emily being married too." I stood up from the table and walked into the kitchen. I went to the tap and filled a glass of water for him, then set it on the table. "Is Emily the reason you're here?"

"Daniel Keim, her husband, is actually my *gut* friend." He took a long pull from the water glass. "When he heard what happened, he left me a message on my farm's shed phone. He said that I should talk to you because you helped him when he was in trouble last year."

This was true. I had helped Daniel Keim and

his family when Daniel's father, Thad Keim, was wrongly accused of murder. I had been the one who discovered that Thad was innocent of the crime.

"You got his *daed* out of jail."

I nodded.

"So, can you help me find out who killed my *daed*?" He looked down to hide the tears in his eyes, but a single tear fell, landing on the white rabbit in his lap.

Chapter 8

I swallowed hard and realized that I should have gotten a glass of water for myself too. "You want me to find out who killed your father?"

"*Ya*, it is what you do," Eli said.

I frowned. "It's not exactly what I do. I make candy and carve chocolate. I don't solve murders for a living. That's police work."

"But you have solved a murder more than once."

I couldn't argue with him there. "Why do you think your dad was murdered? The police and the EMTs today seemed to think that he had a heart attack."

"Because he's been afraid. There have been notes, threatening notes. They've gotten worse in recent days." He swallowed. "He didn't know I found out about the notes."

My brow went up. "Who wrote them?"

"I don't know. I think my *daed* knew, but I can't ask him now. Even if I had asked him, he would have never told me. He could be secretive." He took a sip from his water glass. "It's not the Amish way to share your troubles with your children. It shows weakness."

I frowned. "Secretive" sounded worrisome to me when it was coming from a young man talking about his dead father. "Have you seen the notes?"

He stared at Puff on his lap and said something I couldn't make out. I didn't think it was in Pennsylvania Dutch either. He had only said it too softly for me to hear.

"What was that?" I leaned over the table and stopped myself before I cupped my ear.

He straightened and looked me in the eye. His blue eyes were clear now, and his jaw had a determined set to it. "I have them."

I fell back into my chair. "You have them? You have them with you right now?"

He nodded and reached into the inside pocket of his plain denim jacket. He pulled out a stack of folded papers. There must have been at least ten sheets of paper in that stack.

I gaped as he set the pile in the middle of the table.

"You can read them. Daniel trusts you, so I trust you. That's all I need to know about you."

I marveled at how easy it was for the Amish to put their faith in a person if that person could be vouched for by a trusted friend. How different that was from English society. Would I put all my faith in someone because Cass told me to? I wasn't so sure that I would. I think it was much more common in the English world for each individual to decide independently as to how he or she viewed another person. In fact, we took pride in making up our own minds. That was the very heart of what made us different from the Amish. The Amish valued community above the individual.

In the Amish faith, everything was decided by the community, and personal pride was seen as a sin. If your friend told you to trust someone, you did, no questions asked. If your friend told you not to trust someone, the same rules applied. In the English world, we told children to be different. In the Amish world they told children to be the same.

I was too English to not believe my way of thinking was the better of the two even when I'd seen with my own eyes happy people living the Amish way. People in my very own family were perfectly happy with their lives. The Amish would say that was prideful of me, to be sure.

I picked up the first letter from the pile, and instantly I wondered if I should be touching it. These letters could very possibly be evidence in a murder if Eli was right. At the very least, they were evidence in a suspicious death. Even if Stephen Raber's death wasn't yet being called a murder, I knew Aiden well enough to be sure that he wouldn't rest until he found out how the rabbit farmer had died.

Tentatively, I held the letter between my fingers. I felt a need to get gloves, so that my fingerprints wouldn't appear on the piece of paper. As far as I could remember, I had two pairs of gloves in the house, and they were winter ones, which were put away for the season, and a pair of garden gloves *Maami* had given me. I had tucked the garden gloves in a drawer in the kitchen somewhere. And I doubted that Eli would stick around if I left the table to find out where I had oh-so-cleverly put them.

Carefully, just touching the edges, I unfolded the note and read out loud, " 'You know what you did, and God will have His revenge.' " It was written in English, but that didn't rule out that it had been left by an Amish person. Most Amish could read and write in English because it was the language they learned in school. Pennsylvania Dutch, their native tongue, was an oral language more than written. The Amish Bible wasn't even written in Pennsylvania Dutch, but in old-style German.

I went on to the second note. " 'You made your mistake without repentance. God will have His revenge.' "

I shivered. The notes were harsh in the extreme. I was afraid to go on. There was so much venom in the writing. "Do you know what the notes are talking about?"

He shook his head.

"And how do you know they were meant for your father? There is no name on them. Were they in envelopes with his name?"

Eli shook his head. "*Nee*. I know they were for

my father because I saw him collect them each day for the last two weeks."

"This has been going on for weeks?"

He nodded. "Every morning my father went to the shed phone and came back with one of these letters."

"Are you the only family that uses that shed phone?"

He shook his head. "There are five families on our road who use the same phone."

I nodded. It wasn't uncommon in an Amish community to share a phone within the district. It was another way for the families to share costs and thereby to save money—frugality was a priority in their culture—and it was a way to keep each other accountable so that phone use was not abused. In most districts, the phone was to be only for business or in the case of emergency. That was becoming more and more difficult for church leaders to enforce as the Amish now needed cell phones just in order to do business.

I glanced down at the first note again. The words "God will have His revenge" stood out.

I reread the second note. "You made your mistake without repentance. God will have His revenge."

I picked up a third note. "You will be sorry." This time, there was no mention of God at all. It was short and to the point. There was no vagueness in the implied threat, but could it be counted as a death threat? I wasn't so sure about that.

The notes weren't like ransom letters in the movies where pieces of newsprint were cut out to reveal the message. The notes were printed on white-lined school paper in black ink. As far as I could tell, whoever had done this had made no attempt to hide his or her handwriting. That might help with the investigation if the notes were sent to a lab for handwriting analysis, but did the Holmes County Sheriff's Department have access to handwriting analysis? If they did, would they use it on a case in which they believed the victim had died of natural causes? Even if Aiden wanted to do that, I guessed he would need permission from Sheriff Marshall because of the cost. Sadly, the sheriff wouldn't care how another Amish man had died. He'd be happy if they all left his county.

I set the three notes on the table and picked up a fourth, reading out loud, " 'What you did won't be forgotten. Be prepared, the day of reckoning is coming!' "

I shivered. The message was much in the same vein as the others. The person alluded to something that Stephen Raber had done in the past. What could he have done that would warrant so many threatening notes, and even worse, what would he have done that would warrant being murdered? He'd seemed like such a nice man. But really, could I judge a person's level of niceness on a five-minute conversation? Anyone can be nice for five minutes.

There were a lot of killers whose neighbors later said that "he was the nicest guy." I had even come up close and personal with killers like that. I couldn't let Stephen off the hook because he'd seemed to be nice this morning. Clearly, I knew nothing about him as the notes proved. It seemed to me that his own son knew very little about him either.

I shouldn't go any further. I knew it was wrong to read more of the notes without Aiden present. He would be frustrated with me that I had read any of them. I'd only done it because I knew this might be my only chance. Aiden would not agree with this reasoning.

Aiden had grown up in Holmes County. He knew better than I did how the Amish were, and how, as a general rule, they mistrusted the police. They mistrusted the police because their church elders told them to, which came right back to the riddle of community versus the individual.

"What do you want me to do with these?" I asked as I set the last note I'd read on the table.

"I have told you. I want you to find out who killed my father."

I pushed myself away from the table as if I needed to put some physical distance between us. "You need to talk to the police about these notes.

They are the ones who can decipher what this all means, not me."

He wrinkled his nose. *"Nee."*

"I know that you might not want to talk to the police, but Deputy Aiden Brody is a good man. He will be kind and fair to you. He will take these notes and this case seriously. I'm sure if you're from Harvest, you have heard about Deputy Brody before and will agree that the Amish community respects him."

He sighed. "I don't trust many people unless my friends tell me to trust that person. Daniel told me to trust you, not the deputy. You can give the notes to the deputy, but I don't want to talk to him. I won't talk to him. If there is something he wants from me, it will have to go through you."

I frowned but said, "Okay."

Aiden was going to hate everything about this deal.

Chapter 9

"If I'm going to help you, I need more information," I said.

Eli set Puff on the floor. The large rabbit hopped across the hardwood floor and twitched her nose. She then hopped into the kitchen. I hoped that it wasn't because she thought she would be able to find something to eat in there; I could vouch that there was nothing to be had. I really should go to the grocery store at some point. Possible murder and giant toffee rabbits will make you think of the more practical aspects of living at times.

Eli rested his elbows on the table. "I will answer what I can."

"When did the letters start?"

"I knew about them two weeks ago, but they could have started earlier. I don't know." He shook his head as if to push aside a bad memory. "I should get back to the farm. The rabbits are my responsibility now. My father cared a lot about those rabbits." His voice caught when he said this. He stood up abruptly, and as he did, he knocked over the chair.

Puff bounded deeper into the kitchen, scared off by the noise.

"I'm so sorry." He righted the chair before I

even had a chance to stand up, then bolted for the door.

I jumped out of my seat. "Wait! I have so many more questions. If you want me to help you, I need more answers. Who might have wanted to hurt your father?"

He had one hand on the doorknob. "You have to find that out. Daniel said you could." With that he threw the door open and ran out.

I followed him. "You forgot Puff!" I called to him as he climbed into his buggy.

Eli froze. "You keep Puff for now. I'm not able to care for her. My father gave her special treatment, and I have too many other worries."

Before I could argue, he clomped away with his horse and buggy.

Of course, I could have gathered up the rabbit, jumped in my car, and chased him down to make him take the bunny back. A buggy can't outrun a car, but I hadn't driven the car in six weeks. I wasn't even sure if it had a full tank of gas, or if the battery would start. And who knew how long I would have to chase Eli's buggy.

I let the front screen door slam closed and walked back into the living room. I peered into the kitchen and saw Puff had wedged herself behind the refrigerator. Or at least she had tried to. Her head and front paws were hidden by the fridge, but ninety percent of her was sticking out for all the world to see.

I sat on the floor next to her and patted her rump. By this time, the sun had set, and I was completely drained from the day. All I wanted to do was go to bed and wake up in a rabbit-free house, but I still had those letters to contend with.

I glanced back at the pile of notes. I wondered what the others said. I knew what the right thing to do was. It would be to call Aiden straight-away and tell him about Eli's visit. I most definitely should not read those letters. Aiden would not look kindly on it if I decided to read them before I told him about their existence. But, then again, this might be my only chance. Aiden was very tolerant of my inquisitive nature, but he drew the line when it came to his murder investigations.

Before I read another one of the letters, I knew enough not to get my fingerprints on them. I patted Puff one more time and stood up. I went into the kitchen and searched through the drawers until I found the garden gloves that my grandmother had given me. She thought that since I now had a bit of land, I would want to put in a garden. I might be great with chocolate, but I had a black thumb, so my grandmother's thinking was wishful at best.

I slipped the flower-printed gloves on. The gloves themselves were very non-Amish with that delicate and detailed print. Part of me wondered if my grandmother had bought me gloves like that because they were ones she couldn't wear herself, being of the plain people.

With my gloves on, I picked up the stack of letters that I hadn't read yet and began to go through them. I counted fourteen letters in total, including the four that were on the table that I had already read. Eli said his father had received one letter every morning for the last two weeks. If that was true, and I didn't have any reason to believe it wasn't, that meant fourteen days, fourteen notes. By my calculations, the letter delivery would have begun April first. Could this all be a long-running April fool's joke? That didn't seem likely, considering there were Amish involved. I had never heard of the Amish participating in April Fool's Day pranks.

Everything was feeling off. I had been home less than twenty-four hours, and in that time, there had been death, a break-in at the church, and the son of the dead man had come to my house asking for help. It was all too coincidental to have happened in such a short period.

Puff looked up at me with sad bunny eyes as if to ask what would happen now.

"I don't know," I whispered to the rabbit.

I was about to open the first letter of the stack in my hand when there was a knock on the screen door of the little house.

I screamed, and letters went flying in every

direction, floating down to the hardwood floor like leaves falling from a tree in autumn.

Aiden burst through the door and into the living room with his gun drawn. "Police!"

I threw up my hands. "Don't shoot! I'm your girlfriend."

He holstered the gun when he saw me in the middle of the room surrounded by the fallen letters. He was out of uniform for a change, wearing jeans, a T-shirt, and a light jacket. I wondered if he only had on the jacket to conceal his gun, which he wore in a shoulder holster. "For the love of God, Bailey, by the way you screamed, I thought someone was hurting you."

I winced. "Sorry, but for the record, you were the one who scared me."

He bent down to pick one of the letters up. Before I could stop him, he read the note. "What are these?" His voice was sharp. He picked up another and read it. "These sound like threats. Are they yours? Are they directed at you?"

He looked so upset that I might be the person receiving the letters that my heart constricted. If I hadn't already known that Aiden cared about me, the frightened look on his face would have proven it.

"They aren't mine and they aren't directed at me."

His shoulders relaxed ever so slightly, and he stood up. "If they aren't yours, whose are they?"

"Well, I was just about to call you about that."

He arched an eyebrow. He bent down and picked up another letter. "These threats are very serious. If anyone is getting notes like this, it should be reported to the police."

"That's why I was about to call you, to tell you about these letters." I hoped that I sounded more convincing than I felt.

"Have you read them?" He studied me.

I shifted back and forth. "Not all of them."

"Were you planning on reading all of them?" He narrowed his eyes. "Before calling me?"

I wasn't sure how to answer that question, so I remained silent.

"Bailey, you're wearing gardening gloves, and I know for a fact that you have a black thumb. You've killed every flower I've ever given you."

I blushed. "But I do love flowers and I love receiving them from you. Don't stop giving me flowers just because I kill them."

He smiled and the dimple in his right cheek appeared. "I won't, even when I know I am sentencing those flowers to certain death. The beautiful smile I see on your face when you receive them is worth it."

I couldn't help but smile, and I stooped to pick up the rest of the letters.

Aiden held out his hand.

I may have hesitated just a little, but I handed them over to him.

He took them from my hand. "Whose letters are these? Who gave them to you?"

"That's two different answers. Eli Raber gave them to me."

His gaze jerked up from the pile of letters in his hands. "Stephen Raber's son?"

I nodded. "The very one. He stopped by my house just a little while ago and gave the letters to me. He said he was sure his father was killed because of these letters. Stephen was the one who was receiving them."

"The murder victim, Stephen Raber?"

I put my hand to my chest. "Murder?"

Aiden nodded. "Murder."

It seemed Eli was right about his father's death after all.

Chapter 10

"That's what Eli thought happened to his father, but I hoped that Stephen died of a heart attack like everyone seemed to think earlier today," I said with my hand still on my chest.

"He did die of a heart attack. That is true." Aiden pursed his lips together as if to decide whether he wanted to tell me more. "It's what caused the heart attack that makes his death murder. Stephen Raber had a weak heart, so the lily of the valley he ate stopped it from beating."

"Lily of the valley," I gasped. Even I knew that the beautiful, tiny, bell-shaped flower was poisonous. When I'd worked at JP Chocolates, Jean Pierre had an extremely wealthy customer who thought lily of the valley was beautiful and she wanted us to decorate the candies for her wedding with the live flower because she would have the same blossoms in her bouquet. It took Jean Pierre a long time to convince her that that was a terrible idea if she didn't want to send all her guests to the hospital. What we ended up doing was decorating the candy with lily of the valley flowers made of white chocolate. Much safer and much tastier too.

"Why would he eat that? And how can you know so quickly? Don't toxicology tests and things like that take time?"

"First of all, I am more than a little disturbed that you know what a toxicology report is."

I rolled my eyes. "It's the twenty-first century, Aiden. Everyone knows what those tests are. Watch any crime show on TV or watch the news for that matter."

He sighed. "The report is not back, but the coroner found a piece of candy in Stephen's mouth, and there was a piece of lily of the valley in it."

I froze. "Candy?" I had a very bad feeling about this. Any time when candy and murder were in the same sentence, I felt a tad worried about the direction of the conversation. "What kind of candy?"

"It was toffee, to be specific. It seems that Stephen had a sweet tooth and loved homemade toffee."

"I did notice him chewing on something, but I just assumed that it was gum or perhaps chewing tobacco." Chew wasn't an uncommon vice in the Amish community. I rubbed my forehead. "Toffee. Why did it have to be toffee?"

"You have something against toffee?" he asked.

"No," I said. "Although, I don't like it when it kills people. But the giant rabbit Margot wants me to carve will be made of toffee too. It just seems like a strange coincidence."

He shifted from foot to foot. "I will have to check where it came from. . . ." He trailed off.

"You think it was from my shop."

"It could be, Bailey. It very well could be." He shook his head as if the idea disturbed him as much as it did me. I was certain that it did. Even before he and I started dating, Aiden had had a special kinship with Swissmen Sweets. When he was a young boy, he and his mother fled his abusive father in South Carolina and took refuge in my grandparents' candy shop for a few months while Juliet got back on her feet. He wouldn't want the candy shop involved in a crime any more than I would.

"Let's talk about these letters," Aiden said. "I will know more about the toffee and the lily of the valley when the coroner finishes his report, and yes, that will take a few days just as television has taught you."

I frowned. I wasn't ready to let the conversation about the toffee go, but before I could protest, he went on, "Why did Eli bring the letters to you? He should have given them directly to the police."

"He's afraid of going to the police. I don't have to tell you that some Amish are afraid of the police. It was easier for him to give them to me. I'm not Amish, but my grandmother is. For some Amish, that is close enough when they need to reach out for help, and they know when help needs to come from an English person."

Aiden's frown deepened.

I held out my hand. "Listen, I didn't ask him

for the letters. I didn't know anything about them before he dropped them in my lap. I didn't even know that Stephen was murdered. All I knew was a seemingly kind man was dead. But now that I have read the letters, I wonder how kind he actually was."

"What do you mean?"

"The notes I read commented on something bad Stephen did in his past. It would seem to me that he did something terrible, and if his son is right, whatever it was got him killed."

"Did Eli know what his father might have done?"

"No, and even though he knew about the letters, his father didn't know that Eli had found out about them. Eli never asked his father about the notes. He just watched him collect them from the phone shed every day for the last two weeks."

"What happened that might have triggered this?"

I shrugged. "Got me."

Aiden rubbed the back of his neck. "The secretive nature of the Amish makes my job so much more difficult than it has to be. I wish, just once, that they would question each other. If Eli had had the nerve to speak to his father, or if Stephen had asked someone for help, Stephen might still be alive today."

"It's not their way."

"I know. God knows that I know that."

"I told Eli that I would have to hand the letters over to you and he agreed, but he said there was a condition."

"I don't like the sound of that. What kind of condition?"

I ignored his tone. "He said that he wouldn't talk to you or any other officers about them. Everything has to go through me."

"Nope, not happening," Aiden said, shaking his head. "That's not going to work. I have to talk to him about this. As far as we know, he's the only one other than Stephen who even knew that these letters existed."

"Maybe Stephen's other children knew? Did he have other children?"

"Stephen also had three daughters. They are all married and have homes of their own now. I'll talk to each of them, of course, and ask if they knew about the letters, but I'm not hopeful they did. Each one had been out of the Raber home over a decade."

"I'm not sure that Eli is going to talk to you. I think he can make himself scarce if he needs to. I told you how he disappeared from the square right when Stephen died, and he sneaked up on my house. I didn't even know he was there until he was standing at the front door."

"He broke in to your house?" Aiden's voice was sharp.

"No, I invited him in after I almost whacked him with a throw pillow."

"Bailey, you just moved here from New York City. Don't you know not to let strange men into your home?" Aiden looked as if he might be ill.

"Of course I did," I said. "But New York and Harvest are two very different places. He needed my help."

Aiden rubbed the back of his neck just a little bit harder. "Do I need to remind you that murder happens in little villages?"

He had a point, and I shivered.

Aiden frowned at the letters. "He can't just drop a sheaf of threatening letters and feel like that is the end of it for him. That's just not how things are done."

"But that's how some things are done for the Amish."

He didn't argue with me because he knew that was true. "What else did Eli say?"

"Not much other than the letters." I paused.

"There is something more. I can tell. What aren't you telling me?"

"Well, he came to me because Daniel Keim said that I could be trusted. Daniel told him that I could find out who killed his father."

Aiden pressed his lips together and rubbed his forehead as if he were about to get a migraine. "And what did you say in response to that?"

"What could I say? I said I would tell you about it, but I also said"—I paused—"I also said that I would help him the best I could."

"So, you promised to catch a killer."

"Not in so many words, but I guess that's the gist of it."

He rubbed his forehead. "I feel a headache coming on."

Aiden really looked like he might be ill.

Puff chose that moment to hop into the living room, and Aiden jumped. "What the—!"

This time he scattered the letters in the air.

I stooped to pick up the letters a second time.

"What on earth?" Aiden blinked at the rabbit. "Did you get a pet?"

"No." I shook my head, holding the letters loosely in my hands.

Puff hopped over to me and sat on my foot as if she was in disagreement on the subject.

"He looks like he's claimed you as his own." The dimple was back in his cheek. "Did you buy one of Raber's rabbits?"

I folded my arms and looked down at the bunny. "No, I didn't. This is Puff."

"Like the magic dragon?" Aiden asked.

I held up a finger. "First, I appreciate that you and I have similar senses of humor. Second, no, this is Puff, Stephen Raber's beloved personal pet. Eli brought her with him when he came to talk to me and left her behind."

Aiden sat at the small dining table. I guessed this was a lot for him to process, and it was getting late too. It had been a long day for us both.

"Let me get this straight," Aiden said. "Eli came over here, gave you these threatening notes and a rabbit, and asked you to find out who killed his father and to keep the rabbit?"

I shrugged and looked down at the rabbit on my foot. Puff twitched her nose. "Pretty much," I said, and then I bent and picked up the rabbit. She was quite heavy. I would say even a pound or two more than Jethro the pig. I knew that because for whatever reason, it seemed I toted Jethro around the village almost as much as Juliet did.

I sat across from Aiden at the table with Puff on my lap. I found her weight comforting, and she was unbelievably soft. It was like having the kind of fur muff ladies wore in Victorian days to keep their hands warm.

Aiden arched his brow at me. "How many of the notes did you read?"

"Four. They're sitting on the table right there." I pointed at the tiny pile of letters I had read while Eli was there.

He pointed at me. "I don't want you to be involved in this."

"I am involved, and there is nothing you can do about it. Stephen died in front of my very eyes, and his son Eli came and talked to me about his father's death. He didn't seek you out, and he won't. He told me that. If you want to solve this case, you need me. The Amish trust me."

"They trust me too," he said a bit defensively.

"Not as much as they trust me, and that's because I have Amish roots through my grandparents. I'm sort of an insider even if I have lived most of my life away from here. You have lived here most of your life, but you are English—nothing can change your Englishness. I can help you."

"I don't want your help when it comes to a police investigation. *Ever*. If Stephen was killed the way both Eli and the coroner think, then whoever did this is very angry, angry enough to kill again. If it's the same person who sent these notes, he wanted Stephen to confess to whatever led to the threats. If that person is the killer, we can only assume that didn't happen, so this person, this killer, made candy to poison Stephen. That is not a crime of passion. That is cold-blooded, premeditated murder."

"I know that," I said a bit uncertainly. "But Eli isn't going to talk to you about his father. He barely spoke to me about him, and he came to me for help. It's just not the Amish way."

Aiden rubbed his forehead. "Not the Amish way. How many times have I heard that in my lifetime? The Amish way is not always the right way. It would be best if you realized that the Amish are just people like us. There are good Amish and bad

Amish. They are people who make mistakes and they are people who are capable of murder."

I bit my lip to hold back a smart retort.

"I need to get these to the station." Aiden stood, removed a pair of latex gloves from the inside pocket of his jacket, put them on, and gathered up the letters.

I stood up too and set Puff on the floor. "Can I at least see the other notes? Eli gave them to me."

Aiden pursed his lips together and then sighed. "All right. I shouldn't be doing this, but you might see something that I will miss." Carefully, he unfolded all the notes on the tabletop.

"Are they in any kind of order?" I asked.

"I just set them out in the order that they were stacked, but that was after we both took a turn at throwing them in the air. There's no clear sign to tell in what order they were received."

"I didn't throw them in the air. You scared me!"

Aiden smiled. "Because I caught you in the act of doing something you know you shouldn't have been doing."

I rolled my eyes. "You're showing me the notes anyway."

"You have a point," he said as he set the last note on the table.

I peered at the fourteen notes. It seemed to me that they were written all by the same hand. The print was almost identical. It was very straight up and down and precise. They all expressed the same sentiment—that the receiver, Stephen Raber, had done something terrible and he needed to repent or suffer the consequences.

I removed my cell phone from the back pocket of my jeans and snapped a photo of the notes on the table.

"What are you doing?" Aiden wanted to know.

I checked to make sure the photo was clear and tucked the phone back into my pocket. "I doubt you will let me see these again. . . ."

"I'm just going to pretend that didn't happen."

"Fine by me." I smiled.

Aiden shook his head and started to gather up the notes again with his glove-covered hands. I looked down at my own flowered garden gloves and felt silly for putting them on. If I was going to be around murder investigations so often, I would need to start carrying some of the plastic gloves that we used at the shop for candy making. I wondered if I should bring a few pairs home for circumstances just like this.

He organized the notes into a neat stack and slipped them into an evidence bag. "If you are going to help Eli with this, please at least promise that you will keep me in the loop. If you want to talk to someone, tell me where and when."

I frowned, promising nothing. As much as I wanted Aiden with me, I knew that many of the Amish wouldn't speak about personal issues in front of a police officer. It didn't matter how well-respected he was by the community.

"I'll let you know what I'm up to, so expect frequent text updates."

"I guess I'll have to live with that." He turned and walked to the door.

"You do." I followed him.

Aiden stopped at the door and turned to face me. "You can be so aggravating at times."

I smiled. "I know."

The dimple appeared on his cheek and he leaned in and kissed me. When he pulled away he said, "I really do need to take you on a proper date. It seems wrong that we haven't done that yet. Life always seems to get in the way."

Murder gets in the way, I thought.

I patted his arm. "Aiden, I understand. Murder first, then romance."

He shook his head. "I wish that weren't such a true statement." He gave me another quick kiss and left.

I closed and locked the door behind him, wishing that it wasn't such a true statement too.

Chapter 11

I had absolutely nothing in my house to feed a rabbit. Shoot, I had nothing in my house to feed myself. It was almost nine on a week night. The local supermarket in the village closed at six, and the supermarket in Millersburg had closed over an hour ago.

I filled a bowl with water and set it on the floor of the kitchen for Puff and searched my kitchen for something else to feed her. In the back of my pantry there was a suspect package of rice cakes. It was the best I could do. I removed one of the rice cakes.

"There you go." I held the rice cake toward her.

She looked up at me.

"They are good for you," I said. "It says right here on the package that they are heart healthy and made with whole-grain rice. They will make you strong."

She flattened her body to the floor and bent her ears back.

I sighed. "It's the best I have."

I set the broken up rice cake on a plate and put it on the floor next to the water dish.

Puff didn't move.

There was a knock at my front door. I glanced down at the rabbit. "What on earth is going on? It's the middle of the night."

She didn't respond.

I grabbed my throw pillow off the loveseat again—apparently my go-to weapon of choice—and approached the door. I peered through the peephole again, and this time I saw a short woman in a flowered blouse and long skirt. She had a prayer cap on her head, but she was most certainly not Amish in that outfit. I guessed she was some sort of Mennonite. She appeared harmless.

I opened the door.

She smiled at me sweetly. In her hand she had a basket with honey and jams. "I hate to come over here so late." I would guess the woman was about fifty. Gray wisps were threaded through the dark hair under her prayer cap. "I'm Penny Lehman. I live right next door to you." She pointed at the little white frame house to the left. I could just make it out in the dark. "I stopped by because I saw the police were here earlier, and I wanted to make sure everything was all right."

"Everything is okay," I said. "The police officer who was here is my boyfriend, Aiden, so you will see him from time to time."

"Oh," she said. "You're dating Aiden Brody? Then, you must be Bailey. I'm good friends with Aiden's mother, Juliet. She's very excited about your upcoming wedding."

I inwardly groaned. "Aiden and I aren't engaged."

"Oh," she said, and I was beginning to realize

that "oh" was her favorite word. "Juliet said you were, or at least I thought she said that. Maybe I misunderstood."

Knowing Juliet, Penny hadn't misunderstood her at all, but I wasn't going to say so.

She held out the basket to me. "I've been meaning to bring this by as a welcome to the neighborhood, but this is the first time I've seen you at home."

"I've been out of town on business." I left it at that and took the basket from her hand, noting that it carried an assortment of jams and honey. "This is very kind of you. Thank you for the welcome gift."

"It's no trouble at all." She peered into the house expectantly and I sighed inwardly. I was so tired, and all I wanted to do was go to sleep. However, this woman was my next-door neighbor and I wanted to have a good relationship with her. It seemed the only way I could do that was to let her in. I had a feeling that Penny would remember the slight if I turned her away. I stepped back. "Would you like to come in for a moment?"

She bustled inside the house. "I can't stay long."

I shook my head as I closed the door after her. It was ironic that I had moved out of Swissmen Sweets because I had wanted more time to myself, and here I was having three back-to-back visitors on the first evening I'd returned from New York.

"Would you like coffee or tea?" I asked. "I'm sorry that I don't have anything else to offer." I set the basket in the middle of the dining table, where the threatening notes had been just minutes ago.

"I'm quite fine," she said as she scanned the room. Puff chose that moment to hop out from behind the kitchen wall.

"You have a rabbit!" Penny said brightly. She plopped down on the floor next to Puff and her long skirt fanned out around her. She scratched the bunny in between her ears, and Puff moved closer to her.

It felt odd to be standing, looming over her while she sat on the floor, so I perched on the edge of a dining room chair.

"A friend just dropped her off for me to look after. Unfortunately, I don't have anything to feed her other than a whole-grain rice cake."

"Oh, that will never do for a bunny. Let me run over to my house. I have some carrots and broccoli that she will like until you can get some bunny food. You can find it at the farm supply store in Berlin or in a pet store. The farm supply store would be less expensive for you. I had rabbits as a little girl and have always loved them. I can tell you what supplies you will need."

Supplies?

"But before I do that, let me go grab those

veggies for this sweet girl." She jumped up off the floor like a jack-in-the-box and hurried out of the house.

Puff and I stared at her, wondering what had just happened. Also, I was impressed with her agility. I don't think I could get off the floor as quickly. Puff and I were alone in my little house for less than five minutes before Penny was back. She came through the front door without knocking first, holding a plastic bag of vegetables. She bustled past me into the kitchen.

Puff's ears pointed forward and she quickly hopped after Penny. I guessed she could smell the carrots.

Penny picked up the plate and threw the rice cake into the trash can under the sink. "My house has the same layout as yours, so I knew your trash would be under the sink." She smiled, broke up the carrots and broccoli into smaller pieces with her hands, and set those pieces on the little plate before putting it back on the floor. "There you go, little bunny. That should hold you until we can get you something else."

Puff hopped over and delicately picked up a piece of carrot with her teeth.

Penny put the rest of the vegetables in my empty fridge and brushed off her hands over the sink.

I gaped at her. "Thank you."

She smiled. "It's the least I can do now that we are neighbors. We have to look out for each other since we are both women living alone. I'm a widow, and my daughter moved away to Cleveland. She doesn't visit me much." A sad look passed over her face, but it soon cleared. "So, I am very grateful to have a nice girl like you move in next door."

"I do appreciate the veggies. That will hold us over until I can get to the store."

"When you go, you might want to get a litter box too."

I blinked. "A litter box?"

"I know it isn't pleasant to talk about, but your rabbit will need somewhere to go to the potty."

I grimaced and realized that this little wrinkle should have occurred to me sooner.

"If you put newspapers down tonight, that should be just fine."

I looked down at Puff warily now that I'd heard about the litter box. What other little surprises did this rabbit have in store for me?

"If she is a house bunny, she should be litter box trained just like a cat. Is she a house bunny?"

"I—I don't know. I know her owner was very fond of her. I assume that she lived in the house with him from the way he spoke of her."

"Who is her owner?"

Now I'd stepped into a proverbial litter box. I didn't know Penny Lehman at all, and I didn't know that I could trust her. However, it was a fair question and she saved the day by bringing over those carrots. I noted that only the broccoli was left on Puff's plate. "Stephen Raber," I said finally.

Her mouth made a little O shape. "Oh, I know—knew—Stephen. I heard that he passed away today. It's such a shame. He was such a kind man. He was always so cheerful."

That had been my impression of Stephen too, but I had only known him for five minutes before he died. I didn't think that was enough time to make a fair assessment of his character. "How long have you known Stephen?"

"Oh goodness, it must be thirty years at least. My family had a little grocery store in Harvest that's long since closed. Before he had a rabbit farm, Stephen was a vegetable farmer and supplied a lot of our fresh produce. In the summer, he seemed to be at the store every day making a delivery. He was a good man."

I swallowed. This woman had known Stephen well for over thirty years. Did that mean she might also know about any mistake he had made in his past? "Can you sit for a minute, so we can chat?"

She beamed. "I would love to, but it is after nine and I'm sure we are both tired. You need your sleep." She peered at me over her glasses. "You look all worn out."

I felt all worn out too, but I had to ask her about Stephen in case she knew something about his past. "Before you go, I just wondered if you ever heard of Stephen being in any trouble before, like when he was younger."

She stared at me. "Goodness, no. Everyone loved Stephen. For an Amish man, he was very outgoing. That's why my father liked working with him. He was so friendly and kind to customers when he was in the store. He was happy to answer any questions they might have about his crops. In general, the Amish are more standoffish with people they don't know." She looked down at her dress. "You might think that I'm Amish from my dress, but I'm Mennonite. There's a world of difference there."

"I guessed that you were," I said before I went back to the subject at hand. "So, there was no one who disliked Stephen . . . ?"

She shook her head. "No one that I can think of, and you will be hard-pressed to find anyone to tell you differently. He was well-liked in the community. There will be many people who will be sad to hear of his death." She clicked her tongue. "Not that it was unexpected."

I froze. "What do you mean by that?"

"Oh, it's just that he didn't take care of himself since his wife died. Since then, he's put on a lot of weight and my guess is his poor heart just gave out." She opened the door and turned back to me. "Why are you asking so many questions about Stephen?" Her gaze was curious.

I realized I would have to be careful about what I said around Penny Lehman. It seemed to me that she was a very astute woman.

I shrugged. "No reason. I guess I wanted to learn more about him since I have his rabbit here."

She looked back at Puff, who was in the archway between the living area and kitchen. "It seems strange that you would be taking care of his rabbit if you don't know what kind of man he was." The rabbit munched on the broccoli.

I forced a laugh. "I think you're right. I'm very tired and should go to bed. Thank you very much for stopping by. I love the honey and jams, and I know that Puff loves the carrots and broccoli."

"You're welcome," she said before going through the doorway with a concerned look on her face.

I closed the door behind her and told Puff, "No more guests tonight."

She wiggled her nose in return.

Chapter 12

With everything that had happened my first day back in Harvest, I was afraid I wouldn't be able to sleep. My worry was for nothing. As soon as my head hit the pillow, I was out cold.

The alarm on my phone woke me up far too early the next morning. I grabbed the phone and silenced it and stared at the white ceiling of my new bedroom. It was only the third night I had slept in my new bed. My body ached. The mattress was still hard and needed to be broken in. Even so, I could have fallen right back to sleep had it not been for remembering that Puff-the-Bunny was in my kitchen and might or might not be litter box trained.

I jumped out of bed.

I left for Swissmen Sweets an hour later, happy that Puff had used the litter box that I had put out for her the night before. I was also happy that I had an extra box and some kitty litter in the basement from the time I tried to move Nutmeg with me to the little house. The little orange tabby had wanted nothing to do with that plan and shredded a tablecloth in protest. After that I took him back to the candy shop. He seemed much happier there, where he could socialize with more people.

Before I left for the day, I gave Puff fresh water and the last of the carrots and broccoli. I considered taking her with me, but I didn't know where I would put her. I didn't think it was a good idea to let her loose in the candy shop with Nutmeg there.

I set a line of unpacked boxes to block the opening from the kitchen into the living room. Puff could have the run of the kitchen but nowhere else. I stepped over the boxes and into the living room. When I looked back, the rabbit seemed to be perfectly content with her surroundings. I shrugged. It was the best I could do. I promised her that I would pick up bunny food while I was out and left for the day.

When I walked out to the garage, I noticed a curtain moved in the side window of Penny Lehman's house. I had a feeling that my Mennonite neighbor was going to keep a very close eye on my movements. I also had a feeling it wouldn't be a long time before her rapt attention got old.

I pulled my little compact car out of the garage, and I was happy to say that it started right up even after being out of use for six weeks. Usually, I would just walk to the candy shop, but I suspected with Stephen's murder that I would be going a little farther afield today, and it would be nice to have the car nearby in case I needed to use it.

As I made the five-minute drive to Swissmen Sweets, I thought about Stephen's death and the fact that yet again I found myself in the middle of a murder investigation. Eli had brought me in, and to find out who'd killed Stephen Raber, I needed to find out who had sent those notes. I also needed to find out what Stephen had done to warrant the notes and what happened to trigger the notes being delivered to his phone shed.

I had the windows open as I drove, and as I turned onto Apple Street a light breeze blew, and petals from the apple blossoms floated into my car and around me like snowflakes. On the sidewalk, an Amish woman pushed a plain black stroller down the street and I saw the baby inside kick her legs as if she was dancing to a melody in her head.

I inhaled the sweet scent of the trees and immediately felt calmer. I loved New York. I loved the hustle and bustle there. In New York, I felt alive, as if I could conquer the world, but here in Harvest, I felt at peace. And I was as surprised as any to learn after all the time I'd spent trying to climb to the top of the chocolate world in the city that peace was what my soul truly craved. The new balance I had struck between living in Harvest and going to New York for weeks at a time to film the television show seemed to be the perfect mix for me. I knew that the show might not be picked up for another season and it certainly wouldn't last forever, but I would enjoy this balance for as long as it lasted.

I parked behind an Amish buggy that was tethered to a hitching post on Apple Street and got out of my car.

I walked to the corner of Main Street. The square was quiet now. The white bunnies were still on the green. Some of the rabbits sat in the middle of their fenced-in pen and plucked clover from the grass with their little bunny teeth, but it seemed that most of the bunnies lay curled up in one of the three hutches in the pen. Seeing how well they were set up for Easter Days made me sad all over again for Stephen Raber. Whatever he might have done to cause someone to write those notes, no one could deny that he loved and cared for all of those rabbits as if they were his pets. It made me determined to take care of Puff for as long as I had her even if I didn't quite understand why Eli had given me the rabbit for safekeeping.

It was before nine, the hour when the candy shop would open, but I let myself into Swissmen Sweets with my key. "It's me!" I called. I didn't want to scare my grandmother or Charlotte, both of whom lived in the small apartment over the shop. I had lived there too until just recently. In some ways, I missed the convenience of rolling out of bed and stumbling downstairs to make candies in the morning. But what I didn't miss was not being able to use my hair dryer or having to plug my phone into an outlet in the industrial kitchen because there were none in my grandmother's apartment.

"We're in the kitchen!" Charlotte called from the back of the shop.

I wasn't the least bit surprised to hear it. I knew that they had been up for hours prepping the candies for the day, and there would have to be extras made for Easter Days, not to mention the additional orders we had for Easter itself. Easter was just five days away, so we would have to kick into high gear to finish everything on time.

Nutmeg mewed at me as he met me at the door. I picked up the little cat and hugged him before I set him back on the floor and walked around the counter to the kitchen's swinging door. Nutmeg watched me from the other side of the counter. He knew that he wasn't allowed in the kitchen. Somehow my grandmother had trained him to stay on the public side of the counter. He did have free rein of the apartment upstairs, where he spent a good deal of his time lounging in my grandmother's sitting room window, which looked out onto the square. He liked to watch the world go by. Maybe he was a feline version of my nosy neighbor Penny.

I pushed open the swinging door and found Charlotte and my grandmother sitting on back-less stools around the large stainless-steel island in the middle of the room. They each had a large metal bowl in front of them that they were stirring with wide wooden spoons.

Charlotte smiled brightly at me and a strand of her red-gold hair slipped from the bun at the nape of her neck. "We're making the marshmallow fluff to go inside the marshmallow Easter eggs," Charlotte explained. "Cousin Clara has to keep telling me not to eat it. I just love marshmallow."

I picked up a spoon and dipped it into my grandmother's bowl. I popped the spoon into my mouth. It was perfect.

My grandmother swatted at me. "Not you too. We will never have enough fluff if the two of you keep this up."

I hopped out of range of her next swipe. "It's quality control. We can't let any inferior marshmallow have our name on it."

"That's a good one!" Charlotte exclaimed. "I am going to use it next time. Thanks, Bailey."

I winked at her.

Maami put her spoon back into the marshmallow. "Charlotte has been telling me about many of your adventures in New York. She said she's going to be on the television program quite a bit." My grandmother's wrinkled face folded into the slightest hint of a frown, but it was enough for me to recognize her concern.

When I was given the opportunity to have my own show on Gourmet Television, Linc and the network had wanted to film the Amish community in Harvest as part of it. But my grandmother's bishop, Bishop Yoder, forbade any of his church members to appear on the program. It wasn't the Amish way to be filmed; the ban went back to the biblical injunction not to make any graven images of oneself.

Charlotte wasn't baptized into the church yet and could get away with being on the program without getting into too much trouble, but it was no secret that the bishop and the other church elders were not happy about it. I chewed on my lip. I knew having Charlotte on the show did make it more authentically Amish, but I certainly didn't want to do anything that would impact my grandmother's standing in the district. Unfortunately, since I was her granddaughter, anything that I did or didn't do reflected on her.

I swallowed. "Her part was very small," I said. I gave Charlotte a look.

Her eyes widened. "Oh yes, I don't even say anything. Mostly, I helped Bailey prep for the different candies. For the most part, I am in the background. Right, Bailey?"

That wasn't entirely true, but I said, "right" in any case. The one advantage I had was that no one from the district would actually see the show because the Amish don't watch television. Well, I should rephrase that. The Amish aren't supposed to watch television, but at times they do bend the rules. However, I knew my grandmother and the church elders weren't the type to bend the rules, so I felt my little fib was safe, at least for the time being.

I frowned. "I have a lot of toffee to make if I'm going to get that rabbit of Margot's done." I went to one of our two industrial refrigerators and opened the door. The bunny head and hindquarters that I'd carved out of white chocolate the day before were still there. I closed the door and sighed.

"Charlotte and I can work on the toffee between customers today. You concentrate on carving the rabbit."

"*Danki*," I said, using the Pennsylvania Dutch word for "thank you."

My grandmother smiled as she always did whenever I spoke Amish. Her brow wrinkled. "Was that all you were worried about, dear? You look upset."

"I saw Aiden last night. . . ."

"Oh no!" Charlotte cried. "Don't tell me you and Aiden broke up. That would be horrible. I think Juliet would never recover."

I shook my head. "No, Aiden and I didn't break up."

"Oh!" Charlotte said. "Then you are engaged! How exciting!"

I held up my hands and waved them in the air. "I'm not engaged either!"

"That will make Juliet sad," Charlotte said thoughtfully. "She really wants the two of you to have a June wedding. She even talked to Cousin Clara and me about the possible dessert list. She wanted to know all your favorite treats."

"Let's not rush things. Aiden and I are fine just as we are." I waved my arms some more. Aiden and I had only been officially dating since Christmas, and it was April. I didn't think a wedding was on the near horizon in either one of our minds. His mother had been wanting us to get married for months before we even decided to date each other.

"Emily and Daniel Keim had only courted for a few weeks before they married, and now they are very happy together."

"No offense, but they're Amish," I said.

My grandmother chuckled, and Charlotte made a confused face. I wasn't sure whether the young Amish woman understood how different the two cultures were. Really, if I married before I was thirty years old, I would be surprised. I was twenty-eight, and I was in no hurry. If, and that was a big "if" so early in our relationship, Aiden and I did marry someday, the next thing Juliet would be harping about would be grandchildren, and I was nowhere near ready for that. I thought Juliet should focus more of her attention on her relationship with Reverend Brook than Aiden's and mine. Juliet continued to insist that Reverend

Brook was a good friend, but everyone in the village knew it was more than that.

I thought it was best to change the subject from marriage and weddings. "I saw Aiden on official police business."

Charlotte's mouth made an O shape.

"What about?" *Maami* asked.

"Stephen Raber. It looks like he was murdered."

"I thought he had a heart attack. That was what Margot said when she bustled in here right before we closed yesterday."

"I think that's what Margot wants to have had happened, but Aiden told me it looks like Stephen was murdered. It seems Stephen was poisoned."

Charlotte gasped, but surprisingly my grandmother didn't appear nearly as shocked as her young cousin. I wondered if it was because she'd expected that Stephen would be murdered or because she was becoming accustomed to murders in the little village of Harvest. I thought that either reason was a bad one.

"Aiden just told you this? Usually he is more closemouthed about crime," *Maami* said.

That was an understatement. "Usually he is," I said. "But last night the murder investigation came to me. Eli Raber, Stephen's son, stopped by my house and asked me to solve his father's death. He said that Daniel Keim told him to come see me." I didn't bring up the threatening notes. I knew Aiden wouldn't want to let that information out. I trusted my cousin and my grandmother. However, Charlotte had been known to say too much when she was excited, and murder was something that certainly could get her talking.

"You helped Daniel at Christmas with a similar situation," *Maami* said. "It makes sense that he would tell his friend to see you when he needed help."

"True. I only wish the Amish trusted the police more. Aiden is a good man. They should know that he wouldn't do anything to hurt them. They should go to him, not me."

"We know that." My grandmother set her bowl of fluff on the island. "But the sheriff is still the man in charge of the department, and Aiden has to take directions from him. Until that changes, I think very few Amish would be likely to go to the police directly."

"Are you going to help Eli?" Charlotte asked.

I nodded. "I said I would, but I also told him that I had to talk to Aiden about it. Eli agreed to that just as long as he didn't have to talk to Aiden directly."

"Aiden won't like that," my grandmother said knowingly.

I nodded. "He didn't. I think he will try to speak to Eli. I don't know if he will get anywhere." I moved across the room and removed a giant block of chocolate from the other fridge. The least I could do was get to carving while we talked. "Charlotte, can you help me lift this next piece onto the island?" There was an even larger block of chocolate at the bottom of the fridge. The cold chocolate would be much easier to carve than it would be if it was warm. I would carve the rabbit's ears, nose, eyes, and paws out of blocks of chocolate. However the body itself would be made of Rice Krispies treats. If it was made out of a solid block of chocolate, it would be too heavy to move and we didn't have enough chocolate in the shop for a six-foot rabbit as well as everything else we needed to make from chocolate before Easter. "Also, it seems I'm rooming with a rabbit."

Charlotte helped me lift the block of chocolate onto the island at the count of three. When the chocolate landed on the stainless-steel countertop with a resounding thud, she asked, "What do you mean when you say you're rooming with a rabbit? You speak in *Englisch* riddles. At times, they can be so difficult to follow."

"This one isn't a riddle. It is a fact." I went on to tell them about Eli leaving Puff-the-Bunny with me. I opened the drawer under the island where I kept all my best knives for carving. One of those knives, a very long and curved one, had been a Christmas present from Aiden. When I saw the knife in the drawer, my heart constricted a little. I wanted to solve this murder, but I didn't want to be at odds with Aiden over it. I hoped he would see that we could work the case together.

I removed one of the smaller knives to start and etched lines into the giant piece of chocolate where I planned to make large cuts. "What can the two of you tell me about Stephen? Was he well liked? Did anyone have an issue with him?"

"Everyone loved Stephen." *Maami* shook her head and repeated what Penny had told me last night. "I can't think of a single person who would have a reason to want to hurt him. He was the kindest of men. You saw him with his rabbits. He was so gentle, a gentle giant."

"I didn't know him well," Charlotte added. "But he was always kind to me. Even when I decided to leave my old Amish district and join Clara's, he didn't ask me why I changed or when I was going to be baptized as so many other Amish do. All he said to me was, 'Everyone has to do what's best for him, but you will have to live with the results.'"

I held my knife suspended in the air. *Everyone has to do what's best for him, but you will have to live with the results.* Knowing what I knew about the threatening notes Stephen had been receiving, I believed he was referring to something in his own past rather than Charlotte's decision to change districts.

There was a small frown on my grandmother's face. I knew she must be wondering when Charlotte would be baptized and make a commitment to the church. Charlotte was twenty-one, and by Amish standards, long past due to make up her mind. My grandmother didn't speak a word about it though, and it didn't seem that Charlotte noticed the crease in *Maami*'s forehead.

I sliced my knife into the chocolate. I looked from my grandmother to Charlotte. "Have either of you heard any murmurings about something bad in Stephen's past? Maybe when he was a young man?"

Maami cocked her head. "What do you mean, child?"

I glanced over at Charlotte, who was watching me intently, and knew I shouldn't say anything more. I swallowed. "I just wondered what he was like as a young man. That's all."

Maami thought about this for a moment. "*Nee*, not Stephen. If I remember right, he was baptized very young. He wasn't even fifteen when he made the choice to join the church." She glanced again at Charlotte, who was pouring her marshmallow mixture into an icing bag, which she would use to fill the chocolate eggshells that she had already made for the marshmallow eggs. "He's always been kind and polite. Very friendly."

"What about his family?" I asked.

"He is a widower. I think his wife died two or three years ago. Cancer," *Maami* said. "His wife Carmela was an expert quilter and usually brought home a grand prize from the county fair for one of her beautiful quilts every year. Her death was a great loss to the community."

"I'm sorry, *Maami*," I said, and made another cut into the piece of chocolate in front of me.

She smiled at me as she slid her bowl across the island to Charlotte. "If you want to know more about the Raber family, I suggest you talk to Carmela's quilting circle. I've never been a member of the circle myself because I much prefer to knit, but those would be the ladies who were closest to Carmela and they would know the most about her family."

"That's a good idea," I said. "Do you know where I can find them?"

Charlotte began to fill a second icing bag with marshmallow from my grandmother's bowl.

Maami watched her young cousin for a moment before she spoke. "You could ask Ruth Yoder. She is a member of the circle."

I grimaced. Ruth Yoder was the uptight and persnickety wife of my grandmother's bishop. Because of Bishop Yoder's advanced age, Ruth was able to wield more power in the community than she normally would in an Amish district. She had been highly critical when I came to live in Harvest. She didn't like seeing an *Englischer* working in an Amish business even if I had every right to be there. However, if Ruth was my ticket to learning more about Stephen, then I would have to take it. However painful it might be.

"Where can I find Ruth?" I asked.

"I imagine she will be wandering around the square at Easter Days today," *Maami* said. "She wasn't very happy about the idea of the festival."

That came as no surprise. Margot and the bishop's wife were constantly at odds when it came to events happening in the village. The funniest thing was that if the two powerhouses combined their strong wills, they could very well take over Holmes County altogether, if not the entire world. The very thought of it terrified me, so I was happy with their being on either side of every issue the village faced.

Chapter 13

"If Stephen was poisoned, how was it done?" Charlotte asked as she carefully filled the hollow chocolate eggs with marshmallow.

The sight of all that sugar made my teeth hurt, but it didn't change the fact that I wanted to dip my spoon into the marshmallow bowl again.

"Toffee," I said finally. "Someone put lily of the valley in a piece of toffee and he ate it."

Charlotte made a face. "But that's poisonous. Every Amish child is taught to stay away from it in the woods."

I nodded, regretting that I had said anything since the poisoning wasn't common knowledge yet. "Which is the reason that Aiden is almost certain it was murder. The coroner will run a toxicology report to make sure the lily of the valley was what really killed the poor man."

Charlotte shivered. "How terrible. What a loss. I wonder what will happen to the rabbits. Every time you saw Stephen, he had a rabbit with him."

"Eli will take over the farm," my grandmother said. "He will want to fill his father's shoes. It is the Amish way. As the only son, he was destined to get the rabbit farm eventually. He will take it on without argument, and he's of age."

"How old is he exactly?" I asked. "I guessed twenty."

"A little older than that," *Maami* said. "I think he's at least twenty-five. He was already over twenty when his mother died and that was a few years ago."

My grandmother, Charlotte, and I worked in silence until the shop opened at nine. It was the middle of the week, and even with Easter Days going on across the street, traffic was light in the shop this early in the day, so I decided to take a break from carving the white chocolate rabbit, which was coming together quite nicely, I thought, to see if I could track down Ruth Yoder.

Midmorning, *Maami* sent me across the street to the village square with three heavy boxes of candy that Swissmen Sweets was donating to the day's festivities. I think we were sending over enough chocolate rabbits for every child in the village and maybe half of the adults too.

The actual Easter Days celebrations started at noon each day. It worked out well for Margot because the local schools' spring break was Easter week as well. By the time I crossed the street with my candy offerings, there were dozens of English families with weary-looking parents who already appeared ready for spring break to be over, and it was only Wednesday.

"Bailey!" Margot called from the top step of the gazebo. Fortunately, she didn't appear to have her bullhorn on her, but I heard her loud and clear without it. "Have you brought the candy?"

I lifted the boxes a little higher so that she could see.

"Wonderful!" She hurried down the steps. "Over here, I have Easter baskets waiting where you can put the chocolate rabbits." She guided me around to the back side of the gazebo, where two cafeteria-long tables stood covered with dozens of plastic Easter baskets. There were even more Easter baskets on the grass behind the table. The baskets were full of candy and small toys. "Aren't these great?" she asked, puffing her chest out with pride. "It's all donations too, just like your chocolate rabbits. We're selling them at Easter Days to raise money for the village."

"What's the fund-raiser for this time?" I asked. It seemed that Margot had been spearheading one fund-raiser or another the whole time I had lived in Harvest. Honestly, I thought her talents were wasted on our little town. She should have worked on a presidential fund-raising campaign or something like that in Washington, DC. She had an uncanny ability to convince people to part with their money. It certainly worked on me—I was donating hundreds of dollars' worth of chocolate to her and I didn't even know where the money would go.

"We want to make the downtown area more inviting, so we'd like to add a small pond with a waterfall. It will be absolutely lovely," Margot said.

"You are having so many events on the green nowadays. Won't that impact the amount of space?"

"Goodness no, we wouldn't put it in the green. We need every green inch of the square that we can get. We plan to put it in the park across the street by the new playground."

"Ahh," I said. The new playground was another fund-raising initiative that Margot had spearheaded.

"Go ahead and put those rabbits in the baskets," she said. "I think we already have a line of customers who would like to buy them." She smiled at the cluster of people patiently waiting not too far away from us.

I got to work tucking a cellophane-wrapped chocolate bunny in each waiting basket. As soon as I had the first table done, people were lined up and ready to buy.

Margot set to work collecting money from the parents buying baskets for their children. When there was a lull in the number of people buying baskets, Margot said, "Shouldn't you go back to the shop and work on the toffee bunny? You said it would be done tomorrow."

I was realizing I should have given myself more time. I sighed. There was no point in correcting her now. I would just have to work late at the shop.

"I'll head back in just a minute." I paused. "Did you happen to see Ruth Yoder anywhere?"

Margot patted the top of her curls as if to make sure they were still there and scrunched up her face. "Why? What did she say to you about me?"

I stepped back. "She didn't say anything about you. My grandmother just said she's seen Ruth around the square, and I wanted to talk to her."

"Oh," she said, somewhat mollified. "The last I saw of her, she was muttering about something and walking toward the church." She shook her head. "There is no pleasing that woman."

Some would say the same about Margot, but I stopped myself from telling her that. I placed the last chocolate bunny into the waiting basket, which reminded me of the live rabbits that were still on the square. "Who's been taking care of the rabbits that are here?" I asked.

She handed another customer a basket and collected the money. "Stephen's son, Eli, was here this morning to feed and water them. I haven't seen him since. I have another volunteer keeping an eye on the rabbit pen just to make sure that everything is running smoothly." She frowned. "I do hope that Eli will be back soon because I have been asked by a couple of families if they could adopt one of the rabbits, but without Eli here to sell the rabbits, I had to put them off." Her frown deepened as if the more she thought about this, the more irritated by it she became. "I'm sure he's upset over his father's heart attack, but life must go on."

I grimaced at her cold attitude to Stephen's death. "You think it was a heart attack?"

She studied me. "Is there something you're not telling me, Bailey King?"

Uh-oh. I was certain that if Margot didn't already know that Stephen's death had probably been an act of foul play, Aiden didn't want her to know. "Nothing official."

"Saying 'nothing official' doesn't mean you don't know anything. It just says that you won't say what you know." She pressed her lips together.

"Oh, look," I said. "Here comes another group of families. I'm sure they will all want Easter baskets. I had better leave you to it!" I scurried away from her. I wasn't ashamed to say I might have been running.

"I'll find you and find out what you know, Bailey King. This village isn't that big. Remember that," she called after me.

I groaned. I knew that was true. If Margot wanted to find me, she would. There weren't many places to hide in Harvest.

Chapter 14

After leaving Margot and her Easter baskets, I had no luck finding Ruth Yoder. She might have been by the church earlier in the day, but she most certainly wasn't there now.

Instead of the bishop's wife, I stumbled upon Juliet, who was planting flowers around the church. Jethro was following her, digging up with his snout as many flowers as she planted. Dirt covered the polka-dotted pig's face. Juliet didn't seem to notice or mind the havoc that Jethro was wreaking, so I didn't bring it to her attention.

Juliet hopped up and brushed dirt from her hands. "Bailey, I'm so glad you're here. I was meaning to stop by the candy shop today to talk things over with you."

I winced. "Things?" I asked. Usually when Juliet had a pressing need to speak with me about anything, it was either concerning the wedding that Aiden and I were so not planning, or she needed me to pig-sit Jethro. Neither of these sounded too appealing at the moment since I was rabbit-sitting already, and I never wanted to discuss wedding plans with Juliet for fear of encouraging her delusion.

"Yes." Her Carolina accent sounded more pronounced, so I knew she was upset. "I wanted to talk to you again about the break-in at the church. Aiden is so preoccupied with what happened to Stephen Raber, he's no longer worried about what happened here at the church. I can understand that. Stephen was a nice man, and now he's gone, but the church and Reverend Brook both need to be protected. This is the Lord's house and he is a man of God!"

"I know Aiden hasn't forgotten," I said, coming to my boyfriend's defense.

"I know that's true. My son is the finest sheriff's deputy there ever was." She removed her polka-dotted gardening gloves. The fact that the gloves were speckled in multicolored dots didn't surprise me in the least. "But I know that you have a nose for crime too. Maybe you could take a look at the kitchen. You will bring a different perspective than Aiden had. A woman's eye is a valuable tool."

Now that she mentioned it, I did want to see the church kitchen and take a look at that minor crime scene. Part of me thought it still might be related to the murder. Or maybe that was just hopeful thinking, because if toxic toffee was to blame for Stephen's death, I most certainly didn't want anyone to think that such a horrible thing had been concocted in my shop.

"I'd be happy to look."

"Wonderful." She dropped her gloves in the grass and scooped up Jethro. It wasn't until

124

that moment that she noticed what he had done. "Jethro, did you dig up all those flowers I just planted? You naughty, naughty pig," she cooed, and then hoisted him on her shoulder.

Jethro smiled at me over her shoulder, and I rolled my eyes at him.

I followed the pair toward the church's rear entrance.

"How did they get in?" I asked. "I thought the church invested in new locks." I knew that because, unfortunately, this wasn't the first time the church had been broken into through this very door.

Her face turned red. "Well, it seems the door was left unlocked."

I raised my eyebrows. "Why?"

"Margot and her people have been using our fellowship hall to store things for Easter Days. We don't mind at all. It seems when they left for the night before the break-in, they may have forgotten to lock up behind them."

"How, then, do you know it was a break-in? Couldn't it have been a member of Margot's team who caused the mess?"

She unlocked the door and we walked inside. I followed through the short hallway into the church's large kitchen. It may have been a mess yesterday morning, but now everything was perfectly clean. I knew that Juliet and the other church ladies must have been itching to get in the kitchen and disinfect the place after the intruder.

"Margot insists that it was spotless when she and the others on her committee left for the night. She said she was the last one to leave."

I raised my eyebrows. "So, Margot forgot to lock the church?"

Juliet nodded. "Yes, and she feels awful about it."

I frowned and made a mental note to speak to Margot again about the night she and the committee were in the church. Maybe there was something she would remember that could lead us to the intruder. As I looked around the clean kitchen, I knew there was very little I would be able to glean from the scene. There was nothing left to indicate that anything at all had happened in this room. The church ladies were thorough in their cleaning. "What was the person cooking in here?" I asked. "I can't tell since everything has been put away. You told me yesterday that it was sticky like candy."

"It was candy," she said.

I turned to face her. "What kind of candy?" I asked, but deep in my heart I already knew.

"Toffee."

I left Juliet and Jethro in the church's kitchen shortly after that. I walked into the parking lot and to the edge of the graveyard at the perimeter of the church property to make a call.

Aiden picked up on the first ring. "Bailey, are you all right?"

"Why didn't you tell me it was toffee?"

"Toffee? You mean the toffee that Stephen ate?"

"No, well . . . maybe."

"No, well maybe what?" Aiden asked, sounding exasperated.

I knew he was busy. He didn't have time to play guessing games with me, but I was so frustrated with him for keeping this important fact of the case from me. I took a breath. Aiden didn't have to share *anything* about the case with me. He was the cop; I wasn't. I needed to remind myself of that before I accused him of anything.

Much more calmly, I said, "You didn't tell me that the candy that was made during the break-in at the church was toffee."

He was silent for a moment and asked, "Where did you hear that?"

"Your mother told me."

He grunted into the phone.

"Is that where the toffee was made that killed Stephen?"

"Yes," he said finally. "We tested the samples I took from the church in the lab and it's a match. I'm hoping to get back to the church today to take another look."

"Did you tell the church ladies that? Because

the place is spotless. They disinfected the entire kitchen. You aren't going to find a fingerprint in that room."

Aiden groaned. "I told Reverend Brook not to touch anything."

"I doubt the reverend was the one who cleaned up the mess. You should have told your mother. She was the instigator with spray bottle and scrub brush."

Aiden made a noise that was something between a groan and a squeak.

"You okay?" I asked.

"Yes," he said after a beat. "Just frustrated. The sheriff is not going to be happy with me if he finds out my own mother tampered with a crime scene."

"Oh." I grimaced. I knew that Aiden wanted to avoid trouble with the sheriff at all costs. He was already on slippery ground with his boss. "I'm sorry, Aiden."

"It's not your fault. Don't say sorry for something that you didn't do." He had said this to me countless times, and I was still guilty of it. I supposed I was used to taking responsibility for things that went wrong. It had been my job to do so as Jean Pierre's first chocolatier in New York. If something went wrong for one of the big clients, I had to take the heat. It was just part of the job and a way to test whether I could eventually handle Jean Pierre's position.

Ironically, I knew that I could handle it but chose to give it up for the life I had in Harvest.

"I think," I said, "we need to get together to solve this murder. I can talk to the Amish and you can gather evidence and talk to the non-Amish who may be involved."

"No, Bailey," was all he said.

"Did you know about the quilting circle?" I asked.

There was resignation in his voice. "What quilting circle?"

I went on to tell him what I had learned from my grandmother about Stephen's late wife Carmela and her closest friends in the quilting circle. "You have to admit that I will have much more luck talking to them than you would."

He sighed. "You're right there. I can't believe I'm about to say this." There was a pause on the line. "Okay, Bailey, you have a deal. We will work on this together, but I want you to tell me your every move. You leave Swissmen Sweets, I want a text about it."

I grumbled.

"No complaints. I want you to be safe."

"All right," I finally agreed. "I want to find Ruth Yoder and talk to her about the quilting circle, and I'm going out to Keims' Christmas Tree Farm too."

"Why are you going there?"

"Because Daniel Keim was the one who sent

Eli to me. He must be close to the family or know someone who is closer who can tell us what Stephen did to get himself killed."

"You still think that the death is tied to those notes?" he asked.

"And you don't?" I challenged.

He sighed. "I didn't say that. I don't like the idea of you going out to the Keims' alone."

"Aiden, I go there all the time to pick up and drop off Emily. It won't be a big surprise to any of them if I just happen to stop by."

"I suppose not," he said with resignation. "When are you heading out there?"

"Within the hour, I hope. I have to run back to Swissmen Sweets to make sure that my grandmother and Charlotte can spare me for a few hours. Luckily, we got all the candy done for Easter Days and most of the Easter special orders too. The only big project I have left is the toffee rabbit. I should have it done tonight, although it will be late."

"You'll be working late at the candy shop?"

"Most likely."

"Then, I think you should stay there tonight. There's no sense going home when you have to be up at the crack of dawn the next morning."

"Aiden," I started. "I'll be fine. Besides, I have to go home tonight. I have Puff to take care of, remember? I'm going to stop on my way out to the Keims' farm to make sure that Puff is okay."

"Oh, I forgot about the rabbit," Aiden said. "Just be careful. Text me when you leave the candy shop. I don't care what time it is."

"I think you are being more than a little paranoid."

"Am I? A man is dead, Bailey. He was poisoned by a candy made in a church. Whoever planned this did it in a calculated sort of way. That's not the sort of person you want to mess with."

"No, I suppose it's not," I said quietly, and ended the call.

Chapter 15

I hurried back to Swissmen Sweets, taking the long way around the square to avoid being spotted by Margot. I knew that she would track me down eventually, but I would rather it be later than sooner.

I pushed open the door to the shop and was happy to see a line at the counter. The shop was doing a brisk business as people stopped by to pick up their Easter orders for the end of the week and tourists stumbled in from Easter Days.

As aggravating and demanding as Margot could be with her many ideas to raise the profile of Harvest, no one could argue that her methods didn't get results and tourists into the village.

I helped Charlotte and my grandmother for a half hour, until the line died down. Then I removed my apron. "I'm going to go to Keims' Christmas Tree Farm to see what I can learn from Daniel about Eli."

"Did you find Ruth Yoder at the square?" *Maami* asked.

I shook my head. "She was gone by the time I got there."

My grandmother nodded thoughtfully. "You might have more luck finding her husband's woodworking shop, Yoder Furnishings. It's not too far from here. I'm sure you've passed it many times driving through the village."

"Yoder Furnishings is the bishop's store?" It wasn't surprising that I didn't know it belonged to *the* Yoders from my grandmother's district. Yoder was the number one surname in Holmes County. It was like Smith, but as if all the Smiths decided to move to the same little corner of Ohio. It was hard to drive through the county without seeing the last name on half a dozen buildings. At least to me, it was impossible to see which Yoders were related to which.

"It is their store," my grandmother said. "The bishop is too frail to make furniture there any longer. His boys took over the day-to-day work years ago, but I'm certain Ruth still keeps the books."

"I'm sure she's good at it," I said. Ruth Yoder had a reputation as a stickler for details. She was just the kind of person who would make the perfect bookkeeper, especially since many Amish businesses still kept their books in actual ledgers.

It was taking some work, but I was pulling Swissmen Sweets away from that, and entering our accounts into computer software. It was a long process, and I hadn't got much of it done before I had to leave for the filming in New York. It was yet another project I wanted to complete before I got called away to the city again by Gourmet Television.

"I think I'll stop by the furniture shop after leaving the Keims."

My grandmother nodded. "That does sound like a good idea. Daniel will tell you the truth about his friend, but don't be gone too long."

I raised an eyebrow.

"Margot stopped by while you were out and wanted to see the toffee bunny. I wouldn't let her back into the kitchen. I know how you hate to have your creations critiqued before they are done."

"Thanks, *Maami*," I said, thinking that Margot must have come to the shop while I had been at the church.

My grandmother peered at me over her glasses. "Did you really promise her that it would be seven feet tall?"

I gaped at my grandmother. "No. I said six feet. No one said anything about seven!"

"Well, it seems she found out that the biggest toffee bunny ever made was six and a half feet tall, so she wants yours to be seven. I think she was really looking for eight though."

"Of course she was," I grumped. "That woman is going to be the death of me."

"I'm sure you're not the first one to say so," my sweet Amish grandmother replied with a smile.

Shaking my head, I left the shop to head toward Keims' Christmas Tree Farm.

It was on a remote road that was little more

than loose gravel with overgrown grass on either side. There was no berm to speak of. Even though there were few street signs and even fewer landmarks, I knew the way there because I had visited the farm often in the Christmas season, and I had taken Emily home many times since she and Daniel had married.

Driving down the long street, I felt glad for Emily. I knew she had married Daniel very quickly after a whirlwind courtship, but she appeared to be happy, and after years of being ridiculed and mistreated by her older sister and brother, she was finally out from under their control. Thinking on that, I supposed Aiden was right. The Amish were similar to the English in that way—likely all people were—you had your good, your bad, your indifferent. While I did believe that the Amish had fewer of the societal flaws I had encountered in the big city because their faith instilled in them a strong sense of family and community, driving them to place God and family first, I think there was occasionally a downside to their focus. Such strong adherence to their ways meant that sometimes, if someone didn't conform to the model dictated by their bishop or *ordnung* laws, that person was ostracized or berated. In Emily's case, the girl's brother and sister truly believed they were doing the right thing, that their harsh treatment of her was only showing her the error of her ways. But that kind of punishment smacked a little too close to mistreatment for my comfort. And what of poor Stephen, the gentle rabbit keeper? From the notes he'd received, it was clear someone deemed themselves judge of his actions, and that someone thought to punish him too—and they'd succeeded.

I shuddered and forced the thoughts away.

Emily's family owned Esh Family Pretzel, which was right next door to Swissmen Sweets. I wished I had a better relationship with the shop owner, Esther, Emily's older sister, but when I'd helped Emily get away from her repressive siblings, I'd ended any chance of making up with Esther or the girls' older brother, Abel. It was all worth it to me because now I knew that Emily was living with a loving family.

The Keim family made most of their income around Christmastime, selling the beautiful Christmas trees they grew, but that wasn't enough to last them the entire year, so they also sold cash crops to wholesalers and farmers' markets. Emily said that this year the crop would be soybeans, alternating from corn last year. The Amish farmers alternated crops to keep the soil healthy. It was better for the land that way.

The soybean fields were freshly plowed. It was April, but an unusually warm April. The land could be tilled up and made ready, but it would be a few weeks before the seeds were in the ground. In Ohio there could be frost right into May, and seasoned farmers like the Keims would know better that to taunt Mother Nature by getting too far ahead of themselves. If the weather held, it promised to be a beautiful Easter at the end of the week. My prayer was that the mystery surrounding Stephen's death would be solved by then, so the village could enjoy the holiday without his untimely death hanging like a cloud over our heads. I knew the Amish community, in particular, must be on edge with this sad turn of events.

I turned into the Keims' long, gravel driveway, and the loose pebbles crunched under my compact car's small tires. In the late afternoon, the farm was quiet. Just beyond the large white farmhouse and white barn, I could see the Christmas tree planting. It looked like the Keims had been expanding by planting new saplings on the edges of the more mature trees. I smiled. Tulips and daffodils bloomed in the front garden. I was glad the family was doing well. They had had a very difficult Christmas. I hoped that Easter would be a much brighter season for them.

I knocked on the front door. Inside, I heard the *thunk, thunk, thunk* of a cane hitting the hardwood floor. A few moments later, the front door opened and Grandma Leah's face broke into a grin. Grandma Leah was well into her nineties and was the oldest woman in my grandmother's Amish district if not the entire Amish community of Holmes County, but you wouldn't know that. Except for her cane, which was a recent addition after she took a tumble in the barn over the winter, you would never be able to guess her advanced age. She held herself erect as if she was still on a mission to prove that she didn't need the cane to hold her up.

Thad was Daniel's father and Grandma Leah's grandson. Grandma Leah, Thad, Daniel, and Emily all lived in the big white farmhouse. It was certainly large enough for the multigenerational family. However, Emily told me that she and Daniel were toying with the idea of building their own little house, a *daadihaus*, on the farm to have some privacy. This surprised me. Privacy, at least privacy from other family members, wasn't something the Amish typically valued. I thought it showed a generational shift from Thad's generation to the next and certainly a giant leap from Grandma Leah's time.

"My," Grandma Leah said. "Aren't you a sight for sore eyes? I heard that you were in the city making a television show. What on earth has brought Bailey King to my doorstep?" She leaned forward on her cane. "Is it trouble? It seems the only thing that brings you here when Emily is away is trouble."

I grimaced, wondering if that were true and thinking it just might be. "I *was* in New York, but I'm back now for a little while at least."

"*Gut*. I know Clara would want you home for Easter. It is a time that family needs to be together." She thumped her cane on the floor for emphasis. "Are you here to see Emily? I sent her on an errand to Millersburg to pick up my medicine from the pharmacy. She went in the buggy, of course, so she won't be back for a long while. I hope she wasn't supposed to work at the candy shop today. She told me she didn't have to." She said all this without taking a single breath.

I smiled. "No, I'm actually here to see Daniel. Do you know where I might find him?"

She raised her eyebrows. "Now I know that you are here because of some kind of trouble."

Before I could answer, she went on to say, "It's Stephen Raber's death, isn't it? I should have known that was what it was the moment I heard your car come up the drive. You don't think my Daniel had anything to do with it, do you?"

"No, of course not," I said, but at the same time I wondered why that was her immediate assumption. Did the Keim family have some kind of con-nection with the Rabers that made her think Daniel might have been involved? Eli Raber had gone to Daniel for help after his father died, so the two of them must be close friends. I knew I would have to find out more from Daniel.

"*Gut*," she said. "I don't want my great-grandson tangled up in any trouble again."

For Emily's sake, I didn't want that either. My young Amish friend had been through enough.

"Daniel is in the barn doing chores. You're welcome to visit him there. You know what a hard worker he is, and he won't want to stop his chores to chat. I imagine he will speak to you while he mucks the stalls."

I thanked Grandma Leah and walked to the barn. The flowers from the front garden perfumed the air as I went, and I inhaled deeply, reveling in the scent. Spring in Amish country was beautiful. Spring in New York was beautiful in its own right, but I had never had time to appreciate it when I was in the city, especially around Easter. While others were tiptoeing through the tulips in Central Park, I was trapped in JP Chocolates working fourteen-hour days, sometimes sleeping on a cot in the back room because it was easier than schlepping my tired body home at night. It was amazing to me how my life had changed in the last few months. I couldn't help but wonder what the spring and summer would hold. I hoped no more death. I had had my fill of that.

Red-and-brown chickens flapped their wings and ran ahead of me as I made my way to the barn. They scattered when I reached the large barn door.

It was wide open. I knocked on the barn siding to let Daniel know I was there. "Daniel?"

Daniel Keim was a handsome young Amish

man with round glasses perched on the end of his nose. Only married a month, he was still in the process of growing an Amish beard. At the moment, the beard resembled more of a patch of dirt on the end of his chin than any real facial hair. At nineteen, Daniel had married young by English standards, but in the Amish world he was considered a man at fourteen, so such youthful marriages were not unheard of, although they were becoming less common these days.

Despite their young age, I was happy that Emily and Daniel had found each other. In the time I'd known Emily, I had never seen her truly happy until she married Daniel. They were a good couple. Daniel doted on her every whim too, which didn't hurt.

"Bailey, what are you doing here?" Daniel leaned on the handle of his shovel and pushed his glasses up his nose in a practiced move.

My eyes adjusted to the dim light of the barn. There was a battery-powered lantern that hung from an iron hook on the wall. Even though the sun hadn't set yet, it was dark in the barn, which only had a few windows on the south side of the long building.

"Has something bad happened?" Daniel asked.

I blinked. "Why would you ask that?"

"Because you obviously aren't here to see Emily, and the only other time you come here is when something bad has happened."

Was I like the Typhoid Mary of the Amish community? That wasn't a reputation I wanted to have.

He straightened up and went back inside the stall that he had been cleaning out. "It's about Eli's father, isn't it?"

I followed him over to the stall and rested my arms on the opposite side from where he was working. The smell of straw, manure, and animal sweat floated around me with every shovelful that Daniel dumped into the waiting wheelbarrow. "You were the one who sent Eli to me."

He sighed. "*Ya.* He was very upset, and I didn't know what else to do."

"You could have told him to go to the police." The stall wood dug into my forearms.

He glanced at me. His glasses were slipping down his nose again. "That is not our way."

How well I knew that.

"Why did Eli come to you?" I asked. "You aren't members of the same district."

"But we are still friends, and he knew what happened to my mother." He paused. "He thought I could help. That's when I told him about you."

I bit the inside of my lip. Daniel's mother had been killed just before Christmas. I had discovered who was behind her murder. Considering the Amish aversion to English authority, it made sense that he'd told Eli to talk to me instead of Aiden or the police.

"When was this?"

He frowned. "Yesterday, just after midday. I had finished my supper and was going back out to check the fields when he rode up in his father's buggy."

That must have been right after I'd seen Eli on the square, where his father had collapsed. He must have run straight to Daniel. "What did he say?"

Daniel shrugged and went back to shoveling. "He told me what happened to his father. I thought maybe it was a heart attack. Everyone in the district knows that Stephen had a weak heart. We took up a collection several years ago so that he could have a heart procedure at the hospital."

I nodded, thinking this over. The Amish didn't have health insurance. Their health insurance was essentially their community. Whenever one of them became ill and needed medical treatment, they took up a collection to help the family pay the medical bills.

"But Eli didn't think it was a heart attack," I said.

A calico barn cat wove around my feet.

Daniel dropped another shovelful into the wheelbarrow. "*Nee*. He thought it was something like what had happened to my mother."

"Did he tell you why he thought that?" I moved my leg and accidentally scared the cat away.

"*Nee*, and I didn't want to know. I told him

to see you because I knew you would be the *Englischer* who could help him."

"Did he tell you about any notes?" It was hard for me to believe that Daniel had sent his friend away without asking more questions. If he were English I would have doubted it completely. However, the Amish are far less likely to pry.

Daniel shifted his stance and picked up the shovel again. The metal scraped against the concrete floor of the stall, and I thought he wasn't going to answer me. "He tried."

"Did you read them?"

"*Nee*. I said I didn't want to know about his family's private affairs, so I told him how you had helped Emily and me and sent him to you. I told him that we would pray for him, but we didn't want any more to do with it. Both Emily and I have had enough to deal with these last several months. I told him I was sorry, but we couldn't take anything else on."

Out of the corner of my eye I saw something white dash around the barn floor. I jumped and knocked my right knee against the side of the stall.

Chapter 16

Daniel dropped his shovel. "What has happened?"

I looked down to see what had scared me and expected to see a large white rabbit with a bright pink bow around her neck. "Puff?"

How did the rabbit get here from my house? I wondered.

Daniel leaned over the side of the stall. "Puff? What do you mean? That's one of the barn cats. I think it's Eliza. Emily has taken to naming them all. You know how she loves cats."

I did. Emily's heart had broken when she had to give Nutmeg to me because her brother said she could no longer keep the little orange tabby.

"Oh, for a moment, I thought it was Puff, Stephen Raber's rabbit."

He stepped out of the stall and looked for the cat.

The white cat sat on a hay bale near the cow stall. The large jersey cow mooed as if annoyed by her new visitor.

"It's just Eliza. I'm glad it wasn't the rabbit. I told Eli that I couldn't take his father's rabbit." He clicked his tongue at the cat, and she meowed in reply. I had a sense it was a conversation they had often.

"Eli tried to leave Puff with you?"

He nodded and walked back into the stall to pick up his shovel again. That was interesting to learn. Did Eli not want his father's favorite rabbit at all? I bit the inside of my lip. I hoped that Eli didn't think Puff was permanently rehomed with me. I couldn't take on another pet either. I was away from the county for weeks at a time. I couldn't ask my grandmother to take on the care of yet another animal while I was away. I had already adopted Nutmeg since moving to the village, and now the orange tabby lived with *Maami* full time. I shook my head and resolved to worry about that later.

He shrugged. "He said he needed a place for her to be safe while he sorted things out, but again, I told him it could not be with me. We can't get involved."

I didn't like the sound of that one bit. I thought the best course of action was to ignore his comment. "I know you said you don't want to be involved in what happened to Stephen, but you sent Eli my way, so I need you to help me out a little bit."

"I suppose I did," he said slowly, as if it was something that he regretted doing.

"Do you know any reason why someone would have wanted to kill Stephen Raber?"

He shook his head. "Everyone liked Stephen. I told you about his heart procedure. It was no trouble at all to collect the money he needed to pay his medical bills. Every member of his district and many others, including mine, was willing to contribute. That is our way, but it was also because of who Stephen was. He was one of the friendliest men you'd ever meet. Sometimes, people complained that he would have been better off if he had been born *Englisch* rather than Amish."

I wrinkled my brow. "Why's that?"

"His demeanor. He was friendly to everyone. I'm sure that you've noticed that in general we Amish can be a little standoffish to people, especially to *Englisch* people we don't know."

I had noticed that. Not so much with myself, but with tourists who stopped the Amish on the street and asked them questions. I think I got a pass because of my Amish grandparents. Jebidiah and Clara King were much beloved in the county.

"Stephen would talk to anyone, and he didn't mind being photographed by *Englischers* even if it is forbidden. So"—he paused—"the only complaint against Stephen would be that he was too friendly."

I chewed on this for a moment. "Could he have been murdered for friendliness?"

Daniel was thoughtful. "*Nee*, it's not a *gut* reason to kill someone. It might get him in trouble with his deacon from time to time but would result in nothing more than a smack on the hand. There are many ways to make an Amish man

147

behave before resorting to murder. He might have been shunned if he got too carried away, but for the most part, I think his deacon and bishop turned a blind eye to his behavior because they liked Stephen just as everyone else did."

He leaned over the side of the stall. "Maybe that wasn't the only thing the bishop ignored about Stephen. He treated that rabbit more like a child than an animal." He shook his head as if the very idea was ridiculous. "My wife is much the same way with her cats."

"I got the sense that he cared for all the rabbits, but Puff received extra attention," I mused.

"Eli told me that Puff's mother was killed by a hawk just a few hours after Puff was born."

I made a face.

"Stephen took her into the house and raised her on a bottle. When she was weaned, he should have put her out in the barn with the other rabbits but could never bring himself to do it. Eli was embarrassed by how his father fussed over that rabbit." He shook his head as if Stephen's adopting Puff as a pet was some sort of great failing on the bunny farmer's part.

Could that be the reason that Eli had wanted to unload Puff on Daniel or me? Because he thought his father gave Puff too much special attention? Was he jealous of the white rabbit?

Personally, I liked Stephen even more after hearing how he'd cared for his animals. He sounded like he had been a well-beloved and kind man, which made it all the odder that he should have received those threatening notes. What had he done? Clearly, Daniel Keim did not know. "Where is the Rabers' farm?"

"It's on the edge of Millersburg, not too far from town actually. When Eli and I were young, we used to walk into Millersburg from his farm all the time. It's on Route Sixty-two."

Route 62 was one of the bigger roads in the county, so I knew the Raber farm would not be hard to find. I realized I would have to go there eventually. Maybe sooner rather than later. I wanted to give Eli his rabbit back before I grew too attached. I had a weakness for animals too. Maybe I could convince Daniel to take the rabbit?

"It's funny that you mentioned Eli's trying to leave Puff with you. He left her with me when he stopped by my house to talk about his dad."

"I'm not surprised," Daniel said, and began to shovel again.

"Don't you think she would do much better here on the farm, where she could be around other animals?"

"No. No. No." He shook his head. "I said no to Eli and say the same to you."

"No, what?" I asked with as much innocence as I could muster.

His expression was firm. "I can't take on another animal."

"Neither can I," I said. "I'm rarely home, and I'm in New York for weeks at a time."

"But you have your grandmother and Charlotte to look out for your animals. Don't they take care of Nutmeg, your cat, while you're gone?"

"That's different," I said, even though I knew I was losing ground. "One cat is not as much work as two pets will be, and a cat and a rabbit in Swissmen Sweets would be like oil and water. What if Nutmeg chased the rabbit?"

He laughed. "That would never happen. Puff outweighs Nutmeg by six pounds at least. Besides, I can't keep her without my father finding out. He won't be pleased. He blames rabbits for any problems we might have on the farm."

I grimaced. I knew this was true. All among the Christmas trees, there were rabbit snares to keep the rabbits down on the Keims' farm. It wasn't something I was completely comfortable with, especially after having seen what they could do. I saw a man trapped in one of those rabbit snares once. It was just around his ankle, but he had been in a lot of pain. It was hard to imagine what one of those snares could do to a rabbit like Puff. I could feel my resolve weakening.

Daniel must have sensed it too because he said, "It's only for a few days. I'm certain Eli just needs time to sort out what he should do. You don't want anything to happen to Puff, do you?"

"But I have a cat," I protested, making one last

gallant attempt to get out of this predicament. "Cats and rabbits don't go together. It would be a disaster if the two came together."

"And we have cats all over the farm. You just saw one. Also, Emily told me that you don't live at the candy shop any longer, so the rabbit won't be coming in contact with your cat."

I inwardly groaned. There was no way I could lie to get out of this with his wife as a member of my candy shop staff. "That's true, but I'm not home too often. Puff would be alone for much of the time, so I think I would have to take her to the shop during the day."

"We have chores to do here on the farm, so it would not be like the rabbit had company here either. I don't think she would mind being alone at your house." He smiled. Daniel knew he was winning this argument, which was what I found the most infuriating part of the conversation. He knew he had won before we even got started.

"But there is Grandma Leah—maybe she would enjoy having the rabbit here," I said, making a last attempt to get myself out of rabbit-sitting.

"My grandmother would be too afraid that she would trip over the rabbit if we took it into the house, and she has been feeling poorly ever since her fall and needing to walk with a cane. She can't be tripping over an animal."

I sighed. There was no going back now that

he'd mentioned Grandma Leah's fall. "All right. I'll keep Puff for now."

He smiled, looking very much like Nutmeg when *Maami* let the cat lick from the whipping cream bowl.

Chapter 17

I needed to track down Ruth Yoder to ask her about Eli's mother and her death, but I was closer to the rabbit farm than the Yoder family furniture store where she might be. So instead of going to the furniture store, I headed to the rabbit farm, assuming that I would be able to find it with Eli's description of its location.

There was a large sign on Route 62 in white with black lettering, announcing RABER'S RABBITS. Far back from the road, a small brick home stood with three small white barns behind the house. The barns were much smaller than other Amish barns I had seen in the county. Each one was a third of the size of the Keim family's barn.

To the left of those barns was a huge aluminum grain silo that seemed to have fallen into disrepair. The door to it was open, and there wasn't any grain inside that I could see.

I climbed out of the car, walked up to the brick house, and knocked on the door. As it was an Amish home, there was no doorbell. A large picture window was just left of the door. I peered inside but couldn't make anything out in the dark space. Frowning, I circled the side of the house toward the first barn.

Like most Amish barns, this one wasn't locked, and I easily pushed the heavy door open. The room smelled of sawdust and animals. There were dozens of cages in the space with rabbits sitting in each cage. The animals appeared to be well taken care of, but I didn't see any sign of Eli. The second was much the same, but there were no rabbits. I suspected that this was where the bunnies that were at Easter Days lived. I was about to open the third barn door when a twig snapped behind me. I spun around.

"Are you finally doing something about this?" An English man of medium height with a drooping face scowled at me. "It's about time you people did something."

I still had my hand on the barn door. "Who are you?" I wanted to know. Perhaps my question came off as rude, but I couldn't help it.

"Liam Zimmerman. I've been calling you all night and day hoping to get some type of response. You're from the zoning board, aren't you?"

"I—" I started to say that I wasn't, but he didn't give me a chance to continue.

"I'm glad that one of you has finally come here to do something about Raber's new barn, which is clearly in violation of the county's building codes."

Now that he mentioned it, the third small white barn looked newer than the other two. The edges were a bit sharper and the paint a touch brighter.

"It's good of you to finally show up. I should get more respect from the county. I pay my taxes—unlike the Amish. They are a bunch of freeloaders."

I frowned. This man was touting a common misconception—that the Amish didn't pay taxes. They paid their property taxes just like everyone else. In fact, they owned so much land that many times they paid higher taxes than their English neighbors.

But before I could correct him, he held up a measuring tool that was in his hand. "I'll prove it to you." It wasn't your average tape measure. This was a serious tool for a serious man. The diameter of the measuring tape was at least a foot when it was rolled up.

He handed me what my father would have called the dummy end of the tape, and he started to walk back away from me while I dumbly continued to hold my end like a kindergartner who had been given very specific instructions. "Ten feet. Twenty feet. Twenty-nine feet. And nine inches. See! Do you see?"

"It's less than thirty feet," I said.

"Exactly. He's breaking the zoning law. The building code states that no structure on his property should be within thirty feet of my land. It's as plain as day that he's in violation." His face was impossibly red.

It seemed that I'd stumbled upon a new suspect

for Stephen's murder without even trying. "When did he build the barn?" I asked.

He narrowed his eyes. "I said all that in my formal written complaint. Didn't you even take the time to read it? Typical government employee," he muttered. "A complete waste of my tax dollars. No one wants to enforce the law around here."

"When did he build the barn?" I repeated, pretending that I didn't hear his snide remarks.

"It was a month ago."

I pressed my lips together. Eli had said that his father had started getting threatening notes two weeks ago, and it seemed that Zimmerman had become increasingly angry about the property dispute. Perhaps it had escalated to threats.

For some reason, I had assumed that whatever Stephen had done wrong had happened a long time ago, but there was no good reason to believe that. The transgression could be much more recent. The notes could be from the man standing twenty-nine feet and nine inches away from me. Aiden came immediately to mind. He had asked me to text him every time I went somewhere, and I hadn't included this little detour to the rabbit farm in my texts. He would be so angry if I got hurt.

I dropped my end of the tape. "I'm not from the zoning board. I just stopped by to talk to the Rabers about Easter Days in Harvest. We're both involved in the event."

He glared at me. "You're one of those Amish lovers. I know the type. You all think the Amish are such good, upstanding Christian men and women. I'm here to tell you that they're not."

I frowned, taking personal offense at his comment since my grandparents were Amish and they were the kindest and gentlest people I knew. "Have you seen Eli Raber?"

"If I had seen Eli Raber, do you think I would be wasting my time talking to you? I would tell him exactly what I think about this violation of my land."

"Do the Rabers know about your complaint?" I took a small step back, and every inch of distance I put between this angry man and myself made me feel a bit safer.

" 'Course they know I'm upset. I tell them every day, and they don't do a thing about it. Neither does the county zoning board. They don't give a lick as to what the Amish do. The plain folk run around this county like a pack of wolves."

I blinked. I had never heard the Amish compared to a pack of wolves, and I had heard many comparisons since moving to Harvest. "You spoke to Stephen Raber about this too?"

"Yes," he said in exasperation. "I spoke with him again yesterday morning. He just nodded like he always does, as if he's really listening to me, but I know he's just placating me. He's not going to do anything about this, and if the authorities don't make him do something, nothing will get done. I plan to speak with Stephen when I see him again too. The barn has been up since March, and I will not be ignored." He clenched and unclenched his fists.

He didn't know that Stephen was dead, or he was a very good actor who was pretending that he didn't know. I was surprised. An entire day had passed since Stephen had collapsed on the square. I would have assumed that one of the sheriff's deputies, maybe even Aiden himself, would have come to the Raber farm because it was Stephen's home.

"Were you home yesterday?"

He frowned. "I was away on business overnight and just got back an hour ago. Why do you ask?"

That would explain why he didn't know about the murder yet *if* he was telling the truth. I wasn't ready to tell him, and I knew Aiden wouldn't want me to say anything. "I wondered if you saw Stephen or Eli later in the day."

"I didn't," he said shortly.

I glanced back at the Rabers' property. It seemed to me that Zimmerman had a perfect view of the phone shed and the Rabers' rabbit barns.

He frowned at me. "When I bought my house two years ago, I never thought I would have the trouble I have come across with the Amish. They have been terrible neighbors to me. They cut through the woods behind my home all the time, trampling the plants that I grow back there."

I peered beyond Zimmerman toward the woods that ran behind his and the Raber property. The woods were at least two acres away from the back of Zimmerman's house, so I didn't know why Amish walking through them would have bothered him so much. I guessed at this point just about anything the Amish did would strike Zimmerman as an insult or a threat to his property. However, what really caught my eye was the shed phone building in front of the Rabers' portion of the woods. This must be the same phone shed where Eli said his father received the notes. Were the notes from the man right in front of me? He certainly had easy access to the phone shed. All it would require was walking out his back door.

An Amish phone shed can be any kind of a shed with a telephone landline connecting to it. Many times, the phone sheds reminded me of an old-fashioned outhouse and the Rabers' shed was no exception. The wood was weathered, and the siding ran vertical instead of horizontal across the exterior. The clue that it was a phone shed was the phone line running from the road to the roof of the small building. Eli had said that they shared the shed with other families in the area. I wondered who those families were.

"Are you sure it's not deer going through your portion of the woods?" I asked.

"Deer don't wear size eleven boots. I've called the police about the trespassing more times than I can count, but they seem to be blinded to the Amish as well. Neither the Millersburg police nor the sheriff's department will do a thing about it. It's my life in those woods."

I must have looked confused, so he went on to say, "I'm researching native plants. I was away on business yesterday because I was giving a lecture on this very topic. That's what is back there. I can't learn how the plants thrive in a pristine environment when they are trod upon every few days because people are trying to get to that cursed phone." He pointed at the phone shed, confirming my suspicions about the building. "They don't even look where they step when they are back there. I have seen countless trillium and ferns stomped to the ground by their careless steps."

"Have you asked them to walk around the plants?"

"Yes, do you think I'm one of those men that don't try to resolve their own problems and run straight to the police with every complaint?"

No, I would never think that, I thought sarcastically.

"I have told them countless times, but they don't listen. Without any enforcement from the law, why would they listen to me? I take it as a personal insult. It's disrespectful."

I could see why Zimmerman was upset that Eli was walking through his property when he'd explicitly asked him not to, but I thought he was overreacting just a tad.

"I can tell by the look on your face that you are like everyone else. You don't understand the importance of these native woodland flowers. Trillium, jack-in-the-pulpit, joe-pye weed . . . if we don't continue to plant these flowers, they will be lost, and the bees will be lost too. They depend on these pollinators."

"Can you show me?" I asked.

He blinked at me. "You want to see them?"

I nodded, thinking that whatever was in the woods behind Zimmerman's house could have gotten Stephen Raber killed.

He seemed calmer then. "Maybe if you see it, you will understand. Follow me." He marched in the direction of his property and the woods.

I hesitated for a moment.

"If you want to know about these flowers and plants, now is the time."

Before I followed Zimmerman into the woods, I texted Aiden that I was at the Raber farm and might need his assistance very, very soon.

Chapter 18

I knew Aiden would be furious when he got that text, but I thought it was better to play it safe than sorry. Later, I would deal with Aiden's anger at me for being so careless. As I walked into the woods, I kept my distance from Zimmerman, always maintaining five feet between us. If he noticed this, he made no comment on it.

"The flowers start here." He pointed to a cluster of hundreds of large white flowers, which grew low to the ground.

The sight of them took my breath away. They were so pure and bright white.

"These are trillium, my wife's favorite."

I felt my eyebrow go up. For some reason, I'd thought this unhappy man was unmarried.

Trilliums were beautiful white flowers with three large heart-shaped petals. I could see why Zimmerman would want to save them.

He pointed to another spot on the ground, where a delicate, light purplish pink flower grew. "Wild geranium."

I kept my gaze divided between him and my footsteps. I didn't want to be accused of trampling on the native plants as the Amish had been.

The next plants he stopped next to were simply

thick stalks of green coming out of the earth, with no leaves yet.

"The jack-in-the-pulpit doesn't bloom until June. It's just breaking ground now."

He pointed at the ground. "But look at this one. This is what I have been telling you about."

I frowned. It did look like whoever had stepped on the plant had done it purposely to grind it into the ground. I could see the tread of a boot in the damp earth.

"Does this look like something done by a kind person? The Amish aren't as good as everyone would make them out to be." He sighed. "I might not have put up such a fuss over the new barn if the person didn't come back here and ruin my land. I have to find some way to hold whoever it was accountable for their actions."

"How far away is the next farm? The people who live there must use the Rabers' phone too."

"By foot, it takes ten minutes to walk there if you cut through here. If you were to go by buggy, it would take at least a half hour because you have to go through the entire city of Millersburg. I'm not an unreasonable man. I understand their need for a shortcut, but do they have to disrespect me in this way?"

I nodded and found myself feeling just a little bit of sympathy for Liam Zimmerman. The trampling of his plants did feel intentional. I knew I needed to tell Aiden all this just as soon as I could. The phone in my pocket vibrated against my leg. I removed it and checked the screen. The text from Aiden read, On my way there. Stay put. 5 minutes.

It seemed I wouldn't have to wait long to tell him what I knew.

"It only became worse," Zimmerman said, "when Raber's son started seeing the Amish girl at the next farm. He goes through my woods twice as often now. Hers is the closest farm."

"Eli Raber is courting someone?"

"I suppose that's what the Amish call it," he said with a sneer.

"Who is she?"

"I don't know the girl's first name. I have only seen her around her family farm when I've gone there to tell them to stop walking through my woods. Little good that's done."

"Who is the family?" I asked.

"Last name of the Amish who live there is Beiler."

I frowned. Beiler was a common Amish name, but if they were in the same district as the Rabers, there might just be one family by that name. In all likelihood, my grandmother would know them.

Eli Raber had ruined a man's research project by walking through Zimmerman's land to see his girl. I could understand why Zimmerman might be angry, but was he angry enough to kill over it? If he was, wouldn't Eli be the dead man? And was Zimmerman really angry enough to kill over less than a three inch discrepancy in the zoning code? It seemed far-fetched, and now that we were in the woods, he seemed much calmer. It was clear he loved his land.

"You moved here two years ago?" I asked.

"Two years ago, and it's been a struggle with the Rabers since day one." He scowled. "I think they have been accustomed to going back and forth through these woods and didn't see why that should change when I bought the property. But it's *my* land!"

I thought about the notes I had seen. One had read, "You know what you did. Confess."

Could that note have been from Zimmerman? Confess that the new barn was a few inches too close to Zimmerman's property line? It seemed like an overly dramatic way to get his point across, especially when he said that he had complained directly to Stephen every day about it and had gone to both the Millersburg police and the sheriff's department. Zimmerman didn't strike me as someone who would be stealthy about his dislike of another person. Also, if he complained often enough about it, surely Aiden and the sheriff's department would know exactly how he felt about the Rabers. Still, I had to know for sure.

"You said you gave a lecture yesterday. Did you come home at all?"

He frowned at me. "When?"

"In the afternoon."

"I'm not home in the middle of the afternoon. Unlike the Amish, I have to work to pay my bills. Things aren't just handed to me."

I stepped back. This man's misconceptions of the Amish were worse than I had first thought. "Where do you work?"

"I drive for a local delivery service."

I frowned. "I thought you said you were a botanist."

"I am. I'm working on a study that I hope to publish, but I have to pay the bills. I don't get charity like the Amish."

I bit my tongue to keep myself from correcting him yet again. The Amish didn't accept charity. They shared resources in the community, but they were far too proud to accept charity from an English organization. I wondered where all his ideas about the Amish had come from.

"Do you work by yourself?" I asked.

He glared at me. "Why are you asking me all these questions about me? I thought you were interested in my plants."

I took a step back out of the woods. "I came here because I was looking for Eli."

"And Stephen too, I suppose. Everyone who comes out here is looking for Stephen."

"Who is everyone?" I asked. "Was anyone here recently?"

"For almost two weeks there has been a different Amish person going into the phone shed each day. They aren't the usual people who use the shed. I have never seen any of them before or since."

It was clear to me that Zimmerman kept a close eye on the Raber rabbit farm. Perhaps too close an eye.

"What time of day do they come?" I asked.

"In the morning. At just about five."

"Are the Rabers there when they come?" I asked.

"I would guess so, but I have never seen them go to the phone shed. I leave for work just about then. I can't hang around and see what happens when I need to make money."

"What do the people do at the phone shed?" I asked.

He thought for a moment. "They go inside for a minute or two."

I froze when I heard this. "Are they Amish? Could they just be making a phone call?"

He gave me a dubious look. "Every morning at the same time like clockwork? And different people each and every time? Doesn't seem likely to me unless they were all calling the same person."

I thought about this for a moment. That would be easy enough for Aiden to find out if he asked a judge to subpoena the phone records on the shed phone. I wondered if the phone was in the Rabers' name or in the name of the district.

"Were the people who went into the shed holding anything?"

He shook his head. "I don't know. I'm always leaving for work at that time. I can't be late for my first delivery, so it's not like I can go over there and investigate. Besides, it's still dark that early in the morning. I most likely wouldn't even see them if they didn't go through my woods to get there. I put floodlights on the back of my place to discourage the Amish from going through there. Not that it's done any good."

"Did someone come to the shed this morning?" I asked.

He frowned. "Now that you mention it, no. No one came to the shed this morning, and I was looking for them." His face reddened just a bit. "It's become a habit of mine to look for them when I'm leaving for work."

I shivered. He had said exactly what I expected. In the last couple weeks, someone had come to the phone shed each morning at five a.m., but those visits had stopped today. The day after Stephen Raber died of poisoning. I needed to talk to Aiden. I believed those visits had stopped because Stephen was dead. There was no need to warn him any longer. He'd paid the price for what he had done. Whatever that might have been.

I stared down at the plants at my feet and my eye caught a long bright green leaf that was perfectly shaped. It grew up around a delicate stem. The stem dripped with a line of little green buds. The flower hadn't yet bloomed. That would come later in spring. I swallowed. There were dozens of these plants behind the jack-in-the-pulpits. With a shaky hand, I pointed at the plants. "What are those?"

"Don't you recognize lily of the valley?" he asked.

I did. I recognized it right away.

Chapter 19

"Bailey! Bailey!" Aiden's shouts interrupted my thoughts.

I grimaced. Aiden wasn't going to be the least bit happy when he found out that I'd gone into the woods with Zimmerman.

"Who's that?" the botanist asked.

"Just my boyfriend," I said casually. "I told him I was coming to the rabbit farm today to speak to Eli."

"Bailey!" Aiden's shouts were more urgent now.

I spun on my heel. "I had better go see what he needs." I bolted out of the woods.

Aiden stood next to the Raber phone shed with his gun drawn. When he saw me running out of the woods, he lowered the gun. "Are you all right?"

"I—"

Before I could finish telling Aiden that I was fine, Zimmerman came out of the woods. "What's this? You called the sheriff?"

Aiden had his hand on his gun again and narrowed his eyes. "What's going on here?"

"Oh, I see how it is," Zimmerman spat. "I can call the sheriff's department until I'm blue in the face before I get a response, but if your girlfriend calls, you come running. Figures."

Aiden folded his arms. "What is happening here?"

"I stopped by the Raber farm because I wanted to talk to Eli," I said.

Aiden arched an eyebrow at me. "And?"

"He wasn't here, but I ran into Mr. Zimmerman, who has some strong feelings about his Amish neighbors." I didn't go so far as wiggling my eyebrows at him to make sure that he picked up my point, but I nodded knowingly.

Aiden frowned at me. I think he was about to say something too, but Zimmerman was faster. He held out his hand. "Liam Zimmerman. I've had members of your department here before to deal with the Amish, but never you."

Aiden raised his eyebrows. "Deal with the Amish?"

Zimmerman went on to describe his complaint about his Amish neighbors in detail. I tuned him out. My gaze drifted to the phone shed. Zimmerman had said that a different person came each morning at five to go into the shed, and it stopped this morning. The first morning after Stephen was killed. I needed to talk to Aiden and in private.

"I don't work many property dispute cases, so that's why you haven't seen me," Aiden was saying. "We each have our own assignments in the department."

I shivered because I knew one of Aiden's assignments was homicide. I knew this from personal experience.

"I have the feeling that you're too important to

171

investigate my complaint." Zimmerman glowered at Aiden.

"No, Mr. Zimmerman," Aiden said calmly, as if he dealt with irrational people like Liam Zimmerman all the time. "I'm just telling you why you haven't seen me here before this."

Zimmerman clenched his jaw as if he wanted to say more, but wisely, stopped himself. He wasn't doing himself any favors by being rude to Aiden.

Aiden glanced at me. "Bailey, can I talk to you for a minute?"

I winced. I knew that Aiden wasn't happy with me, and his disapproval was understandable. Talking to Zimmerman alone hadn't been the wisest move I had ever made.

Zimmerman scowled as Aiden led me to the Rabers' phone shed.

I held up my hand when he turned to me. "Before you start, I see your point perfectly."

He arched his brow at me. "And my point would be?"

"You were going to say that talking to Zimmerman alone was a stupid move and that I didn't inform you I was coming here like I promised I would." I held up my hand. "At least I thought to tell you after I was already here. So that should be good for something, right?" I gave him my brightest smile.

"I'm so glad you're all right. You gave me a scare, Bailey."

"I'm sorry," I said, meaning it. Aiden had enough to worry about without adding me to the list.

"I really don't have the energy to talk to you about this right now. Just tell me what you learned from Zimmerman. We can deal with the other stuff later."

That sounded ominous, but I went on to tell him what I'd learned. He glanced at the phone shed.

"And I found the murder weapon." I told him about the lily of the valley in the woods.

He listened quietly and then said, "I need to call this in." He stepped away from me for a moment and removed his cell phone from his duty belt, turning away as he made the call.

He spoke in a low voice, and I couldn't catch most of it, but it sounded official by Aiden's tone. He ended the call and walked back to me.

I looked at him expectantly.

"I called my crime scene guys to come here and look for evidence in the shed. If you're right and this is the place where the letters were delivered to Stephen, then it's a crime scene. They will also get samples of the flowers from the woods. Perhaps there is a remnant of soil in the candy we can match. It will be microscopic though and will take time and money." He grimaced.

I knew he was thinking that he was short of both those things.

"Can you do that without Eli's approval? Go

into the phone shed, I mean. Isn't he the technical owner of the property now? And no one seems to know where he is."

"I have some of my guys on the lookout for him, but that doesn't matter for this part of the investigation anyway." Aiden shook his head. "Most likely it will belong to the Amish district, and I have already spoken to the Rabers' bishop, asking for their cooperation. The bishop promised that the district would cooperate, and that they had nothing to hide. He also said I was free to ask questions about Stephen throughout the district."

I raised my eyebrows. "Isn't that unusual?"

He nodded. "Very. But the bishop was so broken up over Stephen's death, I think he would have agreed to just about anything to have this resolved. It seems that Stephen Raber is greatly missed by his community."

"Does the sheriff know that you went to ask the bishop's permission?"

He shook his head. "No, and he wouldn't have if it's up to me. What he doesn't understand is that you get much farther with the Amish if you give them the courtesy they deserve. The sheriff has never done that or learned that." He frowned. "Most likely he knows it, but he just refuses to honor the Amish in any way." Aiden shook his head.

This was a battle that he had been fighting with

the Holmes County sheriff for over a decade. It wasn't going to be resolved any time soon as far as I could tell. I thought the only way to put an end to it was for Aiden to be sheriff, but he refused to run against his boss, saying it was looked down upon in law enforcement to challenge authority in such a way. That might be true, but there was a time when authority must be challenged. I knew my thinking wasn't very Amish. I supposed that it was good my father had left the faith, so I wouldn't have to make the choice myself later.

A crime scene van pulled into the Rabers' driveway, and I raised my brow. "It seems like they got here awfully fast." Typically, it would take twenty to thirty minutes, if not an hour, to get anywhere in our rural county. I found it suspect that the crime scene people had made it to the Rabers' in less than five minutes.

Aiden pressed his lips together. "Very fast actually."

The SUV came to a stop, and Aiden walked over to it. I followed him. I wasn't going to miss whatever it was the crime scene tech said.

Aiden shook the other man's hand. "Mason, how did you get here so fast?"

Mason removed his aviator sunglasses and tucked them into the breast pocket of his uniform. "We were called into a break-in just down the road."

"What break-in?"

"An Amish farm. Someone broke in to their barn and slashed all the tires on the two tractors. They did a job on the engines too. It was a real mess."

My brow wrinkled. The Amish farm must have been from a more liberal district than my grandmother's community to own gas-powered tractors. However, even more curious was that the sheriff's department had been called about the vandalism. In most instances, the Amish would much rather settle such an issue within their own community.

"Which farm?"

"Their name was Beiler. It was just a small Amish vegetable farm. I spoke to Jud Beiler briefly. He seems completely taken aback over what has happened and has never seen anything like it."

Aiden frowned. "Why wasn't I told about it?"

The tech shrugged. "I don't know. The sheriff said for us to get over there and process the scene."

"But I have told you before that I should be notified of any cases related to the Amish in Harvest while I'm working this homicide. They could be interconnected."

Mason shrugged. "I'm sorry, man. I would have thought that one of the other deputies or the sheriff would have told you."

Aiden clenched his fist at his side. I wondered if he was suspecting the same thing I was—that the sheriff hadn't told him about it on purpose. Sheriff Jackson Marshall wasn't above such a thing at all.

"Was anyone hurt?" I asked.

The young tech looked at Aiden expectantly, as if asking him for permission to answer my question. Aiden gave a small nod.

"No, Beiler says that he's in and out of the barn most of the day and everything was fine when he went to bed for the night. He discovered the vandalism when he woke up in the morning. Someone must have come in the middle of the night and done it."

Aiden frowned. "Did the farmer have any theories?"

Aiden shrugged. "I don't know. It's the deputy's job to ask questions. I'm just there to process the scene."

"Was there a deputy on the scene?" Aiden asked.

"Not that I saw, but he might have been called away."

Aiden's brow furrowed.

"You said it was Jud Beiler on this road?" I asked.

Mason turned to me again. "It is. You know them?"

Aiden watched me as Mason asked this.

It had to be the same Beilers that Zimmerman

had mentioned. It was possible that there would be another family by that name on the same road—there were a limited number of surnames among the Amish—but it wasn't very likely, and Mason's car had come from the direction where Zimmerman had said the Beiler girl Eli was courting lived. "I don't know them, but I think Zimmerman does. He was mentioning that the Beilers are another Amish family that he isn't happy with."

Aiden pressed his lips together. I knew he was thinking what I was thinking. Zimmerman hadn't been happy with the Beilers and their tractor had been vandalized. He hadn't been happy with the Rabers and Stephen Raber was dead.

Chapter 20

I was itching to get over to the Beilers' farm and talk to Jud about the tractor, and from what Aiden said next, I think he knew this. "Bailey, can you sit tight for a minute while I show Mason what I need him to do with the phone shed? And don't get any crazy ideas like going to the Beiler farm," he added under his breath.

He knew me too well.

Aiden led Mason to the shed. Zimmerman stood on the edge of his property and watched them with his arms crossed over his chest. I wasn't sure there was anything the sheriff's department could do to make Zimmerman happy. I wouldn't be surprised if Zimmerman was the type who was never happy.

I wanted to listen to Aiden tell Mason what evidence he needed from the phone shed, but I had already followed them once, and I doubted Aiden would tolerate it a second time. Instead I walked back to Zimmerman.

He glowered at me. "What's going on over there?"

I shrugged. I wasn't going to be the one to tell him that something was going on or that he was most likely a suspect in a murder since the murder weapon grew in his woods. That was Aiden's job, not mine.

"Are they going to do anything about the trespassing on my land or the building infringing on my property?"

"I'm sure the sheriff's department is taking your complaint seriously," I said, and mentally added, *or at least now they will—because there is a murder involved.*

Aiden walked over to us. "Mr. Zimmerman, I'm going to need to ask you a few more questions. Before I do that, I'm going to walk Miss King to her car."

Zimmerman scowled at me. "Your last name is King? Isn't that an Amish name?"

I shrugged yet again. "Not all Kings are Amish."

He frowned as he considered this, which gave Aiden time to guide me by the elbow back to my car. "Go back to the candy shop."

"I can't go back yet. I haven't even tracked down Ruth Yoder to talk to her about the quilt circle."

He shook his head. "Wait and do that tomorrow."

I started to speak, but he held up his hand. "I'm not just asking because I don't want you traipsing all over the county trying to solve a murder." He smiled. "Even if that's a little part of it. I say this because your grandmother asked me to remind you that you need to get back to the candy shop. Swissmen Sweets was very busy when I was there, and Margot has been pestering your

180

grandmother nonstop over the toffee rabbit."

The toffee rabbit. That reminded me of another rabbit, Puff, who was at home and most likely out of carrots by now. I needed to make a stop and get some rabbit food before I did anything else.

I wished my grandmother would call me when she needed help. We had a phone in the candy shop for business, but in my grandmother's mind it should only be used for emergencies, and a candy crisis didn't qualify as an emergency. I would need to talk to Charlotte about calling me when I was out and the shop got crazy. I knew my young Amish friend would be more than happy for any excuse to use the telephone, which she still found to be a novel experience. Charlotte, having grown up in a much stricter Amish community than my grandmother's, had not been exposed to many things. There were also many things she wasn't allowed to do, including playing the organ, which was why she'd left.

I bit my lip. I really wanted to stay and see what happened to Zimmerman, but if Aiden said that my grandmother needed me, I had to go to her first.

"I'll head back to the candy shop now," I said.

He smiled. "Thank you."

I said good-bye to Aiden and walked to my car. All the while, I couldn't help but think that I'd missed something about Zimmerman. He had motive, means, and opportunity for the murder. He was the perfect suspect. If he was the killer, then why wasn't he keeping quiet now? He didn't have to tell everyone how much he hated Stephen, and I didn't believe for a second that he knew Stephen was dead unless he was the world's best actor. I wished I could stay and be there when Aiden told him what had happened to his neighbor and questioned him about the lily of the valley growing in his woods.

But I had two rabbits to deal with. One needed to be fed and the other needed to be made. Shaking my head, I climbed into my car.

Instead of heading to the center of Harvest, I made a detour to Millersburg. It was the county seat and still very much a small town rather than a city. There were no cities at all to speak of in Holmes County. The closest true city was Canton, which was about forty minutes to the north on Interstate 77. I went to Millersburg because it was the only place nearby that boasted a pet shop. Hoping to make a quick trip, I ran in and scooped up everything the employee working there said a rabbit would need.

I drove back to my little house and found Puff waiting for me in the kitchen. She looked up at me with her big blue eyes, her ears halfway up, which I interpreted to mean she was hungry. "Don't worry," I said to the rabbit. "I have everything here you need." I filled a bowl with the rabbit food from the store and replenished her water dish.

She hopped over to the water and began to drink. I put all the other supplies in the kitchen. I hated to leave her again, but I needed to get to the candy shop and deal with the toffee rabbit. If all went well, I would be done with the rabbit tonight. The sooner I displayed it in the square's gazebo, the better. Then Margot would leave me alone.

Puff curled up on the pillow that I put on the kitchen floor for her, and I could see how she'd gotten her name. Her ears, nose, and paws were tucked into her sides, forming a circle, so that all I could see was her pristine white fluff. I took a photo of her with my smartphone and texted it to Cass with the caption, New roommate.

She immediately texted back.You adopted a pillow.

Rabbit. Fostering not adopted. Long story.

I'll call you tonight when I get home. I want deets.I can tell I need wine to hear this one.

She didn't even know the half of it. When Cass found out that I was involved in *another* murder investigation, she was going to hit the roof of JP Chocolates.

With the rabbit safely tucked in the kitchen

with her toys and food, I left my car in the garage and walked to Swissmen Sweets.

As I walked to the candy shop, my mind wandered back to Stephen Raber. What could he have done to motivate someone to kill him? I couldn't believe that it was building his barn three inches too close to Zimmerman's property line. The oddest thing about the afternoon was that there had been no one else on the Raber farm when I got there. Where was Eli? And where was the rest of the family? I knew how the Amish dealt with tragedy. I had seen it firsthand when my grandfather died. When *Daadi* passed away, the community gathered around *Maami*, barely leaving her alone for a moment. There was always a woman from her district sitting with her. There was always a man from her district doing some of *Maami*'s chores.

But there was no one on the Raber farm. No one there doing the chores or giving comfort to the family. I found this very odd, especially since everyone I spoke to mentioned how well-liked Stephen Raber was.

It was close to seven now and the sun was setting. The streets in the village were empty. The villagers, both English and Amish, were home for the night around this hour in Harvest. Most of the shops closed at five on weekdays, six on weekends. That had been one of the hardest things for me to get used to when I moved to

Holmes County. In New York almost everything was open well past eleven at night. Honestly, there were a vast number of businesses that catered exclusively to a night-owl crowd, so that old adage about the city that never sleeps was entirely true. With my long hours at JP Chocolates, I could attest to that. If it wasn't for late-night deliveries and 24/7 food stores, I'd have subsisted only on chocolate. And I'd never admit this to Jean Pierre, but no man or woman could live on chocolate alone. Here in Holmes County, not being able to even order a pizza after seven o'clock was a bit of an adjustment for me.

I smiled as I thought about the times that Cass had visited me in Holmes County and had been flabbergasted at how everything closed so early. At least when I'd moved here, I knew that was the case because of the summers I had spent with my grandparents as a child. For Cass, it was completely foreign.

I heard a scraping on the sidewalk behind me as if someone was dragging a paper bag across the ground. I stopped in my tracks and looked back. Normally, something like that wouldn't bother me, but I was more than a little on edge after Stephen's murder, and there usually wasn't anyone out in the village this late. I scanned the area behind me. The gas-powered lampposts were flickering on, and the last rays of the sun were fading. There was enough light to see by, but I didn't see anything. There wasn't a soul on the street.

I shook my head. I was being jumpy. It was most likely a stray cat or maybe even a white-tailed deer that had wandered into the village proper. Goodness knew there were plenty of deer in the county. I had a fear of hitting one with my car every time I drove at night, which was one reason I'd decided to walk to the shop. I knew it would be completely dark when I finished piecing together the toffee rabbit.

Or maybe it had been a raccoon. I had seen some *giant* raccoons since I'd moved to the country. I gave them a wide berth. I loved where I lived, but I hadn't completely acclimated to all the wildlife just yet. The most I had to deal with in the city was the occasional angry squirrel or pigeon. Holmes County had a whole slew of wild animals.

I walked a few steps and heard nothing more. I went on my way again; the animal or whatever it was must have moved on because the sound was gone. I turned the corner onto Main Street. The air was perfumed with the scent of apple blossoms. The white rabbits in their pen on the green across from the candy shop looked like puffed white pieces of cotton against the dark grass. I knew where Puff was, but I didn't know what would happen to these rabbits or the ones that were back at Stephen's farm. I hoped no one would think that I should take them. Puff was more than enough for me.

I let myself into the candy shop. As I stepped inside, my grandmother and Charlotte were coming out of the kitchen.

"Bailey," my grandmother said. "You were gone so long. We weren't expecting you back tonight."

Nutmeg was at my feet and he meowed until I relented and bent down to pick him up. When I did, the cat stopped fussing and snuggled under my chin.

"Aiden told me that Margot has been driving you crazy over the toffee rabbit."

"Has she ever!" Charlotte said. "I think she's been over here just about every hour looking for you."

I grimaced. "I told her that it wouldn't be done until tomorrow, but I had better finish it tonight no matter how late I have to stay up. I have a feeling Margot expects that the toffee rabbit will be on the square ASAP."

"I can guarantee it," Charlotte said. "She told me to tell you at least eight times."

I groaned. "This is probably a situation where it's best just to get it over with, and the pressure might help me to work. My head is all jumbled up over what happened to Stephen Raber. I went to the Christmas tree farm and spoke to Daniel, and then I went over to the Raber farm. No one was there. I found it strange. I learned that Eli was courting a girl from the Beiler farm, but I didn't get a chance to get over there and talk to her."

"I didn't know that," Charlotte said.

I shrugged. "I hope Aiden will tell me more. I'm sure he's been to that farm by now." I stopped myself from mentioning the vandalism on the Beiler farm. I didn't want my grandmother to worry about Amish being targeted in the county.

My grandmother shook her head. "I believe the Rabers' community is gathering at one of his daughters' houses. Eli was the only one who was still living with Stephen. Maybe they thought they could support the family better where there was more family."

That made me feel a little better. "I have a lot to sort out. I think working will help."

My grandmother smiled. "You are your *gross-daadi*'s granddaughter because when Jebidiah was stressed out about anything, he threw himself into work. Some of the most productive times at the candy shop were when Jebidiah was puzzling about things outside the candy shop."

I smiled, knowing that she was likely thinking of *Daadi*, and his lack of ability to sit still. That did sound like my grandfather and like me.

Chapter 21

Charlotte started to yawn and covered her mouth. "We made a lot of toffee. There are trays and trays of it cooling in the kitchen. I've never seen so much toffee in my life."

I smiled. "Thank you for doing that. I appreciate your both staying up so late. I know you have an early morning."

Charlotte shook her head. "We made so many trays of toffee, I lost count, and don't get me started on the Rice Krispies treats to make the rabbit's body. I feel like I have marshmallow in my hair."

Maami shook her head. "It's a good thing that tomorrow is our wholesaler's delivery day. We're running low on so many things."

"Even cocoa to make chocolate everything," Charlotte said.

"We can't have that," I said. "Chocolate is our business."

"I could stay up and help you out more," Charlotte said. Even as she said this I could see her eyes drooping closed. She had been up since the wee hours of the morning and would have to get up at the same time the next day. I couldn't ask her to stay up with me, especially after she and *Maami* had made all the toffee I would need to put my rabbit together.

"No need," I said. "It's just a matter of carving the Rice Krispies treats you made and assembling all the pieces now. I shouldn't be up too late."

Maami patted my hand. "We know you could use the help, and it is our job to help each other."

I hugged her. "You both go to bed. I'm going to work for an hour or so and then head home myself."

My grandmother's brow wrinkled. "Why don't you spend the night here? It's very late, and I don't like the idea of you going back to that house all by yourself." She frowned. Although she would never say it, I think my grandmother was disappointed when I moved out of the candy shop. I think in her mind I should have lived there as long as I worked at the shop just as she and my grandfather always had, but I couldn't do that. I was still a city girl at heart and I needed my space. I always needed a place to plug in my hair dryer. Neither of those things were options in my grandmother's apartment over the shop.

I wrinkled my nose. I'd spent too many nights sleeping on the floor or on a small cot when I shared a room with Charlotte. I wasn't eager to repeat that experience. Besides, I needed a good night's rest too. I didn't know what else Margot had in store for me at Easter Days. I knew better than to think the giant toffee rabbit would be the end of it.

I shook my head. "I don't mind. Really. I worked

more late nights that I can count back in New York."

My grandmother looked like she wanted to argue with me more over this, but Charlotte stifled a yawn. "Well, good night, Bailey. I'm eager to see the rabbit in the morning."

"Me too," I said with a laugh. "I hope I can pull it off."

My grandmother reached out and squeezed my hand. "You will do well, but I will pray to the Lord to give you energy to sustain you through this night of labor."

"*Danki, Maami*," I said.

She smiled. "You are a *gut* girl. How blessed am I to have you and Charlotte here to help me with the shop. Your *daadi* didn't know what would happen to me or the shop if something happened to him, and I know it worried him. He would be so pleased to see what you have done. He would be so pleased that you are still able to live your New York dreams and help me too. The Lord had been very *gut* to us."

I swallowed the lump in my throat. "He's been very good," I said, and for the first time, I almost believed it. I didn't have the unshakable faith of my grandparents. My only exposure to God had been through them. After growing up Amish, religion was a topic that my father refused to talk about. The longer I was in Holmes County, the more I realized all that he'd rejected when

191

he left. I know I would have not been born if he'd remained Amish since my mother wasn't Amish, but at times, I could see the pain on my grandmother's face when she talked about my father and how he fell away from the faith.

I handed Nutmeg to Charlotte. The cat usually slept in her room at night now that I lived outside the candy shop.

My grandmother tucked a lock of my hair behind my ear just as she had when I was a little girl. "I know that it is not Amish of me to say, but I am very proud of you, and your *daadi* was so very proud when he was alive too."

I watched my grandmother and Charlotte shuffle up the stairs to bed. It had been a trying day. Now all I had to do was construct a giant rabbit. Should be easy, I thought, and then I laughed at myself.

I pushed through the swinging door into the kitchen. My grandmother and Charlotte hadn't been kidding. They had made a *lot* of toffee. There was toffee in metal trays on every surface of the kitchen. There was even a tray precariously balanced on the edge of a mixer. I moved that off and set it on one of the two empty stools. I had hoped to sketch out my plans for the rabbit, but it was clear to me I wouldn't be doing that in the kitchen.

Earlier, I had carved the rabbit's ears and paws out of solid white chocolate. Now, I needed to tackle the giant Rice Krispies treat balls that Charlotte had made for the head and the body of the rabbit. The three Rice Krispies treat balls were each the size of a college dorm room refrigerator. If they were stacked one on top of the other, they would easily be six feet. The rabbit's ears were two feet themselves. Instead of a six-foot rabbit, I would give Margot an eight-foot one and the platform the rabbit would be standing on would add another foot. The rabbit would appear to be eight feet tall. It would easily top eight feet. Go big or go home. I started to feel excited about the project and it reminded me of my old competition days for JP Chocolates.

But to carve the Rice Krispies balls, cover them with white-chocolate fondant, and assemble them, I would need a lot more space. I decided the front room was my only option. I rolled up my sleeves and got to work. The first thing I did was move all my pieces and the tools I would need to the front room. Then I covered one of the small dining tables with wax paper, set one of the Rice Krispies balls on top of it, and started to carve out the lower half of a very large Easter bunny.

While I worked, I tried to push thoughts of murder out of my head, but they continued to creep in. Where had Eli Raber been today when I went to his farm? At the Beiler farm, where his girlfriend was, or at the home of one of his sisters? I didn't know why it bothered me so much that Eli hadn't been there.

And then there was the issue of Zimmerman and the lily of the valley. It took all my will power not to call Aiden and ask him what he'd learned from the botanist when the murder weapon was brought up.

I sighed. Margot wanted a toffee rabbit, and I would give her just that. There would be toffee all over the rabbit, but I decided to use broken bits of toffee to mimic the bunny's fur. My grandmother and Charlotte had saved me a lot of time by making the toffee, and I was grateful for that. I knew I would have to make it up to them. I couldn't wait to tell them about the trip I was planning, for them to go to Pinecraft.

Tap, tap, tap came on the window. I dropped my carving knife on the floor. I froze, wondering if I had just woken my grandmother and Charlotte upstairs. There was silence, and I gave a sigh of relief. They both needed their rest, just as I did. I glanced at the long, plain clock on the wall. It was after midnight. I hadn't realized I'd been working so long.

Tap, tap, tap came again.

I scooped up my sketchbook and the lantern and looked out the window. There was a dark shape there. My breath caught. Then, the form stood in the light from the gas lamppost. It was Deputy Little. The young deputy knocked on the pane again and, when he saw me sitting there, he waved.

I sighed and got up. I went to the door and unlocked it. "Little, what on earth are you doing here?"

"I'm glad I found you, Bailey," he said, slightly out of breath. "When I couldn't find you at your house, I got worried."

"Worried why? Why are you looking for me?"

"Deputy Brody was called away to Millersburg on a suspected robbery, so he asked me to check on you. I've been looking for you all over the village."

"It's most likely I would be here."

"Yes." He nodded. "I should have thought of that. I just didn't think you would be here so late in the day. You keep cop hours at the candy shop?"

"Hardly," I said, since I knew the kind of hours that Aiden kept. I couldn't begin to compare my work schedule to his. It wasn't unusual for him to get multiple calls in the middle of the night, which meant he had to leave his warm bed to fight crime.

"Why did Aiden tell you to check on me?"

"The notes you gave him," he whispered. "He's worried that those notes you received might make you a target. He's very protective of you." His Adam's apple bobbed up and down as if he was embarrassed by his last statement.

195

"That's sweet of Aiden and you for coming out here to check on me, but as you can see, I'm fine. Besides, I don't have the notes any longer. Aiden does, so I can't be a target."

He looked as if he didn't believe me.

I smiled. "Thanks for stopping by, Little. You can report back to Aiden that I'm perfectly fine, and unless you have any ideas about how to create a giant rabbit out of toffee, I suggest you leave and attend to more pressing police business. If you stay here, I can guarantee I'll put you to work making candy rabbit fur."

He glanced at the table. "What are you doing?"

I told him about the giant white chocolate-and-toffee rabbit I planned to create.

He frowned. "That sounds complicated." He backed away as if he thought I'd be true to my threat about putting him to work. It was a wise move because I wasn't kidding.

"If you are all right," he said, "then, I'll be on my way."

I smiled, happy that I had successfully scared off the deputy. "I'm just fine, Little. Don't worry so much. You're too young for an ulcer."

His forehead creased. "Do you think I'm in danger of getting an ulcer?"

If anyone was, it would be Deputy Little, but I wasn't going to tell him that when he looked so horrified at the prospect. "I was just teasing."

He backed toward the door. "Okay," he said

as if he didn't quite believe me. "Deputy Brody isn't happy that you are mixed up in another investigation."

"To be honest, I'm not happy about it either," I said with a sigh.

He tipped his hat to me like a deputy would in the Old West and went out the door. I watched through the front window as he walked to his cruiser.

I sighed and turned back to make the giant rabbit.

Chapter 22

I yawned and stared at the giant bunny standing on a rolling flat in the middle of the front room of the shop.

Overall, it had been a good call to construct the rabbit in the front of the shop. All I would have to do now would be to roll it across the street in the morning with Emily's and Charlotte's help. The rabbit was lifelike and standing on its hind legs. I'd decided to go with a lifelike rabbit as opposed to a cartoon version because I thought it might be more palatable to the Amish.

The bunny stood eight feet high from the tip of its ears to its toes. The toffee fur idea had worked out beautifully. It looked like real rabbit fur, which was a good outcome since I didn't have any other ideas. I decided to lightly cover the rabbit in plastic, taking care not to mar its fur. I would try to get to the candy shop early the next morning, so we could move it out of the way before too many customers arrived. The rabbit took up quite a lot of floor space.

By the time I cleaned up the kitchen, made a few extra trays of candy to make up for all the time I had missed in the shop that day, and set the chairs upside down on the café tables, it was well after midnight. Every muscle in my body ached as I walked out through the front door and locked it behind me. Part of me was sorely tempted to take my grandmother's advice and sleep at the shop for the night, but my warm bed was calling me.

I wrapped my arms around myself when I went outside. I had a long-sleeved shirt on, but no jacket. It was still April, and the days had been warming in the last few weeks. I inhaled the scent of the apple blossoms from the trees and the hyacinths that bloomed on the square. The rabbits across the street all appeared to be sleeping, from what I could see by the lampposts' dim light. I almost went over to check on them but thought better of it. If the bunnies were sleeping, I didn't want to wake them. I walked back to my little house through the quiet streets of Harvest.

Just as I had when I'd arrived at the candy shop that night, I heard a scraping sound behind me.

I stopped, and the sound stopped too. I began to walk and the sound returned, but much more faintly this time. I paused in the middle of the sidewalk again and looked behind me. There was nothing there, and the sound was gone too. I started walking, and the sound didn't return. I shook it off as nothing, or maybe it was one of those giant raccoons. My mind was playing tricks on me because I was tired and because I had only been back in Ohio for a day and was tangled up in a murder again.

Finally, I reached my little house. I walked up the drive to the back door. I usually entered the house through the kitchen. I walked into the backyard and was passing the unattached garage when a hand sprang out from seemingly nowhere and spun me around. Before I knew what was happening, my face was pressed up against the rough wood siding of the garage. "I want those notes back. Where are they?"

I was pressed up so hard against the rough siding, I couldn't talk.

"Where are the notes?" the raspy voice asked again.

"I don't have them," I gasped.

"Don't lie to me."

I couldn't breathe. "I . . ." The man was pushing so hard against me that I thought my ribs might crack. I couldn't get the words out.

"What?" the voice wanted to know.

"—Can't talk," I rasped.

He loosened the pressure on me just a bit.

I coughed. "I really don't have them."

"I don't believe you."

"It's true. I gave them to the police."

"You were instructed not to give them to the police. They were never supposed to go to the police."

"I'm not that great at following directions." I pushed back, and immediately regretted it because he tweaked the arm that he was bending behind my back just a little bit more. Pain radiated out from my elbow.

"You get those notes back from the police or you will be sorry."

"How am I supposed to do that? They are part of a police investigation now, part of the evidence."

"You're a smart girl. You'll think of something." He yanked my arm again and I bit down on my lip to keep from crying out in pain. "Don't make me come here again."

"Even if I got them back, I don't know who you are. How would I even give them to you?"

He laughed. "You think you can trick me into showing myself to you? How dumb do you think I am? You get the notes, and I will find you." He pressed hard on my back, pushing himself off me. "I want those notes. If you want your grandmother to remain in good health, you will get them for me."

"Bailey! Bailey King! Are you all right?" Penny's voice rang out in the night.

The man pushed me hard against the garage, and I thought my ribs would crack.

"Bailey!"

Then, just when I thought my back would snap in two, the pressure ended and the man was gone.

I turned around and slid down the side of the garage. I cradled my arm against my body. Would he really hurt *Maami*? I shivered. Why wouldn't he? He'd attacked me tonight, and presumably, he was also the one who'd murdered Stephen Raber. I didn't think he would have many qualms.

"Bailey!" Penny called again, a little more urgently.

I saw a swath of light move across the back-yard.

"Over here," I croaked.

The flashlight beam hit me directly in the eyes. "What on earth are you doing on the ground like that, girl?"

My entire body shook, and I started to cry.

Chapter 23

"Oh, honey," Penny said, kneeling in front of me. "What happened to you?"

"A man jumped me."

"Jumped you? Here? In Harvest?" she said with disbelief. "No one gets jumped in Harvest. This isn't the big city."

"But it happened," I said, trying to stand up.

Penny helped me to my feet. "I'll call the police."

"No," I croaked, willing my voice to go back to normal. "I'll call Aiden. The man is gone now, and it would be better to call Aiden directly."

She clicked her tongue as if she wasn't happy with this idea but picked up my purse and helped me to the back door of the house. When my hands were shaking too badly to unlock the door, Penny took the keys from my hand and unlocked it for me.

We stepped into the kitchen, and I closed and locked the door behind us. Puff hopped over to me.

Penny clicked her tongue again. "You go sit in the living room, and I will bring you some tea and an ice pack."

"The tea is—" I started to tell her where the tea was in the kitchen.

"Hush," she reprimanded. "Go sit down and call Aiden. I know my way around the kitchen."

I nodded and shuffled into the next room. After I settled on the loveseat, I made the call. "Aiden," was all I managed to say.

"Where are you?"

"At home."

"Are you safe?" he asked. He sounded fully awake even though I knew I must have woken him up.

My voice hitched with a sob before I could smooth it over.

"I'll be there in two minutes."

"Y-you don't have to come here. I can tell you what happened over the phone."

"I'll be there in two minutes," he repeated, and ended the call.

I struggled to my feet because I knew Aiden would be true to his word. My arm ached, but overall, I was physically all right. Emotionally, not so much. The threat against my grandmother had shaken me.

Penny bustled into the living room with Puff hopping behind her. She had a steaming teacup in one hand and dripping ice cubes wrapped in a dish rag in the other. She spun around as she looked for a place to set the teacup. The only table in my front room was the small dining table. She clicked her tongue and set it there. "I would like to put it closer to you, but it seems that I can't."

"The table is fine," I said.

"I looked in the freezer for some frozen peas or an ice pack to put on your face, but all I found was ice." She handed the dish rag of ice to me.

It dripped on my legs. "I haven't had time to go shopping since I got back from New York. I mean shopping other than for what Puff needed."

"Yes," she said. "I see the rabbit is well stocked now."

My arm throbbed, and the cheek that had been pressed up against the garage stung. I placed the ice on my cheek, hoping there wouldn't be a giant bruise or black eye on my face in the morning.

"Thank you, Penny, for everything."

"It's no trouble—it's the neighborly thing to do."

I adjusted the rag on my cheek and winced. "How did you know that I might be in trouble?"

She flushed. "Oh well, I'm a light sleeper, and I thought I saw some shadows out of the back window of my house."

So she had been watching my house. Maybe to see when I came home and what I was up to. That would bother me more if she hadn't just saved me from further injury or even being killed.

I heard Aiden before I saw him. He had his siren blaring as he came down the street. I stood up. I wanted to be the one to meet Aiden at the door. I didn't want the first person he saw to be Penny.

Aiden was making his way up the walk when I opened the door.

With no other greeting, he asked, "What happened to your cheek?"

I touched my cheek and felt the raw skin there. The skin was clammy and damp from the ice. "Is there a bruise?"

"It's all red. It looks like a rug burn."

I grimaced.

"Why are you wet?"

"Ice." I stepped back to let him inside the house.

"Deputy Brody, I'm so glad you're here," Penny said.

Aiden pulled up short when he saw Penny standing there.

"Aiden," I said. "This is my next-door neighbor Penny Lehman. She came to my aid tonight."

"Oh, it was just the neighborly thing to do," Penny said modestly, but she had her chin tilted up with pride. "I could tell that Bailey was in trouble, so of course, I came running."

Aiden looked from me to Penny and back again. "What happened exactly?"

Before I could answer, Penny said, "Why, didn't Bailey tell you that she was attacked! Right in her own backyard. A man jumped her!"

I inwardly groaned.

"Jumped her?" Aiden asked.

"People can get jumped in Holmes County just like any other place," I said.

"I know that," Aiden said quietly, and I shivered.

"Penny, did you see who attacked Bailey?"

She sighed. "I'm afraid not. I just heard a commotion from the backyard. The voices were low, but I had a sense there was trouble. Whoever it was ran away before I made it there with my flashlight."

Aiden nodded. "Thank you for all you did tonight. Bailey and I are both in your debt." He glanced at me, then back to Penny. "I think you should go home and rest after your ordeal. If it's all right with you, I'm going to send a deputy to your house."

"Oh," she said excitedly. "I'm happy to help any way that I can. I will go home and make some notes about the evening to avoid forgetting anything."

"Good plan," Aiden said in his most cop-like voice, and then to my great amazement, I watched as he trundled Penny out the door. He stood outside in my yard until he saw she'd made it safely inside her own house.

When we walked back into my living room, Aiden's face was stormy, and I knew I was in for an earful.

Aiden closed the front door. "Do you have a first-aid kit?"

I nodded. "It's under the sink in the bathroom." I started to get up from the loveseat.

"Sit down," he ordered.

"I can get it. I'm not helpless." I stood.

"No one said you were." He sighed. "Sit down, please. I'll go get it and you can tell me what happened while we get you fixed up."

I sat back down on the small loveseat with a *thud*. Normally, I would protest to prove how tough I was, but I had to admit I wasn't feeling all that tough at the moment. All I could think about was the threat against my grandmother and what might have happened if Penny hadn't investigated the noise. I jumped out of my seat and went to the window. How did I know the man was really gone and that he wasn't headed to Swissmen Sweets right that very moment to attack my grandmother?

I stepped away from the window. "Aiden!"

Aiden came back into the living room carrying the red first-aid kit. "What? Did something happen?"

"I hope not." I went on to tell him about the threat to my grandmother. "If I don't get those notes back from you, I know he'll hurt her."

"Bailey, you know I can't give you those notes back even if I wanted to. They are evidence in a homicide."

"But *Maami* . . ."

"We'll keep a close eye on your grandmother and you. Let's verify that she is all right. I'll send Little over there to be a night guard for her and Charlotte."

I frowned. "I know my grandmother, and I know

that she won't like having an *Englischer* who's practically a stranger in her home."

"Little can stay in the candy shop. If he's on guard, he shouldn't be sleeping in any case."

"I'm going with you if you plan to check on my grandmother tonight. I don't want you or Little scaring her or Charlotte. It would be better for me to go inside the shop first and make sure they are all right. I'm sure they're asleep."

Aiden nodded. "That's a good plan. Go pack a bag. I'll be waiting for you down here."

"Pack?" I asked.

"You're spending the night at Swissmen Sweets."

"But—"

"You're spending the night at Swissmen Sweets or you're spending the night with me. You aren't staying here alone."

Puff knocked into the boxes that corralled her in the kitchen as if she was pulling off a jail break. Maybe that was her plan.

"I'm not completely alone," I said, nodding in her direction.

"Rabbits don't count. You can't stay here because I would worry about you. I would stay with you here, but I never know when I will be called out. I don't have enough deputies to put one both here and at Swissmen Sweets." He pointed at my cheek. "And anyone who could do that to a woman can't be trusted."

"Puff has to come with me."

"I expected that," he said. "Now, pack up. Little should be at the candy shop by now."

"Tell him to wait outside until I get there. I don't want Charlotte and my grandmother to be upset," I said. I rubbed the back of my neck. This was one of the times when it would be much more helpful if my grandmother had a cell phone or even just a landline in her apartment. All it would take was one short phone call to verify that she was okay. Unfortunately, the only phone was in the candy shop and my grandmother turned the ringer off every night, so that it wouldn't wake them up. The only way to reach her and Charlotte at this late hour was to go into the shop. "It will take me three minutes to grab what I need," I said, heading to the stairs that led to my bedroom. "Can you pack up Puff's stuff?"

He blinked at me. "Puff has stuff?"

"You have no idea," I said as I ran up the steps.

Aiden insisted on carrying my overnight bag and Puff's overnight bag to his SUV while I carried the heavy rabbit out of the little house and locked the door behind us. It was close to two in the morning now, and the street was completely quiet. The house directly across from mine had one light on, and I saw the curtains move. I groaned. I had a feeling that my midnight escapade with the police would be the talk of the neighborhood. I hadn't known Penny long, but I sensed that she was going to love passing on every tiny detail. It was good that we were going to my grandmother's tonight. If not, she might hear about the attack through the Amish grapevine before I even had a chance to tell her myself.

Aiden put our bags in the back of the SUV. "You can put the bunny back there too."

I shook my head. "I'll hold her." I was comforted by Puff's warmth, and she seemed to be calmer settled in my arms.

Aiden didn't argue; he simply opened the front passenger door, and Puff and I took our seat.

To walk between my house and the candy shop took about twelve minutes. To drive there, it was about two or a little more if you got caught at the stop sign waiting for a buggy to cross before you turned onto Main Street. There were no buggies out tonight. All the Amish had long since gone to bed. It made me wonder if the person who'd attacked me was Amish or English. I knew it was a man by the feel of his body and his voice. I wished I had been able to turn my head just for a moment to catch a glimpse of him. I hated knowing that there was a faceless man out there lying in wait to catch me unawares again, or worse, my grandmother.

Aiden parked the car in front of the candy shop. "Stay put. I'll get the door for you."

I waited for Aiden and noticed that Little's cruiser was already there, but I didn't see the young police officer in the car. He might have been close by, but it was so dark at this time of night it was hard to see anything that wasn't directly under the gas lamppost.

Aiden opened my door just as there was a loud crack from the direction of Swissmen Sweets.

"Was that a gunshot?" I yelled.

"Stay here!" Aiden slammed the door closed on me and ran toward my shop with his gun drawn. I could see him speaking into his cell phone as he went. I knew he must be calling for backup.

I dropped Puff on Aiden's driver's seat and said, "Stay here," just as Aiden had to me. She flattened her body onto the seat. Clearly, the rabbit had no interest in being a hero. All I could think about was *Maami* and Charlotte. I knew that the shot must have woken them up and they would be terrified. Unless they were . . . I couldn't even let myself complete the thought. They were fine. Scared, I was certain, but fine.

I ran toward the shop. All the lights came on in the front room. Through the large display window, I saw Charlotte and *Maami* in their nightclothes, and Aiden and Deputy Little.

As far as I could tell, no one else was in the room, and Aiden no longer had his firearm out. I opened the door and stepped inside just in time to hear Aiden say, "Good job, Little, you shot the chocolate rabbit dead."

I turned to the chocolate bunny and saw the right side of his face was gone.

Chapter 24

I stared at the fractured head of the rabbit and spotted where its right ear used to be. "You shot my toffee rabbit?"

Little looked as if he was about to cry. "I came through the back of the shop and saw it in the middle of the front room. I thought it was an intruder and it wouldn't respond to any of my commands to get on the floor."

"Maybe because it's made out of sugar," I said. "It doesn't speak English."

"Bailey," Aiden quietly admonished.

"Aiden, that could have been my grandmother or Charlotte. They could have been killed."

Little turned a sickly shade of green when I said that, and Aiden pressed his lips together. Aiden knew I was right.

"I didn't know what else to do. Deputy Brody said that the candy shop had been threatened. I thought this was the intruder he was expecting."

"So you shot it?" I cried. I still couldn't believe that Little could be that stupid. Didn't they teach officers to shoot as a last resort?

Little licked his lips. "I couldn't find the light switch to verify who it was."

I would give him that there weren't many light switches in the shop. That was on purpose because it was an Amish business. There was one by the stairway leading up to my grandmother's apartment, so that she could turn the lights off as she went upstairs, and there was one in the kitchen. But in my mind, that still wasn't an excuse to blow the head off my toffee bunny. "So, it's better to shoot first and ask questions later?"

"We are going to have to remove the bullet from the wall," Aiden said. "Any time a deputy uses his firearm, we have to gather the bullet for evidence and file a report." He glanced at Little before he walked over to the wall and started to cut the bullet out of the wood with his pocket-knife.

Little folded his arms as if he suddenly felt a chill, and I felt a little bad for yelling at him. "I know it was an accident, Little."

He gave me a small smile.

I rubbed my forehead. "Margot is going to freak out."

Maami patted my hand. "Charlotte and I will help you fix the rabbit. She'll never have to know. Among the three of us we can get him put back together before morning."

"But you need your sleep. You and Charlotte have only three hours before you have to get up to make candies for the shop," I said.

"I could never get back to sleep now," Charlotte said. Her eyes were as big as dinner plates.

I grimaced. I felt the same way. "All right. I could use the help."

My grandmother smiled. "*Gut.* And while we work, you can tell us why the deputy came into the candy shop and what has happened to your cheek."

I was afraid she was going to ask me that. "Okay, but first I have to get Puff from Aiden's car. We're sleeping over for the night, assuming that we sleep at all."

Aiden removed the bullet from the wall and tucked it in an evidence bag. He put the knife back in his pocket. Little watched him with more than a little fear on his face. Aiden noticed and said, "It will be all right, Little. No one was hurt, and that's the most important thing."

Little swallowed, and his Adam's apple bobbed up and down. He was clearly relieved. Aiden was his idol, and he was the last person Little would ever want to disappoint.

I went out the door, and Aiden followed me to his departmental SUV to collect my bags and the rabbit. His face was cast in shadow by the gas lampposts that marched up and down Main Street. "You will have to come down to the station tomorrow morning."

I pulled Puff out of the car and then I straightened up and turned to him, holding the rabbit to my chest. "Why?"

He cocked his head, and I could tell that his dimple was about to appear in his cheek despite the seriousness of everything that had happened

215

that night. "Bailey, you were attacked. You have to file a report. You're lucky that I didn't drag you to the hospital to have you checked out to make sure you're all right."

"I am all right."

He sighed. "I believe you, but you still have to file a report because if I catch the man who hurt you, I plan to throw him in jail and lose the key. Also, you have to realize that whoever did this is most likely our killer, and if that is the case this is more evidence against him."

I hadn't thought of that. "All right. I'll stop by in the morning. Will you be there?"

"If at all possible, I will try to be there when you come in."

I nodded. It was the best I could hope for. Aiden never knew what his workday looked like. Every one of them was a complete surprise. He told me once it was the boring days that he loved best, when the most he had to do was give a few speeding tickets to motorists, but it seemed to me that those boring days were becoming far less frequent.

Aiden reached forward and scratched the top of Puff's head. The rabbit closed her eyes and leaned in to his caress. It appeared that I wasn't the only female who was enamored of the handsome sheriff's deputy, and I was certain there were others too. "I'm going back to your house to take a look around the garage to see if there are any foot-

216

prints or if your attacker left any evidence behind. One of my crime scene guys will meet me there."

"You know Penny will be up watching you."

He smiled. "I don't doubt it, but this is one of those times when I'm grateful for a nosy neighbor." He moved his hand from the top of Puff's head to my cheek just below the scrape that the rough garage siding had left there. "If anything had happened to you, Bailey, I would never get over it. I—I care about you a lot."

"And I care about you," I said with a tightness in my chest. For a moment, just the briefest moment, I thought he was going to say that he loved me. The problem was I couldn't be sure I was ready to say "I love you" back.

He dropped his hand and leaned forward, giving me a quick kiss on the lips. "Let's get you back inside. You have an Easter bunny to bring back from the dead."

"I'm afraid I do," I said.

Aiden dropped the bag just inside the door to Swissmen Sweets and then left to meet up with the crime scene tech. Little settled at one of the small café tables in the front of the shop. I saw that my grandmother and Charlotte had made him as comfortable as possible with his own pot of coffee and a large chunk of fudge to keep him occupied.

Maami rolled up the sleeves of her housecoat. "It's time for damage control." Her comment made Charlotte and me laugh, which I think had been the whole idea.

It took what remained of the night, but Charlotte and *Maami* were true to their word—we got the rabbit put back together again. Thankfully we had just enough white chocolate left to fix the fracture in its head and for me to carve a brand-new ear for the giant sculpture. Charlotte and my grandmother had made more than enough toffee, so after we replaced the toffee fur on the rabbit, you would never know that it had been shot.

The wall to the right of the stairway leading up to the apartment was another story. There was a crack in the trim from the bullet's impact, but my grandmother assured me that a carpenter from her district would be able to fix it.

Around five in the morning, I shooed my grand-mother and Charlotte upstairs to catch a few hours' sleep.

Maami shook her head. "You need rest after what you've been through."

"You two have worked so hard since Charlotte and I got home," I said. "It's my turn to mind the shop. Besides, I'm too wired to sleep. The least I can do is get the candies ready for the day."

"If you're sure," Charlotte said with a yawn.

"I am," I said. "Off to bed with both of you."

It took a little more coaxing, but finally I was able to convince them to go to bed. I knew they really must be tired to go at all. When they left me alone in the kitchen, I fell onto one of the backless stools, physically exhausted but mentally wide awake. I listened to the creaks as the old building settled, and any sound from the outside made me jump. I realized that I was more shaken up over the attack than I had let on. Little was in the front room of the shop, standing guard over us for the night. I didn't want to go out there and tell him how scared I was. Because I had a feeling that the young cop wouldn't know how to handle my fear, and he would most likely call Aiden. Aiden had enough to worry about. He didn't need to add my nerves to his list.

I closed my eyes and repeated the different kinds of chocolate, which I had memorized as a young chocolatier at JP Chocolates. The list had become a bit of a mantra for me when I was stressed: "White chocolate, milk chocolate, dark chocolate, sweet chocolate, semisweet chocolate, bittersweet chocolate, cocoa, couverture, vermicelli." I let out a breath. "Okay, King," I told myself. "Get to work. Nothing distracts you like work."

There was a ring and buzzing, and my eyes flew open. It took me a moment to realize where I was.

My unhurt left cheek lay on the stainless steel island in the middle of the candy shop's kitchen. There was a bowl of buttercream in front of me. Some of the mixture oozed over the side and onto the island. I touched my head and realized it had oozed into my hair. I must have laid my head on the island for just a moment and fallen asleep.

I picked up my phone, which thankfully had survived the buttercream attack. " 'Lo?"

"Bai, are you still in bed? It's after eight." Cass's voice was accusatory. Anyone who worked at a candy shop knew about the early hours.

"Not in bed. I never went to bed."

"What's with the all-nighter? I doubt there was some kind of Amish rager that you had to stay up for."

"It's a long story," I said.

"I'm free for the next seven minutes. Hit me with it."

I sighed and gave Cass the short version of the last few days, ending with my attack in my own yard.

"Where the heck was Hot Cop? I told that boy to protect you! I trusted him."

"Aiden came the moment I called him."

She grunted as if she wasn't quite happy with this. "I'm going to text Hot Cop and tell him to keep an eye on you."

"Please don't do that. Aiden has more than enough on his plate."

"You can't stop me. If anything happens to you, he's the one that I will hold accountable."

I prayed nothing would ever happen to me because I had seen Cass many times when she was mad. It was a sight to behold. Thankfully, she had never been angry at me, at least not yet.

"Promise me you will be careful." Her tone turned serious. "I need you to be careful."

"I will," I promised.

"Good. My seven minutes are up." And with that she ended the call.

I did my best to wipe the buttercream from my hair, but I think I only made it worse. I stumbled through the swinging door to the front room of the shop. Little was gone, but my grandmother and Charlotte were moving around the room, filling shelves and cases with the candies that I had made throughout the night.

I blinked. Both of them appeared to be impossibly well rested even though I knew they hadn't got much more sleep than I had.

"Bailey," *Maami* said. "We're so glad you are finally awake. We saw you sleeping there and thought it was best to leave you alone. You looked so peaceful, and you did a wonderful job with the candies, my dear. You must have been inspired. Some of the chocolates you made look like little works of art."

"I tasted one of the peanut-butter-fudge lambs you made, and they are delicious. Can you teach me how to weave a chocolate basket?" Charlotte asked. "That looks like it's fun to do."

I rubbed my eyes. "It is fun to do, and of course, I'll show you just as soon as I figure out what day it is."

"Go to bed, Bailey. You did a great job getting the candies ready for the day." My grandmother studied me. "I can tell you worked very hard last night. You need your rest. Everything you made is wonderful."

I touched my hair, forgetting the buttercream tangled in it. "Not everything. I can think of a bowl of buttercream we can't use."

"One lost bowl of buttercream won't make a bit of difference. Emily will be here soon to help us."

"But what about the toffee rabbit? I have to take it over to the square," I protested.

"Go to bed, Bailey," *Maami* said, her voice sounding as stern as I had ever heard it. "The toffee rabbit and Margot Rawlings can wait a little while longer."

I wanted to argue with her but couldn't work up the energy to do it.

"Charlotte, help Bailey to bed," my grandmother directed.

Two hours later my cell phone alarm went off. I groaned as I rolled onto my hurt shoulder. I rolled to the other side and rubbed the abrasion on my cheek onto the pillow. If I had forgotten what had happened the night before, my aches and pains certainly came as a reminder. I moved my leg, and my foot hit something solid at the bottom of the bed. I sat up and saw a white and orange ball of fluff lying there. Puff's ears popped out from the pile of fur, and Nutmeg raised his head and began to groom the bunny's cheek. And here I had been thinking that the bunny and the cat wouldn't get along. Puff was twice the size of the little cat, so maybe that's what made Nutmeg decide she was a friend, not prey. "At least you two are one less problem to worry about," I muttered.

I showered, washing the buttercream out of my hair, and got ready for the day. Even just those few hours of sleep made me feel much better.

Hair still wet because there was no hair dryer in my grandmother's home, I went downstairs and found Emily wandering around the front of the shop looking under the tables and around the side of the counter.

I smiled at her. "If you're looking for Nutmeg, he's upstairs bunny-sitting Puff. I think the two of them are best friends. You are welcome to go up there and see him. Last I saw, they were in Charlotte's room."

"You have Stephen Raber's rabbit?" she asked, and the sunlight coming in through the front window of the shop reflected off her honey-gold hair. Emily was one of the most beautiful women I had ever seen, and since she'd married Daniel she had a happy glow around her that made her even more beautiful.

I nodded. "Did Daniel tell you I stopped by your farm?"

"*Ya*, but he said nothing of the rabbit." She cocked her head. "And why is there a giant chocolate bunny in the middle of the shop, and what happened to your cheek?"

I touched my cheek and winced. My sad attempt to cover the abrasion with makeup clearly hadn't worked. "I'll tell you while you and Charlotte help me move the rabbit to the square."

Twenty minutes later, Emily and I carefully rolled the toffee rabbit out of Swissmen Sweets while Charlotte followed behind us carrying the head. Charlotte held the door as Emily and I guided the rabbit to the curb. With a light *thump* we were about to roll the platform from the sidewalk to the street when a horse and buggy went by. The buggy driver stuck his head out of the buggy and stared at us.

"Move along," Charlotte said. "This is just another normal day in Harvest."

I laughed because she was right. I thought New York had oddities, but that was before I moved to Amish Country.

The buggy passed, and we bounced across the street.

"This is a really bad idea," Emily said.

I glanced back at her and she was chewing on her lip. "Don't worry—we're almost there."

"Careful. Watch out for the horse droppings," Charlotte warned.

I wrinkled my nose. The last thing I needed would be to roll over that.

"Should we be concerned that no one on

the square is staring at us like we're crazy?" Charlotte asked.

"I think they are just used to weird things happening since Bailey moved here," Emily said.

"Gee, thanks," I teased.

Our progress was painfully slow, but we finally made it to the opposite curb. "Now what do we do?" I asked.

The curb was only four inches off the ground, but the rabbit and the rolling platform easily weighed over one hundred pounds. I doubted that the three of us could lift it up.

Apparently seeing our dilemma, a group of Amish men who were setting up for Easter Days took mercy on us and lifted the rabbit up onto the curb.

I frowned. "The platform won't roll on the grass, so we will have to carry it over to where Juliet is standing."

About twenty yards away Juliet, holding a tired-looking Jethro under her arm, waved at me from a spot next to the white gazebo. On the grass next to her was a raised platform that came nearly two feet off the ground. I had called her earlier that morning and said we needed to borrow a small riser from the church. I was relieved to see that she'd come through with exactly what I wanted. Now, it was just a matter of getting the toffee rabbit over there.

"It's not a problem," said one of the Amish men

who had red hair and no beard. "We can carry it there. You ladies stand back."

"We can help," I said.

He shook his head. "You just make sure that the path is clear. We only want to do this once." He said something in Pennsylvania Dutch to the other men, and together they lifted the giant rabbit off the rolling platform and painstakingly carried it over to the still platform. They set it delicately in the middle of the platform and turned the rabbit so it faced Main Street.

"Thank you so much," I said to the men. "I don't know what we would have done without your help."

"It was no trouble." He winked at Charlotte, who blushed. This made the man smile as he went back to work.

Before I could comment on the redheaded man, Juliet set Jethro on the ground and clapped her hands together. "Oh, Bailey," she said in her sweet Southern drawl. "It's such a vision. You have a real gift."

"It will look even better when its head is attached." I climbed up on the platform, Charlotte handed me the rabbit head, and I slid it over the wooden dowel rod that I had imbedded in the middle of the rabbit's throat to hold the head in place. I stood back. It didn't look half bad. All I had to do was add some pieces of toffee around the seam to hide it. The rabbit stood proudly at eight feet tall. Charlotte ran back to the shop to grab the toffee we would need.

I smiled. "Thank you, Juliet."

At my feet, Jethro sniffed the base of the sculpture, which made me just a tiny bit nervous. When it really came down to it, I didn't trust the pig much. He was a troublemaker through and through, and he would get away with a lot less if he wasn't so darn cute. He wiggled his tail and walked behind Juliet.

"You will have the most glorious desserts at your wedding."

I blinked at her. "Did you say my wedding?"

She smiled. "You don't have to be coy with me, my dear. We're practically family now. You can tell me whatever plans you have with my sweet boy."

"Uh," I said, and looked around, hoping Emily would lend me a hand, but she had already run back to Swissmen Sweets. Smart girl. I wished I had made a quick getaway too.

Instead of seeing my Amish friend, I spotted Eli Raber refilling food dishes and water in the rabbit pen. I was relieved to see him. Part of me had wondered if he'd left the village altogether after he visited me at my home with that stack of threatening notes.

Charlotte returned with the toffee.

"Thanks. Between the two of us, we should be able to do this quick." Quick was what I wanted because I needed to escape Juliet and her wedding talk.

"There's still time for a summer wedding," Juliet went on to say as I set toffee into the rabbit's neck. "Reverend Brook is a very busy man, but Aiden is an upstanding member of the church. He would be able to find the time to squeeze your wedding in. After the wedding, of course, you will have to join the church. It's best for a couple to attend church together."

I was only half listening to Juliet because I noticed that Eli wasn't alone tending to the rabbits. There was an Amish man and a young Amish woman with him. I guessed that she was close to Eli's age. I couldn't help but wonder if this was the girl he was courting. She didn't look particularly comfortable around him, but that wasn't unusual with Amish courting couples out in public. They were being watched by this district very carefully to see if they were a good match. Anyone would be nervous under that kind of scrutiny. I knew I would be.

The girl was very pretty. Tall, a bit taller than I, and I was five nine. She stood very straight and her dark hair was tied back into the traditional Amish bun at the nape of her neck. A small white prayer cap was pinned to the top of her head. A wayward strand of hair fell over her brow as she bent down to fill the rabbit water dishes with a watering can.

I put the final piece of toffee on the rabbit and stepped back.

"It looks perfect, Bailey," Charlotte said. "Like a real rabbit."

I handed her the toffee tray. "Thanks. Can you take this back to the shop?"

She glanced over at Eli and smiled at me knowingly.

"Bailey," Juliet said. "Are you even listening to me about the wedding?"

"Yes, Juliet," I said.

Charlotte chuckled as she walked back to the shop. I think she might have been enjoying hearing Juliet pester me about marrying Aiden.

Juliet smoothed the sleeve of her pink-and-green polka-dotted wrap dress. "Have you thought about a wedding party yet?"

"Wedding party?" I squeaked. "Not at all." This was the truth. I hadn't thought of a wedding yet either, but I didn't want to completely ruin her day. "Juliet, can we talk about this later? There's someone I need to speak to."

"I'm starting to think you don't want to talk about the wedding, Bailey!" she called after me.

I didn't bother to reply.

Chapter 25

"Eli?" I said as I approached Stephen's son.

The young Amish man looked up at me from where he was crouched in the pen filling the last few remaining food bowls.

He stood up. "You told the police about the notes."

"I told you that I would," I said.

"Now, there is no way out of this."

"No way out of what?"

The Amish man whom I had seen with Eli earlier stepped over to where we stood. "Is there anything else you would like Katey and me to do, Eli?"

"*Nee*, but *danki*. You have been a great help. My father would have been so pleased to see his neighbors helping like this."

"It's our pleasure," the man said, and he glanced back at the young Amish woman standing a few feet away. She had a tote bag over her shoulder and a book clenched to her chest. Her round glasses perched on the end of her nose. She could not have looked more uncomfortable if she tried. The man studied me. "Who are you?" His question was blunt, which wasn't unusual for the Amish, who weren't fans of idle talk.

"Bailey King. I run Swissmen Sweets across the street from here with my grandmother."

He nodded. "I heard there was an *Englisch* granddaughter who had come to stay."

"And you are?" I asked, mimicking the Amish directness.

"Jud Beiler."

I swallowed. Beiler. He had to be the Beiler whose tractor was vandalized the day before. I shot a glance at Katey. That must mean that Katey *was* the girl that Eli was courting, the one he trampled all over Zimmerman's wildflowers to reach.

Katey stared down at her feet as if making eye contact with me was just too painful. I thought there was something more happening here than the general Amish shyness around strangers.

I turned back to her father. "I was sorry to hear about what happened to your tractor," I said.

"How did you know about that?" His voice was sharp.

His harsh reaction surprised me. "You know how people talk in this village, and there are people in and out of the candy shop all the time telling us the news in the community." For some reason, I didn't want to tell him that I had heard it from the crime scene tech. I didn't want the Amish to think the sheriff's department gossiped about their affairs. Then, they would be even less likely to call the police for help.

He scowled.

I glanced at Eli. "I still have Puff." Even as

231

I said this, my heart ached just a little. There was something in me that didn't like the idea of giving Puff back to Eli. At least not giving her back until I knew she would be well cared for. The rabbits I had seen at Raber's Rabbits had been all right, but I was concerned for Puff to be there alone so often. She was a special bunny and needed extra care, and I thought tearing her away from Nutmeg might upset her. Inwardly, I rolled my eyes. Who was I kidding? I had grown attached to the white cotton ball.

Eli flushed. "I can't take her today."

"That's all right," I said quickly. I wondered if the relief showed in my voice. "I could keep her if you want. . . ."

Eli appeared pained. "*Nee*. I will take the rabbit when Easter Days are over."

I frowned and told myself to worry about giving Puff back later.

Beiler looked me up and down, and I had the feeling that he was regarding my English clothing with disapproval. "I knew your grandfather. He was a *gut* man."

"Thank you. Are you in the same district?" I asked.

He shook his head. "*Nee*. We are in Eli's district. I respect your family, but their bishop is far too liberal." He said this as if he had a bad taste in his mouth. "My daughter and I are here today to help Eli with the rabbits after the loss of his father. Our families are neighbors."

The girl flipped through her book, and her father frowned. She must have noticed because she snapped the book closed.

"Are you a farmer too?" I asked.

He shook his head. "We grow vegetables, but I'm a carpenter by trade. I sell furniture to the stores that cater to *Englischers*. I can set my own hours that way, which is why we are able to be here today."

"It's very kind of you to help your friend," I said.

"Eli's more than a friend. Katey, my daughter, and Eli are set to marry in the summer. We have been waiting for this union for a long time. I'm sorry that Stephen won't be here to see it."

I glanced at Katey again, and a strange look passed over the young Amish woman's face. She looked down at her book again as if to hide her reaction. Eli smiled at her, clearly not seeing her odd expression. It could be just me, but I didn't think Katey was as enthusiastic about their marriage as he was.

I turned back to Jud. "You know the family for a long time?"

Jud nodded. "I knew Stephen when we were children. We ran around together." He laughed. "We had some wild days during *rumspringa*, but we both put that behind us to do the right thing and be baptized." When he said this, he looked at his daughter again, and annoyance crossed his creased and suntanned face.

If Jud had been Stephen's friend while they were in *rumspringa*, he might also know what Stephen had done to receive those threatening notes. I wanted to ask him about the notes, but now wasn't a good time. The green was filling up with English and Amish volunteers to set up for Easter Days. I didn't know if the man who'd attacked me last night was among them. I shivered to think that man could be here. He could be any one of them.

As usual Margot had no shortage of volunteers. I really thought she was wasting her talents in our little village. She should recruit for the US Army or the Catholic Church so that there was never a shortage of soldiers or priests. I was certain they would have far more than they needed under her watch.

I was searching my mind for a way to bring up the notes without being overheard when I heard Juliet call my name. She waved at me from beside the toffee rabbit. Margot Rawlings stood next to her looking my creation up and down with a critical eye.

"It looks as if Margot would like to talk to you," Eli said.

Probably so, I thought forlornly.

Juliet hurried over to me. "Bailey, Margot wants to speak to you about the rabbit you made." She pulled up short. "Oh!" Juliet clasped her hands.

"Look at all those adorable rabbits. Jethro just loves those little animals." Before anyone could stop her, she set the pig inside the pen with the rabbits. "Go on, sweetie. Play with the bunnies."

One of the smaller rabbits jumped toward him. Jethro scurried to the middle of the pen to get away. That's when he realized his mistake. He was much farther away from any hope of escape from the pen, unless one of us went in there after him. I wasn't willing to do that. The bunnies were harmless. I was pretty sure, mostly sure. But in my opinion, one or two bunnies were cute. Thirty bunnies were intimidating. I was sort of like Jethro in this regard.

Jethro stared at the cluster of rabbits all around him. I wouldn't be the least bit surprised if he passed out from terror.

"Juliet, I don't think Jethro likes being in there," I said.

She waved away my concern. "Don't be silly. He loves being around animals of any kind. You know the friendship he had with Melchior, the camel that was here at Christmas."

I didn't think it was fair to compare one camel to a pile of rabbits. I had a feeling Jethro would agree with me on that point. The polka-dotted pig stood in the middle of the rabbits with a look of panic on his face.

"Aren't they adorable together?" Juliet removed her phone from the pocket of her pink polka-dotted dress. Juliet almost always wore polka dots to match Jethro. She said it was part of their "look." She had become even more obsessed with her pig when Jethro signed on to be in my cooking shows.

She snapped photos of Jethro and the rabbits, and one of the white bunnies walked over to the little pig and snuggled next to him. This seemed to calm Jethro, and he lay on the ground. Moments later he had five bunnies snuggled up next to him. "Oh! This will be perfect for his Instagram!" Juliet exclaimed, and snapped more shots. "We just started. Cass said it would be a good idea to build his social media platform."

I suppressed a laugh. The last time Cass was in Harvest, she had appointed herself as the pig's talent agent. Truth be told, I wasn't the least bit surprised to hear that Jethro had an Instagram account. I would have been more surprised if Juliet said he *didn't* have one.

Juliet noticed me staring at them and smiled. "We're getting Jethro more social media outlets, so that he can get more acting jobs." She frowned. "I'm not saying that your show isn't a good start, but Jethro has so much to offer. He has so much star power to lend to companies and causes. The sky's the limit. Cass said he really has the potential to be in the movies." She waved her hand through the air. "Can you imagine, Jethro's name in lights?" She sniffled. "It chokes me up just thinking about it."

"You need to remove the pig from the pen," Eli said with a scowl. "You must go in and get him."

Juliet looked down at her pretty dress. "I can't climb in there with this dress on. We'll have to wait until he is ready to come out. From the looks of it, that won't be anytime soon." She shrugged as if this were of no matter.

Eli shook his head. "You have to remove the pig."

I looked heavenward. I knew how this was going to end even before it started. "I'll see if I can get him out."

Juliet beamed at me. "Would you? Oh, you are the sweetest girl. I knew that Aiden made the right choice when he chose you."

"Just get the pig out. I don't have time for this." Eli paced back and forth in front of the pen.

"Okay, give me a second."

The side of the pen was only two feet from the ground. I stepped over it. So far, so good. No one moved. I didn't breathe. I felt the collective eyes of the bunnies watching me. I could be wrong, but I felt the eyes of all the Amish on the square staring at me too. If Cass could see me now, she would never believe it.

"Hey, Jethro." I gave the pig a little wave.

His bunny minions stared at him. It might just be my imagination, but they appeared to fluff up their fur a little bit. This was going to be even harder than I'd thought.

I waved at the bunny minions. "Hey, bunnies."

They stared at me with their blue and red eyes. I found the ones with the red eyes the most disconcerting.

I took a step forward. The five bunnies around Jethro stood up. I took another step. They put their ears back against their heads. I didn't know bunny language, but when Nutmeg did that, it was never good. I took another step, and they bared their teeth. Really not good.

"Jethro," I said as soothingly as I could. "Can you tell your friends I'm harmless?" I swallowed. "Please."

I took another step. Nothing happened this time. I was just inches from Jethro now. I could pick him up in one scoop. But I had to build up the nerve with all those sneering rabbits.

"Get him out!" Eli shouted.

It seemed to me that the young Amish man's patience had hit its limit.

I leaned over to pick up the pig, and he took off. Ugh. I ran toward him and tripped over two of the bunnies and fell flat on my face. The bunnies hopped away unharmed. I groaned and spit grass out of my mouth. Jethro walked over to me and pressed his cold snout in my ear.

"Oh see," Juliet cooed from somewhere overhead. "Jethro really loves you, Bailey."

Sure he does, I thought.

Chapter 26

Margot Rawlings patted the mess of curls on the top of her head. "What happened to you?"

I couldn't bring myself to look down at my clothes. If they looked as bad as they smelled, I knew it wasn't pretty. "Jethro." It was all I really had to say. Everyone in the village knew Jethro.

"Well, I'm glad that the toffee rabbit fared better. You know, Bailey, while you were playing with Jethro and the bunnies, I was looking at your sculpture."

I winced and prepared myself for her critique. Would I have to wheel the giant candy rabbit back into Swissmen Sweets and start over? I couldn't bear to ask my grandmother and Charlotte to make more toffee. They had already spent too much time on it. I waited.

Margot took a deep breath. "And I think it's just wonderful!" She grinned. "I wouldn't change a thing about it. An eight-foot rabbit. I should have known you would go above and beyond."

"Ten with the platform," I said with a smile.

"It's so lifelike, and I love that you used the toffee to make it look like the rabbit has real fur."

"Thank you," I murmured, still surprised that Margot was happy with my creation.

"I like it so much that I think I will want you

to make a sculpture like this for all our events on the square."

"Umm . . ." I liked sculpting chocolate, but there was an event on the village square almost every weekend now that Margot had taken over the village social committee. Before I could explain to her how ill-advised that was, she said, "And I'm so sorry that you were there when Stephen died." She cocked her head. "Or maybe he died because you were there?"

I gaped at her. "What are you talking about? I didn't have a thing to do with Stephen's death."

She patted my hand. "I know that you weren't the one who killed him, but you must admit, you are around quite often when someone gets killed." She looked me up and down. "Should I be worried?"

I frowned.

"I'd known Stephen Raber for many years. I still can't believe this happened to him." She leaned in. "And between you and me, I don't know what will happen to his farm."

My brow shot up. "I guess I assumed that it will be Eli's."

"It will, of course. The Amish almost always pass property down through their children, but I don't know if Eli will keep the farm. Stephen hinted to me that Eli didn't enjoy taking care of all those rabbits."

My mind immediately went to Puff. What

would happen to her if Eli decided he didn't want to farm rabbits any longer?

Margot shrugged as if it was no matter. "At least they will be here for the rest of Easter Days. I'm sure Eli will wait for our celebration to be over before making any dramatic decisions."

"Did Stephen and his son get along?"

Margot shrugged. "They seemed to."

That wasn't a very convincing answer. I frowned. Should I be considering Eli as a suspect in his father's murder? He had the most to gain from his father's death. He would inherit a farm and could potentially turn it from a rabbit farm into whatever he wanted it to be. He was getting married soon, so maybe he thought he needed the farm to impress or provide for his new wife. However, none of that changed the fact that he'd come to *me* for help in finding his father's killer. In fact, he was the one who'd put it into my head that Stephen was murdered in the first place. Why would he give me those threatening notes if he was the one behind them? None of it made sense.

"I'm sure Eli will be fine," Margot went on. I had been so preoccupied with my own spinning thoughts, I hadn't realized that she was still talking. "He surely will be married soon, so that will alleviate some of the pain of losing his father."

I wasn't so sure about that, and I wasn't so sure there would even be a wedding. Every time the wedding had come up in conversation, she had looked pained.

"Oh, there's the reporter from the Millersburg paper. They are going to do a feature on Easter Days." She wiggled her fingers at me. "Got to run. You take care, Bailey."

I watched as she scurried across the green to an English man in a polo shirt. Her short curls bounced all the way.

Easter Days started at noon, so within the hour the green would be full of tourists. Juliet and Jethro had disappeared. I assumed they had gone back to the church to load the photos of Jethro and the bunnies into his Instagram account and to show them to Reverend Brook too. That reminded me of the break-in at the church.

I looked down at my clothes. The first thing I would have to do was get cleaned up. I left the square and stopped by the candy shop just long enough to tell my grandmother that I was running home to change.

Maami handed a last customer his change. After he walked through the door, she said, "Do you think that's a *gut* idea? Can't you just get cleaned up here?"

"I only packed one set of clothes and I forgot that I have to file a police report about what happened last night. I have to get cleaned up before I do that at the sheriff's department. I'll be back in two hours, tops. I promise. Besides, I don't want to be afraid to go to my own home in broad daylight."

Maami pressed her lips together. "It seems that your mind is made up."

"You can wear one of my extra dresses," Charlotte offered.

I smiled at her. "That's very sweet of you, but I'd feel much more comfortable in my jeans."

Before I left the candy shop, I went up to my grandmother's apartment to check on Puff. I found Nutmeg and the rabbit sitting next to each other on the bed in a content half doze. If I thought it would be hard for me to hand Puff over to Eli, it was going to be just as hard for Nutmeg to give her up.

I left the candy shop through the kitchen's back door with the hope of not running into too many people. My clothes were muddy and grass-stained and I chose not to think of what else might be on me. The rabbits had been in that pen for days.

As I snuck through the alley to avoid being seen on Main Street, the back door of Esh Family Pretzel opened, and Esther Esh stepped out with a bag of trash, headed toward the Dumpster. She saw me and pulled up short.

"Hi, Esther," I said.

She frowned, but my words must have spurred her into action because she walked over to the Dumpster and dropped the sack inside. "What are you doing back here? Are you spying on me?"

I raised my eyebrows at her. "No, I was just heading home to change." I gestured at my clothes. "I had a little mishap."

"It seems to me that you have many mishaps, Bailey King." She wrinkled her nose.

Sometimes it was hard for me to remember that Emily and Esther were sisters. Emily was sweet and kind, and Esther, decidedly, was not.

"I'll just be on my way then." I walked around her, giving her a lot of space.

"I saw you across the street with Eli Raber," she said.

I turned. "Do you know Eli?"

"*Ya,*" she said, and went through the back door of the pretzel shop without another word.

I could be wrong, but from her reaction, I thought Esther might have known Eli very well indeed.

Chapter 27

"Bailey King! I need to talk to you!" a voice shouted from a buggy rolling down Apple Street.

I lowered my head. At this rate I would never get home for a shower. I stopped in the middle of the sidewalk and waited for the buggy to come to a halt. The bishop's wife, Ruth Yoder, climbed out of the buggy. She was a broad woman in a plain blue dress and white prayer cap. Even though she was out for a drive, she didn't have a bonnet on. "What happened to you?" she asked, and stared at my stained shirt and jeans.

"Jethro," I said, giving her the same answer that I had Margot.

She nodded as if that was enough. She and Margot might be on opposite sides of every debate that came into the village, but they could both agree on Jethro being a troublemaking pig. Everyone in the village could except for Juliet, of course, who believed her pig was above reproach.

"Can I help you with something, Ruth?"

"I heard about what happened to Stephen Raber, and that you were there. I want to know."

"Margot was there too. She would be a good one for you to talk to," I said, taking a little pleasure in that suggestion. It was well-known that Margot and the bishop's wife didn't care for each other.

Ruth scowled at me. "Why would I talk to her, when I can come to you? There is no telling what that woman will say to get her way."

"Why are you so interested in Stephen Raber? He is not even a member of your district."

She frowned at me. "His wife was a *gut* friend of mine and a member of my quilting circle. It was a great loss to us all when she passed away two years ago." She closed her eyes for a moment. "It still breaks my heart to even think about it." She pressed her lips together. "I didn't reach out to Stephen much after Carmela died. I regret that now, so I want to know what is going on. The rumor is he was murdered."

I nodded. There was no point in denying it. If Ruth knew, it was the talk of the Amish gossip mill, I was sure.

"Since you knew Carmela so well, who do you think would do this to Stephen? Was there anyone who disliked the family?"

She shook her head. "Everyone loved the Rabers. Stephen and Carmela were the perfect couple. After Carmela passed, Stephen was still well-liked. He took *gut* care of Carmela in her final days, and as her close friend, I was grateful for that." She glanced away for a moment. "I'm wondering now what will happen to the farm. Now that both Carmela and Stephen are gone . . ."

"I assume Eli will get it. He's the only son."

"That's the problem. Eli is not the only son. Stephen has another son."

I blinked at her. "I thought he had three daughters, all of whom were married and had families of their own."

"He does, and two sons. Eli and the three girls are from his second wife. He had one son with his first wife, Ethel. I would say that his eldest son must be in his thirties by now."

"Well, where is he? Does he work on the farm too?"

She shook her head. "*Nee*. He's *Englisch* now. He took off from the community when he was only twelve."

I blinked at her. "What happened to Stephen's first wife?"

She cleared her throat. "Terrible accident on the farm. She was killed in the grain silo. Something in the silo broke and the grain fell on her." She looked down. "She was smothered to death. Stephen stopped farming crops after that and moved on to rabbits. He married Carmela three months after his first wife died."

I cringed. I remembered seeing the old silo on the Rabers' farm. What a terrible reminder for the family of what had happened to his first wife. Also, I winced at how quickly Stephen had remarried. That marriage sounded awfully fast to me, but I knew things were different in rural Amish communities. Stephen would have needed someone to keep his home and care for his son while he worked his farm.

Ruth must have seen the look of distaste on my face because she said, "Carmela and Stephen were very happy together. Many said that they were a better match than Stephen and Ethel."

"Did Stephen know where his first son went after he left the Amish?"

She shook her head. "Not according to Carmela. They never heard from the boy again after he left. It got to the point that Stephen didn't even want to hear his name."

"What was his first son's name?"

"Casey."

"Would Casey have a claim to the rabbit farm?"

"I would think so," she said.

"Did Stephen have a will?"

She shrugged. "I don't know, but I doubt it. It is not our way."

I bit the inside of my lip. It was true that most Amish didn't bother to write a will. Perhaps it was because they put less value in material things. However, it made things that much more difficult for the family left behind if there was some kind of dispute.

"Do you think that Casey will come back and claim the land as the eldest son?"

"If he hears about it, he might." She pressed her lips together as if the very idea made her ill.

I wondered if Aiden knew any of this. It

sounded to me like Casey, wherever he might be, was a prime suspect for the murder, but how would anyone find him? If he'd run away from the Amish when he was only twelve, no one would even know what he looked like now. Because he'd grown up Amish, there would be no photos of him from his childhood to age up using computer software. That was assuming he was still alive. I shivered to think what would happen to a young boy who ran away from the Amish. He would have left his community with nothing. How would he even know where to go or what to do at such a young age?

"I want you to come to our quilting circle meeting tonight," Ruth said, interrupting my thoughts. "So you can meet Carmela's closest friends. I think it will be important for you to do that to understand the Raber family and to find out who did this to Stephen. As you can imagine, we're all beside ourselves over it."

I stared at her. Ruth looked like she was about to cry. I had never seen the softer side of this tough woman. "Ruth, are you all right?"

She sniffed and straightened her back. Her face went back into its typical grimace as if she was angry with herself for allowing her mask to slip even for a second. "I'd like you to come to the meeting."

I wanted to go to the quilt circle meeting. I thought it would be a good way for me to find out who might have written those notes. If Carmela had been close friends with these women, she might have told them what Stephen had done to receive the threatening notes, but what I didn't understand was why Ruth wanted me there. In the past, she hadn't been pleased with my snooping into crimes that impacted the Amish communities in Holmes County. Why the sudden change of heart?

"Why do you want me there?" I asked.

"Because you have found several criminals before, and because Carmela was my friend and she loved Stephen very much. I would like to know what happened to him for her sake."

I nodded. "I'll come."

She started to untie her horse from the hitching post. "*Gut*. We will be meeting at Millie's. She lives on a little hobby farm on Pear Street here in Harvest."

I knew where the street was, but I didn't know who Millie was. "Millie's?" I asked.

"Millie Fisher. She is a returning member of our quilting circle. She was a member for a long time but moved away after her husband died. She moved back to Harvest right after Christmas." She recited the address to me. "It will be at seven o'clock sharp." She stepped back to the buggy. "Be sure that you're on time. We don't abide lateness in the circle."

I didn't think Ruth abided much at all.

She flicked the reins and left me standing on the sidewalk, feeling confused by what had just happened. I had never expected Ruth Yoder to ask me for help. Ever.

Chapter 28

I walked the rest of the way home without incident, and the house was just as I had left it. I cleaned up fast, drove to the sheriff's department, and filed my report about the attack. Aiden wasn't there when I filed the report and the deputy who interviewed me wasn't one for idle chitchat.

I headed back to the candy shop. I was itching to go to the quilting circle meeting and learn all I could about the Raber family from the ladies, but that wouldn't happen until this evening. As I wove through the tourists who were starting to crowd the walks of Main Street, I was happy to see that at least half a dozen people were admiring the toffee rabbit. Maybe I *would* make more of these for the village . . . just not every weekend.

I stepped around a family stopped in front of the cheese shop. As I came around them, I saw Charlotte sitting on a milk can in front of the candy shop with Puff in her lap and Jethro at her feet. Happily, Jethro was attached to a leash.

"What's going on here?" I asked.

"Juliet said that she had an important meeting to go to with Reverend Brook, so she dropped Jethro off."

"Where's Nutmeg?" I asked, wondering if the

little orange tabby was jealous that Puff had so quickly made a new friend.

"Oh—" Charlotte waved my concern way. "He's fine. Emily is working today so he wanted to stay inside with her."

That made sense. The little cat was very attached to Emily. That reminded me of the strange encounter with Emily's sister in the back alley.

"If you're okay out here, I'll go in."

She waved good-bye just as an English family walked up the street.

"Mommy, can I pet the piggy?" a little girl asked.

"If it's okay with the lady," the mother said back.

"You can, and you can pet our special bunny too. This is Puff and she's a sweetheart," Charlotte said. "We have chocolate bunnies inside on sale that look just like Puff!" I heard Charlotte tell them.

I smiled to myself. Just a few weeks in New York, and she was becoming quite the saleswoman. I might have created a monster.

Maami was in the front of the shop when I went in, and there was a short line of customers. I stepped behind the counter, threw on my apron, and pitched in. When the last customer left, I turned to my grandmother. "Where's Emily?"

"We had a shortage of chocolate bunnies and she's whipping up a few dozen of them."

I nodded and went through the swinging door into the kitchen. Emily sat on one of the stools around the giant stainless-steel island, pouring melted chocolate into plastic molds shaped like Easter bunnies. From there, the molds would be put into one of our three industrial refrigerators to set.

"Do you have any more pig chocolate bars working?" I asked. "I think Charlotte would do well selling those outside the shop since Jethro is here."

Emily laughed, and I was so happy to hear the sound. There was a time when it was difficult even to get a smile out of her. "We can make some up quick. Charlotte's training to be a mini-Bailey. Always selling, always trying new things, always hustling."

I winced. "I don't know if that's a good thing."

She looked up at me. "Some Amish would say it's not, but Charlotte is Charlotte and she would be trying new things even if you weren't here. She admires you. When you aren't here, and we are working, she talks about you all the time."

I smiled. "I'm very lucky to be working with both of you. My grandmother and I both feel that way."

She shook her head and stirred the melted chocolate to keep it from sticking to the bowl. "Not lucky. Blessed. Luck is an *Englisch* idea, not an Amish one."

I smiled and filled my own bowl of chocolate from the large vat in the corner. "I can start on the pigs." After I collected the chocolate into the bowl, I grabbed the plastic pig molds, sat on the stool opposite Emily, and set right to work as I said, "I went to see Daniel yesterday."

"He told me that too, and he told me that he sent Eli to you. I wish he hadn't." She didn't look up from her task as she said this.

"Why?"

"Because I know you, and you will want to see if you can solve the murder."

"Of course, I want to solve the murder. I want to help Aiden the best way I can."

She studied me. "Do you think it's a good idea to do this, Bailey? You've gotten yourself into much trouble before. I'm forever grateful for what you did for Daniel and me, but I don't want to see you hurt."

"I'll be fine."

She rolled her eyes. "I think you've said that before when you haven't been fine, and Charlotte told me that someone attacked you last night." She pointed at me. "And I can see the bruise on your face. You were hurt, Bailey. You could have been killed."

I grimaced. "That's beside the point."

She arched her brow at me. "Is it? Maybe you should leave all of this to Aiden."

That was probably true, but I made no comment on it. Instead, I asked, "Do you know the Rabers well?"

"Not too well," she said, slowly and carefully pouring chocolate into the next mold. "Eli is Daniel's friend, not mine." She wouldn't look at me as she said this.

Silently, I poured chocolate into the pig molds for a few minutes. Emily got up and put her tray in the fridge and gathered up a second mold and more chocolate. When she was seated again, I said, "I saw your sister today in the alley."

Emily took in a quick breath. Her siblings hadn't spoken to her since she'd left the pretzel shop and married Daniel. I knew it was a sore subject, but I had to find out what Esther's connection was to the Rabers.

"Esther told me that she knew Eli Raber."

"Everyone knows everyone else in the village. You should realize that by now," she said, a little more defensively than the comment warranted. "I don't want to talk about my sister," she added quietly.

"I can understand that, but if there is anything I should know about her and that family, I would appreciate hearing it."

"My sister didn't have anything to do with what happened to Stephen." She looked up from her mold with tears in her eyes.

I set my bowl down. "Emily, what's wrong?"

"You can't know what it's like to be cut off from your family. Maybe they were unkind to me, but Abel and Esther were the only family I had for a long time. Daniel keeps telling me that I have his family now, but it's not the same. They will always be his family, and I will always be different from them in some way."

I bit my lip. I had to think of a way to mend the broken Esh family. I hated seeing Emily like this. I pushed the thought aside. I was a fixer, and I wanted to fix everything. I thought that was how I ended up in most of the scrapes I found myself in, and likely why I was dealing with murder yet again. Heck, it was likely why I'd dealt with the men I dated before Aiden. But I couldn't fix everything, and I shouldn't try to fix a family that didn't want my help. "Your family isn't always determined by your blood relations. I consider Cass my family."

"It is different for the *Englisch*," she said, and wiped her eyes with a paper towel.

"It's not," I argued. "Isn't that what being Amish is about? Community? Your district and the Amish community become your family. Daniel is right to say you have his family now, but you also have Charlotte, *Maami*, and me, and all your other friends in the district. Just because two people on the planet are too stupid to see what a wonderful person you are, that doesn't make them right. Two shouldn't outweigh the dozens of people who love you."

Tears gathered in Emily's eyes again. "Do you really believe that?"

"Of course I do." I smiled. "And be careful not to get any tears in those chocolate rabbits."

She laughed and dabbed the paper towel on her eyes once more.

We worked in silence for a few minutes. My pigs were coming out well. I was debating whether I should mix some white chocolate in to make them look more like Jethro but was afraid Juliet would say I was infringing on Jethro's merchandising opportunities. Stardom had certainly gone to both of their heads. Juliet's more so than the pig's.

"Esther wanted to marry Eli, and my brother forbade it because Eli was from another district," she blurted out so fast I thought that I misheard her.

I looked up from my molds. "Eli and Esther were going to get married?"

She nodded. "It was right after our parents died, and I think most of it was Abel wanting my sister home to take care of the shop and the house. That was many years ago. I was still young, and I wasn't as much help."

For the first time, my heart softened toward Esther just a tad. All this time I'd thought she had been unkind to Emily because she was cruel, but maybe that cruelty stemmed from the pain of being trapped in a life she didn't want. Now that Emily had escaped that life, it seemed to me Esther would be even angrier at her sister even though that anger was misplaced, and she should put it on her brother.

I disliked Abel more by the second. The oldest Esh sibling was lazy, and as far as I knew, he only did odd jobs around the village when he felt like it. Esther and Emily had done most of the work to keep their family going, and now, Esther had to do it all alone. No wonder she was mad at me for encouraging Emily to follow her heart. I supposed that Esther could leave too, but I doubt that had ever occurred to her. She'd worked at the pretzel shop for so long, it was very likely that she didn't see any way out.

Then I remembered what I'd learned on the square about Eli's upcoming wedding. "Does she know that Eli and Katey Beiler are courting?"

Emily sighed. "I'm sure she does. She and Eli courted so long ago that I'm sure she is over him."

I wrinkled my brow, remembering the look on Esther's face. I wasn't so sure. At the very least, thoughts of what might have been must keep her up at night from time to time. I remembered the expression on Katey's face; she hadn't looked happy either. You would think she would be thrilled by her upcoming wedding, but she appeared sick over it. I thought there was something more to it than prewedding jitters.

"I wonder what I'll learn tonight from Ruth Yoder's quilt circle."

She stared at me. "Ruth Yoder invited you to her quilting circle? The bishop's wife, Ruth Yoder?"

It was a fair question. Ruth Yoder was a common name in Holmes County, where every fourth person was a Yoder or at least related to a Yoder. That went for all the Amish and English residents of this county.

"Yep, she asked me. Trust me, I was just as shocked as you are. She said she was close friends with Carmela, Eli's mother, and wants me to find out what happened to Stephen."

"Wow." Emily shook her head. "These are weird times in the village."

I agreed with her on that. "Anyway, the quilting circle meets at seven at Millie Fisher's house."

"Millie Fisher!"

I blinked. "Umm, yeah, is that name supposed to mean something?"

She laughed. "With your nosiness I can't believe you have lived in the village for so long and don't know who Millie Fisher is. Millie is the one you go to when you are stuck in love." She touched her cheek. "She's the village matchmaker."

I blinked at her. "Come again?"

"You heard me," she protested. "She is the village matchmaker. If you have trouble finding a spouse or if you aren't sure that someone is the right person for you, Millie is the one the Amish in Harvest talk to. She's so good that people from other districts go and see her. I know of a girl whom Millie found a spouse for in Wyoming!"

"The Amish use matchmakers?"

"Sure. Some do, not all. It depends on what the bishop of your district says, of course. But most districts in Holmes County, unless they are very strict, trust Millie. She just has a knack for knowing whom *Gott* wants you to marry." She blushed. "I was thinking about talking to Millie myself until Daniel started courting me. I know you have Aiden now, but I've heard that she's even matched a few *Englischers*." She cocked her head. "Maybe she could help your friend Cass?"

"Umm, I think it would be best to leave Cass's love life up to Cass, for everyone's sake."

Chapter 29

I spent the rest of the day working at Swissmen Sweets, updating the new Web site I'd made for the shop, placing orders, and running over to Easter Days with more chocolate rabbits every few hours. When six thirty rolled around, I realized if I didn't leave soon, I would be late for the quilting circle. I had a feeling that Ruth would not look kindly on my tardiness. I closed my laptop computer and put it back on the shelf in the storage room where I kept it. My grandmother wasn't fond of having a computer in the shop, so I kept it hidden away when I wasn't using it. I came out of the storage room to find Charlotte flipping the café chairs on the top of the tables and my grandmother sweeping.

"I have to go to Millie Fisher's house," I told them. "Then I'll head home for the night. I'll be back to the shop bright and early tomorrow."

Maami pursed her lips together. "I think you should stay here until the murderer is caught. You may think you are fine, but I am reminded of what happened to you last night every time I see the scrape on your cheek."

"I will be fine. I'll be alert. Whoever did this can't get into my home. Also I have a very vigilant next-door neighbor in Penny. I'm sure she has been watching my house all day long."

"It's not safe," my grandmother insisted.

"You're going to have to trust me. I can take care of myself. I have for a very long time."

Maami shook her head. "I will never understand the *Englisch* need for independence. At heart, this is where the Amish and *Englisch* differ most."

I knew she was right, and I understood why she wanted me to stay with her and Charlotte at the candy shop. However, I couldn't live in fear. I would be afraid enough to be careful, but I would not allow myself to be stifled by fear.

"You're going to the matchmaker?" Charlotte asked with big eyes.

I smiled gratefully at her, thankful for the change of subject. It was evident that *Maami* and I weren't going to agree about my sleeping arrangements for the night. "I am. Emily told me that Millie is the village matchmaker. I didn't even know there was such a position."

Charlotte nodded seriously. "Of course there is. Not everyone is able to find their own match."

"So it's like eHarmony for the Amish?" I asked, smiling.

"I don't know what that is," Charlotte said in all seriousness.

"Never mind."

She chewed on her lower lip. "Is something wrong with you and Aiden that you have to go to her for guidance? Did you break up?"

"Nothing is wrong with Aiden and me. I'm not going there for a consultation, and we didn't break up."

"Why are you going to Millie's house then?" *Maami* asked, much more calmly than Charlotte had.

"Ruth Yoder's quilt circle is meeting there tonight, and she invited me to talk to the ladies about the Raber family."

"That's even stranger," Charlotte said. "Ruth Yoder doesn't like you."

"Charlotte," my grandmother admonished.

"What?" she asked. "Bailey knows that."

"I do know that," I agreed. "I should get going. I can't be late."

"No, you can't. Ruth Yoder would never forgive you," Charlotte said.

That was comforting.

Puff hopped over to me. "What do I do with her? I can't take her to the circle."

"Stop by after the meeting and take her home with you. I would feel better if another creature was in that empty house with you. And here." *Maami* handed me a white candy box. "It's ill-advised to go to any meeting with a room full of Amish women without something to offer."

"What's in here?" I asked.

"Marshmallow-filled eggs."

A clear winner. "They will welcome me with open arms if I have these."

"Be careful tonight. Don't let anything happen to you," my grandmother said. "I wish you would spend the night here again."

"I'll be fine, and I can't be afraid to sleep in my own home." I gave her a hug. "I will be careful. I promise." As I went out the door, I texted Aiden to tell him where I was headed, just to be safe.

Thankfully, traffic was always light in Harvest after five since that's when most of the shops, including Swissmen Sweets, closed. I made good time driving out to the county road where Millie lived.

There were several Amish homes along the road; they were easy to identify as Amish because there were no power lines running to any of the houses. The power lines marched up the street, but none of them were diverted to any of the homes. Even if I didn't have the address of Millie's house, I would have known which one was hers by the sheer number of Amish buggies parked in the front along the drive. I counted six, and that made me realize this was a rather large quilting circle. I was glad that my grandmother had packed a big box of marshmallow-chocolate eggs. A small one wouldn't have cut it.

I stepped out of the car and, from across the lawn, two goats ran toward me. One was brown and white and the other was black and white. Both had short horns that bent backward. The black-and-white one jumped in the air.

I pressed my body against the car. They seemed friendly enough, but I didn't want to meet with the business end of either of them.

"Phillip! Peter! Leave that poor *Englischer* alone!" a clear, strong voice called from the front porch of the white frame ranch.

The goats pulled up short and ran toward the voice. I edged around the side of the car to see a petite Amish woman in a plain lavender dress and white prayer cap that was all but lost in her blond-but-turning-white hair.

Phillip and Peter danced around the woman as she walked toward me.

She smiled, and her entire face lit up. Her lively dark eyes reminded me of hot chocolate. I suddenly felt at ease even with the prancing goats. "Don't you worry about these two knuckleheads. They're just goofballs and like to greet everyone who comes to my home."

I found myself smiling too. "I think that was the first time I've ever been charged by goats. It's not something that would have happened to me in New York."

She laughed. "I'm sure that's true. I'm Millie Fisher, and the ladies are already inside settling into their quilting. Ruth told me that you were coming so I thought I had better get out here and warn you about my security detail, but I see that they've beat me to it."

"You have a lovely home," I said, meaning it. A

swing hung from a giant oak tree in the front yard just to the left of the ranch style house. Flowers and vines poured out of the window boxes. I noticed a small white frame outbuilding behind the house. I assumed that's where Phillip and Peter lived.

"Thank you." She smiled. "The boys and I like it."

I raised my eyebrows. "The boys?"

"Phillip and Peter. It's just the three of us here now," she said with a hint of sadness, and I wondered what Millie's story was. "Let's go inside. The ladies are all looking forward to meeting you."

I followed her up the walk. The goats walked behind us like a pair of dogs, but when we reached the steps, they galloped off together toward some new adventure.

I stepped into the home and was surprised to see the layout of the house. It was one big room with an open floor plan, which wasn't the typical Amish home. I could see the kitchen, which had an enormous island that at the moment was covered with food and treats—it was the right call to bring the chocolate-marshmallow eggs—a small breakfast nook in the corner, and a large living space with a black potbelly stove where a fireplace might have been.

The stove wasn't on at the moment, and all the windows were open. A light spring breeze blew through the windows, fluttering the simple white curtains and bringing in the sounds of Phillip and Peter playing outside. Other than Millie, there were five Amish women of all ages sitting around the room.

"Allow me to make the introductions," Millie said. She pointed at each woman and said her name. I tried to make a mental note about each woman and to pair some rhyming detail with each person's name, but in my current frame of mind, I knew I would forget them just as soon as I left. Oh, who was I kidding? Even in the best frame of mind, I wasn't good with names. Faces, however, I never forgot, which made me wish again that I had seen the face of my attacker. If I had, I know Aiden would have been able to track him down. I tried to put the attack out of my mind, and in my head I recited the types of chocolate just as Jean Pierre had taught me. It seemed to help. I had an uncanny memory for all things chocolate as well as faces.

Ruth Yoder sat on a plain wooden rocker and stood up when I entered the house. "I am glad you're finally here." She did nothing to soften her admonishment.

I glanced at the time on my cell phone. I was one minute late. Actually, I had arrived early and would have been in the house on time if it hadn't been for the goats.

"Calm yourself, Ruth," Millie said with a

chuckle. "Bailey was getting acquainted with Phillip and Peter."

Ruth sat back down with a sniff. "You and your goats, Millie Fisher. I still don't think it's decent for you to live by yourself with only those two for company."

An expression I couldn't read passed over Millie's face, but then it was gone.

"What do you have in the box?" a rail-thin Amish woman asked. She had rosy cheeks and dark brown hair and held a plate of food on her lap.

Ruth wrinkled her nose and opened her quilting basket. "Iris, don't you think you have eaten enough already?"

Iris didn't seem to take offense to Ruth's comment and shrugged. "*Nee*, my husband and son are on a construction job in Cleveland and won't be back until late tonight. Cooking for one is no fun." She held up her plate. "This is my lunch and dinner."

Millie smiled. "You're welcome to stay here as long as you like, Iris. You can keep the goats and lonely me company." She gave Ruth a pointed look.

I had the feeling that I had stepped into the middle of a long-standing argument between Ruth and Millie, and I wanted nothing to do with it. I had enough problems with the murder investigation. I held up the box. "Chocolate-covered marshmallow eggs from our shop."

"Oh," Iris said, and waved me over to her. "I'll take one. I love those. They are perfect for my sweet tooth."

I opened the box, and Iris selected two of the eggs. She winked at me. "One is for later."

I grinned. "Go for it."

"Can we begin?" Ruth asked. "We have a lot to discuss, and we should all be working."

"Don't worry, Ruth. We're all here for the same reason," Millie said, before glancing at me and clarifying, "For Carmela."

Ruth choked up. "*Ya*, for Carmela."

I felt my brow go up in surprise as I realized that Ruth had really loved Carmela Raber. She had clearly been a close friend. I didn't know why it surprised me that Ruth had friends.

Maybe it was because everyone I met, including my own grandmother, found her so aggravating.

Millie took the white candy box from my hand. "Why don't you take a seat there by Iris, and we can get started. Would you like anything to eat?"

I shook my head. "No, I'm fine."

"We will pack up a care package for you and Clara before you leave. My motto is no one leaves my home hungry."

I smiled and settled on the pine bench next to Iris. The Amish woman winked at me.

Ruth removed cut pieces of cloth from a basket at the foot of her chair and laid them over her lap.

She also removed a spool of thread and a tomato-shaped pin cushion from the basket. The other women seated in the room—except for Iris, who was still working on her snack—did the same.

"We just started a new quilt today for my niece who is getting married. Her wedding is not for several weeks, so we are just beginning the piecing," Millie said. "Would you like to help?"

I waved my hands. "I can't sew. The only craft I'm really good at is candy making."

"You're also *gut* at finding killers," Ruth said. "Which is exactly why you're here."

Chapter 30

I wasn't sure how I felt about being the sleuth for the Amish, but that seemed to have become the role I had fallen into.

Millie handed me a lemonade in a mason jar. "You should at least drink something. We also have water and iced tea if you'd prefer."

I accepted the jar. "No, this is fine. Thank you."

"What do you want to know about Carmela?" asked a fortyish Amish woman with a straight nose and wire-rimmed glasses. "I'm Raellen. I live next door to Millie." She smiled at me. "This is a nice place to come when I need a little peace and quiet from the children."

"How many children do you have?"

She smiled. "Nine. They can be a handful."

I blinked. I could barely imagine having one child let alone nine, but Raellen seemed to take it in stride. She was a stronger woman than I was—that much I knew.

"Well," I began. "Ruth asked me to come here to learn about Carmela and Stephen. She thought that if I knew more about them, I might be able to find out who would want to hurt Stephen."

"I don't know why anyone would want to hurt Stephen Raber," Iris said as she dabbed a napkin to the corner of her mouth. "He was just the kindest man, and he'd been through enough. A widower twice over. I don't know many men who would be able to stand that with such a cheerful attitude as he had."

"It was his rabbits that kept him happy. He doted on them," another woman in the group said. "He was especially fond of that large rabbit he carried around the village like a pet cat."

Puff. I decided not to mention that Puff was currently living with me.

"He should have cared less about his rabbits and more about his son," Raellen said. "I know for a fact that Eli did most of the work on that farm. At least now he will be the one who inherits it."

"Maybe," Ruth Yoder said. "We can't forget that Casey might come out of the woodwork."

"That's Stephen's eldest son?" I asked. "From his first marriage?"

Ruth nodded. "That's right. The boy ran away, and if he's still alive, he could come back and lay claim to the Raber farm. Unless Stephen had a will, it would go to his eldest son. That would be Casey."

"Couldn't Eli dispute that?" I asked. "If Casey ran away from home when he was twelve, can't Eli prove that he was the one who lived and worked on the farm?"

"It would all have to go through probate court, and this is an *Englisch* institution," Millie said as if she were speaking from experience. "If Casey came back as an *Englischer*, which we must assume he became, he would use *Englisch* law to take Eli's place."

"But could he really be alive? He left at twelve years old. It's hard to believe that he would have survived," Iris mused.

Ruth shrugged. "No one has heard from him in over twenty years."

"If he is alive, I would guess that he's a long way from here and doesn't even know his father is dead," Raellen said.

"I think the same," Iris agreed.

"What was Stephen like when he was younger?" I asked, thinking of the threatening notes. What were the notes about? How long ago had he done something that would offend someone so deeply that he or she would write those notes?

"He was always a kind man." Iris looked at Millie, who was standing next to the potbelly stove appearing pensive. "You seem to have something on your mind, Millie. . . ."

"I never thought that Stephen and Ethel, his first wife, were a good match."

Ruth pursed her lips together. "Here we go again with Millie and her matchmaking."

"I know when someone is ill-fitted for another person. Everyone has talents given to them by *Gott*. This is mine."

"I don't believe you can know who is meant

for whom. Only *Gott* can know that," Ruth said.

Millie smiled at me. "As you can imagine, this has been a long-standing debate between Ruth and me. We will never see eye to eye. It all comes down to comfort. If you pay attention, you can see who puts another person at ease and who has the opposite effect. Have you ever walked into a room and seen someone there you loved and suddenly felt like everything would be all right? That's a real match."

Ruth muttered something under her breath.

"And I'm not just speaking of a match in romantic love, either. A friend or family member can have that kind of effect. There are many kinds of matches in this life and not all of them have to do with marriage."

Ruth shifted in her seat.

Millie noticed too and one of her blond brows arched, although she didn't press Ruth further. She turned back to me instead. "But you asked what Stephen was like when he was younger. He had always been a kind man, but it was clear to me that he wasn't truly happy until he married Carmela. His life with Ethel was difficult. She was a hard woman, and she was disappointed with their lot in life. I don't think she was happy with an Amish farmer."

"Carmela was the opposite of that," Ruth said, sounding a little choked up again. "She was the kindest woman. She would do anything for anyone. It wasn't a surprise to anyone that Stephen married so soon after Ethel died. He had a three-month-old son and a farm to run. No one blamed him for that."

"Not even Casey?" I asked.

Iris leaned forward. "Now that you mention it, that might have been a reason for Casey to want his father dead. He lost his mother when he was young and must not have felt as if he fit well with the new family. If he had, why would he have left so young?"

"Why did he leave?" I asked.

Everyone looked at Ruth.

Her face reddened. "I don't know. Carmela never wanted to talk about it. She said it was too painful for her husband."

There was something else I had been thinking about since the day of the murder. "Ruth." I cupped my lemonade jar in my hands. "The day Stephen died, I saw you on the square."

"I had nothing to do with his death!" Ruth snapped.

I held up one of my hands. "I'm not saying that you did, but I saw you there with a woman, an English woman. You were clearly trying to convince her to leave the square. Who was that?"

Ruth's face turned a bright shade of pink. "I don't know why that conversation has any bearing on what we are talking about today."

"Just tell her, Ruth," Millie said in a no-nonsense

way. "We don't know what we will say that might lead to who killed Stephen."

Ruth narrowed her eyes. "It was that terrible Sybil Horn. She was on the square, and I knew that I had to tell her to leave."

Several women in the room nodded, but I was still completely in the dark. "Who's Sybil Horn?"

"She takes children away from the Amish," Raellen said in a half whisper, as if saying it was inviting Sybil into her home to snatch her own children.

"She kidnaps Amish kids?" My mouth fell open.

"*Nee*," Millie said. "And, Raellen, it's not fair to say such a thing." She turned to me. "Sybil helps Amish who wish to leave the faith."

I frowned. "What do you mean?"

"Sometimes when young Amish people decide to leave their community," Millie said, "they have nowhere to go, and that's where Sybil comes in. She helps them find a place to stay in the *Englisch* world. She also helps them acclimate to being *Englisch*. There are many Amish communities that are still very far removed from *Englisch* life, and the young people who leave those communities don't know how to handle all they will face in their new world."

"She was at the square looking for young people to pull away from the faith," Ruth said. "So, I told her to leave. We don't want her kind in Harvest."

Millie pressed her lips together as if she was forcibly holding her tongue. "I've spoken with Sybil, and I think that she is a *gut* person. She is just trying to help young people. She's former Amish herself. In my opinion, it's better for a young person to leave the faith and be *Englisch* than force themselves to be Amish and make everyone around them miserable."

"You would think that," Ruth muttered.

As Millie spoke I couldn't help but think of my father, who'd left the Amish life and faith to marry my mother. I liked Millie more for her open-minded opinion of the people who leave the Amish way. At times, I had been criticized by the Amish when they found out my father had fallen away from the faith. Even so, I still didn't know what all this had to do with Stephen Raber. With every passing minute, I felt less and less confident that Aiden and I would be able to find his killer.

Chapter 31

The women quilted for another thirty minutes as they told me what they could about Carmela and Stephen, but I didn't think anything they said would help me find Stephen's killer. I was beginning to feel anxious to leave. They their quilting to keep their hands busy, but since I didn't quilt, I felt I was sitting there wasting time.

Just when I thought enough time had passed that I could give my excuses and leave, the group began to break up. I stood too.

"Bailey, if you would wait just a little while, I will pack up some of the leftover food for you and your grandmother. Charlotte Weaver too. I heard that she's living with Clara," Millie said.

"She is," I said. "But you really don't have to do that."

"I insist. All you need to do is wait a few minutes."

That was easier said than done. I felt I was getting nowhere with Stephen's murder and wanted to talk to Aiden and see what he'd learned that day—if he would tell me.

The women shuffled toward the door. During the meeting, night had fallen. Even so it seemed to me that none of them were in a rush to go home. Ruth stepped over to me with her quilting basket hooked over her arm. A bright yellow quilting square peeked out of the basket. "I want you to remember something, Bailey King."

I straightened up. "What's that, Ruth?"

"Carmela was my dearest friend in the world, and she loved Stephen so very much. You would be doing a personal favor to me if you found out who did this to him."

"So the killer can go to jail?" I asked.

She shook her head. "I don't believe in the *Englisch* justice system. Too many times, the wrong person is punished for crimes he didn't commit." She said this as if she was speaking from experience.

I realized there was a lot about Ruth Yoder that I didn't know. Yes, she was the aggravating bishop's wife and a stickler for the district's many rules, but how did she get that way?

"You know I will do what I can," I said. "And Aiden will too."

She nodded.

In the time that Ruth had been talking to me, the other women had left, leaving Millie and me alone in the house.

"It was *gut* of you to come. I know that Ruth can be a little demanding, but she has a *gut* heart and she has been my faithful friend for many years through many dark times."

I wanted to ask her what those dark times were,

but she said, "I have your food all packed." She held up a canvas bag. "Let's go outside." With her other hand she grabbed a gas-powered lantern from the side table.

I followed her outside, and as soon as we stepped onto the porch Phillip and Peter came galloping around the house. Thankfully, there was enough ambient light from Millie's lantern and the clear sky to see them. I didn't want to accidentally run into the business end of their horns, or their hooves for that matter. I wasn't sure which goat was which, but the black-and-white one leaped in the air when he saw Millie.

As if sensing my unasked question, Millie said, "That's Phillip. He's the more excitable of the two."

As the goats ran around us in a circle, I decided that they both looked pretty excitable to me.

She handed me the sack of food. "You had better put that in your car before the boys get a whiff of it."

"Thank you." I accepted the sack.

"That's why I got these two fellows." She held the lantern high as we walked to my car. Now, there was only one buggy in the yard, which I knew must be Millie's. "When I bought this place a month ago, it was all covered with brambles. I bought the goats to help me clear the land and eat the brush. I thought I would give them to my niece when I was done with that project, but

I came to realize that I love their company and funny antics."

Phillip rolled in the grass and Peter leaped over him.

I grinned. "I can see why." I opened the car door and set the food on the front passenger seat. "Thanks for letting me visit your home."

"It was my pleasure. I have always been fond of Clara. It was nice to meet her granddaughter."

I smiled. "Why did you leave Harvest?"

"I've been in Michigan for the last ten years, caring for my ailing sister," Millie said. "She passed away over Christmas, so here I am back in Harvest in my old district."

"I'm so sorry for your loss." I frowned, wishing I hadn't pried into what must be a painful past.

She smiled. "Thank you. I'm glad she is no longer in any pain. As hard as it is for me here on earth without her, I know she is much better off in our Heavenly Father's warm embrace."

I frowned. I was surprised that Millie spoke about God in such a loving way. Most of the Amish I had met stressed the fear of God over His love. It seemed to me that Millie's God was one I would much rather meet than that of the others.

She studied me for a moment as if she was trying to decide something. Then she nodded as if she'd come to some sort of conclusion, and said, "I wanted to talk to you after the other ladies left because there's something you should know. I think Sybil Horn might have more to do with all this than I led Ruth to believe. I like Sybil and think she's a *gut* person. As you could tell, Ruth is of a different opinion."

"Why do you think Sybil is involved?"

"I was in Millersburg yesterday and saw her with Katey."

My brow shot up. "Katey Beiler. Katey, who is betrothed to Eli Raber?"

"Oh, they are promised now. I didn't know that it was for certain." Her face fell.

"Is it bad that they want to marry?"

She looked at me with those dark eyes. "I don't know that they both want to marry."

"Oh," I said.

Millie shook her head. "They aren't a good match."

I frowned. "How do you know?"

She laughed. "I know because it's my gift."

"Like a magical gift?" I asked.

"*Nee.* Don't let the bishop or Ruth hear you say that. Magic is not something we Amish think of or believe in." She smiled to take the bite out of her words and her cheeks turned a soft pink color. If I didn't have a wonderful grandmother already, I might have adopted Millie on the spot.

Phillip walked over to her and she rested her hand on the top of his head between his horns. "I understand human nature, especially when it comes to love. It is the gift the Good Lord gave to me. He asks us to use the gifts that He provides for us and so I do," she said as if it was as simple as that.

"When did you know that Katey and Eli weren't a good match?"

She scratched Phillip's head. "I've known for some time, but I haven't said anything. I don't always use my gift even when I see trouble in the future." She smiled at me. "I'm still Amish through and through, and we are raised not to meddle in others' affairs unless we are asked to help."

"Someone asked you for help?"

"Katey came to me. She said that her father had decided she was to marry Eli, and she was still unsure of him. It's not uncommon for young people who are struggling to come and seek me out for guidance."

"So, you are a kind of relationship coach or therapist?"

She laughed. "Those are *Englischer* terms. I'm just a matchmaker. I can match young and old couples together. I can see what they are too scared or smitten to see, what the other person is truly like in their heart of hearts."

"It does sound like quite a gift."

A dark cloud fell over her face. "It is. It is a great responsibility."

Before I could ask her what was wrong, her face cleared.

"What did you tell Katey when she came to you?"

"That I didn't think they were a good match and that she should speak to her deacon about it."

"Her deacon instead of her father?"

She pressed her lips together. "There's something off about Jud Beiler, and there always has been since his wife died. My own husband died about the same time, and I think we have mourned differently. I would never tell another person how to mourn—it's a very private affair—but it does become harder to hold my tongue when someone becomes bitter. It seems to me that is what has happened to Jud."

It was funny, but now that she mentioned it, I realized I had thought the same thing about the Amish man.

"I think you need to talk to Sybil," she said simply. "She may have the answers you seek."

"Where can I find her?"

"She has a loft on Route Thirty-nine in Millersburg. It's only a few steps away from the county courthouse. It's very easy to find." She slipped her hand into her apron pocket and pulled out a little slip of paper. "I have written the address here for you."

I took the piece of paper from her. "I should tell Aiden about this," I mused.

"Tell him after you speak to Sybil," she advised.

I raised my eyebrows. It wasn't very Amish to

advise a woman to do something without telling a man.

"I say that because I think Sybil will be more comfortable talking to you alone about what she does, and she certainly won't say anything about Katey if the police are there."

I nodded and folded the piece of paper, tucking it into the pocket of my jeans.

She smiled. "I am glad you want to tell Deputy Brody about it though. That confirms what I already know."

"What's that?"

"You've met your match, my girl. He's the one you've been looking for."

My breath caught.

She patted Phillip on the head one more time. "Go play with your brother," she told the goat, and, as if he understood her completely, he leaped away and chased after Peter. The pair of them careened around the side of the house. She turned back to me. "I suggest that you stop worrying about the day when the two of you break up and think of your future together. If it falls apart, it will be because of your fear. I have seen it happen before, and my heart broke for that couple who were meant to be but were unable to enjoy their love for fear of losing it."

I shivered as I realized that she expressed my worst fear, losing Aiden. I was so fearful of it, in fact, at times I found myself holding him at arm's length, believing that would lessen the pain when it ended. Because part of me thought Aiden was too good to be true. It was just too hard for me to believe a man like him could love me. I had had a very rocky road when it came to relationships, and I would be lying if I didn't say I was waiting for the other shoe to drop with Aiden.

"You know what to do, dear. You always have." With that she turned and walked back to her house.

Chapter 32

It was close to nine by this point, and I knew there was no sense in trying to track down Sybil Horn at this late hour. Nine might not be considered late in New York, but in Holmes County, it might as well be midnight.

I had told my grandmother I was going to stay at my own house tonight, but now that darkness had fallen, fear prickled at the back of my neck. I drove back to the center of the village and called Aiden.

"Where are you? Are you all right?" he asked without even saying hello.

"I'm driving back to the village from Millie Fisher's house. I—I think I want to spend one more night at the shop for *Maami*," I added quickly, unable to show any weakness, not even to Aiden.

"For *Maami*?" he asked.

"She really wants me to be there. I don't want her to worry."

"I think that's wise." There was a smile in his voice. "No one wants to make Clara worry."

I started to say something, but he interrupted me. "Bailey, I have to go. I have a call coming in from the department. If I can possibly drop by and see you at the shop before it's too late,

I will." He said good-bye and then hung up.

I parked my little car in its usual spot on Apple Street and walked the short distance to the candy shop, ever mindful of all the sounds of the night. The tiniest rustle of the blossoms on the apple trees made me jump.

My grandmother opened the front door to the shop just as I came up the walk. I had a feeling Aiden had told her I was coming. "I'm glad you're here."

I smiled and held up the sack. "I couldn't possibly eat this all myself, so I thought it would just be easier to eat here and spend the night. That way I can get a jump on things in the morning."

She gave me a knowing smile.

I stepped into the shop and found Charlotte and Deputy Little in the front room. Charlotte grinned. "Deputy Little is going to keep an eye on us again tonight." She blushed ever so faintly and then turned away. I wondered if I'd imagined the blush.

"What's in the bag?" Little asked.

I set the sack in the middle of the table. "All kinds of goodies. I think Millie gave me all the leftovers from the quilting circle. It was meant for the three of us in the shop, but there is enough here for an entire Amish district."

"Oh, is that sweet potato pie?" Little asked.

I scooted the pie tin over in his direction.

"That's my very favorite," he said.

"I'll get some dishes," Charlotte said, and went into the kitchen. She was back a minute later with plates, napkins, and silverware.

I smiled at her. "Thanks, Charlotte."

She nodded, which was unusual for the typically bubbly Amish girl.

Everyone loaded up their plates, and even though I had eaten more than my share at Millie's farm, I filled up a plate too. I was a sucker for sweet potato pie just as Little was.

I was about to take my first bite when there was a knock on the window, and I turned to see Aiden waving at me. I dropped my fork back on my plate and met him at the door. When he stepped into the room, I immediately felt calmer, as if everything would be all right, just the way Millie said a person feels when it's a perfect match. Aiden was my perfect match.

"You guys eating?" Aiden asked eagerly.

"Are you hungry?" Charlotte asked.

"Always," Aiden said. "Investigating really brings out the appetite."

"I can attest to that," I said.

Aiden shook his head as if he'd just accepted that for a fact. I think it was the best he could do.

Charlotte hopped up to get another plate from the kitchen.

Aiden clapped Little on the shoulder, and I saw the other man relax. I supposed in guy code Aiden was telling Little that all was forgiven from the night before even though no words were used.

Aiden stood up after eating. "Thanks for the food. It's going to be a long night at the station. I want to go over a few things again related to the case."

"Can I help, sir?" Little asked.

Aiden shook his head. "No, I would much prefer that you stay here and keep an eye on the ladies from Swissmen Sweets."

Charlotte was cleaning up the food and packing it away. Even with five people sharing in the meal, we had leftovers.

Little nodded and picked up his plate. "I can do the dishes," he said.

Charlotte's mouth fell open. "We can't let you do that. You're a guest."

"Maybe, but I can't just sit here while you do all the work."

Charlotte looked as if she might protest again, but *Maami* said, "We would love your assistance with the dishes, Deputy Little. It is my least favorite chore."

Little smiled and gathered up the remainder of the plates and silverware. He went into the kitchen. *Maami* and Charlotte followed him with the leftover food.

When Aiden and I were alone, I asked, "Did you talk to the Beilers' about their tractor?"

He nodded. "I did, but they weren't that forthcoming by the time I got there. I have a feeling that Jud Beiler regretted calling the police, so he started to downplay the whole incident."

"How did the person who slashed the tires get to the tractor?"

Aiden sighed. "The shed it was in was unlocked, which is typical of an Amish farm."

"Did the Beilers have any idea who might have done it?"

"Jud Beiler didn't. He wouldn't let me talk to his daughter, Katey. I still would like to, but I have to speak to her away from her father."

The mentioning of Katey Beiler made me think of how strangely she'd behaved at Easter Days. The girl had been uncomfortable. It was painfully apparent she didn't want to marry Eli, and I would have known that even if Millie had not confirmed that Katey and Eli were a bad match. "If you are going to talk to any of them, I would start with Katey." I went on to tell him about her engagement to Eli.

Aiden's brow went up. "I didn't know the families were that close. What else did you learn today?" he asked. "Did you learn anything at the quilting circle?"

"I did," I said, and I went on to tell him about Casey, Stephen's son, and his first wife, Ethel, but as Millie suggested, I didn't mention Sybil Horn just yet. I wanted a chance to speak with her before Aiden and his officers got to her. Millie was right; she would be more forthcoming with me than she would be with the police. She had grown up Amish after all.

"I knew that Stephen was married before and he had a son from that marriage." He rubbed the five o'clock shadow on his chin. "It's an interesting theory that he might come back to claim the farm as rightfully his."

"Can he do that?"

Aiden shrugged. "With an attorney, he can try, and he just might win. It's not like Eli would hire an attorney against him. That's not the Amish way."

"That's what Millie said."

Aiden studied me. "It seems to me Millie Fisher is a wise woman. I'm looking forward to meeting her sometime soon."

"You would like her." I glanced back at the kitchen. "Did you know that she is the match-maker for the village?"

"Oh?" Aiden asked.

I looked up at him. "She said that we are a perfect match."

"I'm glad Millie can reassure on that point." His lips brushed mine. "But I already knew it. I knew that since the day I met you."

"You didn't show it the day we met," I said.

He smiled. "I knew you were the kind of woman who had to make up her own mind about a person. I had all the time in the world to wait for you, Bailey King."

Chapter 33

I went straight to bed after Aiden left and was up the next morning at four. I was determined to beat Charlotte and my grandmother downstairs so that I could make most of the candies for the day. They both had been working so hard in the shop, and it was time to reward them.

By the time *Maami* came downstairs at five thirty, I had all the fudge made and had restocked the marshmallow eggs and chocolate bunnies and pigs. The bunnies and pigs were cooling in the refrigerator.

Maami pulled up short as she came through the swinging door. "Bailey King, what on earth are you doing?"

I was cleaning the large island with vinegar and water to prep for the next batch of candy. I wanted to make taffy because I'd noticed that we were running short. "What does it look like I'm doing?" I asked with an innocent smile.

Charlotte walked into the kitchen too. "Wow. Bailey, did you do all this?" She blinked. "Now I know why Jean Pierre wanted to make you head chocolatier."

I laughed. "You've both been working so hard, and I know that between the toffee rabbit and

Stephen's death, I haven't been pulling my weight around here since I got home. I just want you to know that the shop and the two of you are important to me, and I want to do my part."

Maami's eyes brimmed with tears.

"I'm glad you're both here because I have some news." I grinned.

Charlotte clapped her hands. "Aiden asked you to marry him!"

I shot her a look. "Nooo . . . You are almost as bad as Juliet about that."

"I can't be that bad," Charlotte said, looking aghast at the very idea.

"In two weeks, the two of you are going to Florida for a week of fun in the sun!"

They blinked at me in unison and said nothing.

"I booked you a trip on the Amish bus that goes to Pinecraft and rented a little bungalow for you by the beach."

"But what about you?" *Maami* asked, seeming to have finally found her voice.

"I'll stay here and mind the shop. You take care of it when I'm in New York, *Maami*. It's the least I can do for you and for Charlotte too."

"We can't accept this," my grandmother said. "It will be too much work for just one person."

"Emily will be with me, and this is my gift to you."

Charlotte grabbed my grandmother's arm. "Oh please, let us go, Cousin Clara. I have always wanted to go to Florida, and this might be my only chance."

Maami looked from Charlotte to me and back again. "It's already paid for?" she asked.

"In full," I said. "Not at all refundable."

Maami's eyes glistened. "Then, I suppose, Charlotte, we must go to Pinecraft."

Charlotte jumped up and down. "This has been the very best year. First New York and now Florida!"

Maami said nothing more but pulled Charlotte and me into a three-way hug.

I spent the rest of the day working at the candy shop. I did everything I could to make the day lighter for my grandmother and Charlotte. Finally, *Maami* couldn't take it any longer and shooed me out the door just after lunch. "Go, Bailey, we know you are dying to do some of your snooping."

She couldn't be more right, and the first person I wanted to snoop on was Sybil Horn.

As I drove into Millersburg, my cell phone buzzed in my pocket, telling me I had a text message. A message from Aiden. Where are you?

Millersburg, running an errand, I texted back. He didn't need to know that the errand was related to the investigation, at least not yet.

Millersburg was the county seat of Holmes County. No one would consider it anything other than a small town. The county seat had about forty thousand residents, and unlike other places in Holmes County, almost all of those residents were English.

The center of town was marked by the giant courthouse with its domed clock tower and sculpted lady of justice looking down on the street. There was a small green next to the courthouse with a large statue of a Civil War soldier. That was about as un-Amish as you could get, having a military statue as the focal point of the town. The statue overlooked the intersection of the county's two main routes, Route 39 and Route 62. I didn't know whether Millersburg had been chosen to be the county seat before or after the roads converged there.

I parked on the street across from the courthouse and removed from my pocket the scrap of paper with Sybil's address that Millie had given me the night before. I studied the paper. The address should be straight ahead. I glanced up and saw a girl look up and down the street and turn the corner in the direction I wanted to go. She had long brown hair that fell to her waist and was tethered at the nape of her neck in a ponytail. She wore a T-shirt, jeans, and round wire-rimmed glasses. There was nothing about her that would have caught my attention except for her face. I was certain that Katey Beiler had just turned the corner, and she was wearing English clothes. I hurried after her and was within twenty feet when she went through a window-less door into a flat-faced brick building that I suspected dated back to the turn of the twentieth century.

I walked up to the door where she had dis-appeared and pulled the scrap of paper from my pocket to be sure. I was right. The address matched the one carved into the side of the building. Was this what Millie wanted me to see, but was unable to tell me? That Katey Beiler was going English? Why hadn't she just told me that? And no wonder the girl didn't want to marry Eli. If she did, she would be Amish forever.

I stood there for a moment wondering what I should do. Should I try to speak to Sybil now, when I knew Katey was in there?

I always had the option to call Aiden and tell him what I had seen, but what good would that do? There was no English law that said a young Amish woman couldn't dress like an *Englischer*.

I decided at least to see if I could take a peek into the building before I knocked on the door and asked to speak to Sybil.

The door was large, old, of dark wood. It looked like something out of a British castle, not a door one usually saw in Amish Country, where blond wood and plainness was the norm.

There was a keyhole, and I peered through. All I could see was the inner working of the lock. The keyhole, unlike the ones in most Saturday morning cartoons that I had grown up watching, didn't give me a clear view into the building.

I shook my head and was about to straighten up when the door flew open. I fell inside the building flat on my face. Before I could get up, someone pulled me by the arm and slammed the door behind me. I was trapped.

Chapter 34

A man loomed over me. He wore jeans and a polo shirt and had a full, close-cropped beard. I guessed that he was in his thirties, and he most definitely was not Amish. "What are you doing here?" he wanted to know.

"I . . . I . . ." I scrambled to my feet, and much to my relief, he didn't stop me. When I stood, I noted that I was just a couple of inches shorter than him, but he outweighed me by quite a bit if the biceps barely restrained by his T-shirt were any indication.

I took a step back and put my hand on the door handle. I started to open the door. Clearly, I wasn't wanted here, and this was a case when I knew better than to overstay my welcome.

"Leaving already?" the man asked. "I thought you would want to learn more."

I still had my hand on the door. "Learn more about what?" I asked.

"Did you hear about what we do here and want to see if it was a good fit for you too? I know it can be scary to leave, but this is the best place for you to come once you make that difficult decision."

I squinted at him. "Leave what? What are you talking about?"

He cocked his head. "You're still on the fence,

I see. There's no pressure here. We don't want to convince you either way. It's your decision, but we want you to know that there are places like this you can reach out to if you decide to go. You don't have to feel like you're in it alone."

I felt as if I was in some kind of self-help promotional video. "I'm not looking to leave anything. I'm here to talk to Sybil Horn."

He stepped back. "Are you a reporter?"

I cocked my head. "No, but would it matter if I were? Do you have something to hide?"

"No, we don't," he said with a scowl. His demeanor had completely changed. "What's your name?"

"Bailey King." I had a sneaking suspicion that I had seen him before, but I didn't know where. Holmes County was small. I could have seen him anywhere, at the market, on a walk, or out at a restaurant. However, my gut told me that it was fairly recent.

"Why do you want to speak to Sybil?"

I thought it would be best to be straight with this guy or he was never going to let me out of the entry. "My Amish friend Millie Fisher told me to talk to her."

His face cleared. "Millie is a nice lady. Sybil is in the back of the building." The man walked down the hallway. He turned when I didn't follow him. "If you want to see Sybil, you will have to follow me."

I chewed on my lower lip. Aiden's voice in my head was telling me not to go, but I couldn't leave until I'd spoken to Sybil. After that, I would call Aiden, I promised myself.

As we moved down the hallway, I asked, "What's your name?"

"Adam."

"Adam what?"

"We only use first names here."

This was getting weirder by the second.

Adam stopped in front of a closed door. He slowly opened it and pushed the door halfway in. I was trying to guess what might be in there. Was Katey inside the room too? Was she all right? All sorts of terrible scenarios played out in my head. I should have called Aiden the moment I saw Katey go inside this building. This was a case where curiosity just might have killed the chocolatier.

He pointed into the room. "Go ahead and look. I think it's the best representation of what we do here."

I didn't like the sound of that. I didn't like it at all. I hesitated and then peeked around the door frame. The overhead light was on as well as a green desk lamp in the middle of a table. Katey sat at that table bent over a piece of paper with a pencil in one hand. She made a mark on the paper in front of her and then pushed it in the direction of the person sitting across from her.

The stranger was a dark-haired woman in her fifties, I would guess. She picked up the piece of paper that Katey gave to her and studied it. She set it back on the table and picked up a pencil of her own. She began to make marks on the paper. "That's good, but you divided by two when you should have used four." She wrote something on the paper. "See how that makes the equation easier to do?"

Katey studied the paper. "*Ya, danki*. I think I know what you want me to do now."

"Sybil, you have a visitor sent here by Millie."

Katey jumped out of her seat with a look of panic on her face. "What are you doing here? Did my father send you?"

I held my hands up in surrender. "No, no one sent me. I was in Millersburg and saw you walking down the street."

She narrowed her eyes. The fear was gone, replaced by anger. "You followed me here? Who do you think you are?"

"I came here to speak to Sybil. I didn't know that it would be the same place you were going."

The dark-haired woman stood. "I'm Sybil." She had a regal demeanor about her and had long thin fingers that were perfect for playing the piano. She held her chin high. "How can I help you? Do you want to get your GRE too? I see that you are already in English clothes, but I don't think you're ready quite yet to leave the Amish way. I can see you might be trying too hard with your clothes."

I looked down at my outfit. What was wrong with what I had on, and what wasn't so English about it? I was the most English person in the room. I had lived in the biggest city in the world most of my adult life. Where did she get off telling me that my outfit was trying too hard?

She must have seen the expression on my face. "I think you would do better with something simpler like what Katey is wearing, and then maybe you can move on to more advanced English clothing."

"I'm not Amish. Why would you think that I'm Amish?"

She blinked. "Because Amish are the only ones who come here for help."

"I'm not Amish," I said for a second time.

Adam shifted his stance. "Sybil, this is Bailey King."

"Oh." Recognition registered in her eyes.

"Millie Fisher said I should talk to you."

She nodded. "If you come on recommendation from Millie, I know it's for a good reason. Adam, can you continue the lesson with Katey while I chat with Bailey?"

Katey's cheeks turned bright red and a small smile curved her lips. Adam smiled too. I saw more emotions pass between the two of them than I had ever seen between Katey and Eli.

Perhaps I had met the reason why Katey didn't want to marry Eli. If she wanted to be with Adam she might have to leave the Amish—and that could be precisely why she was here.

Adam sat down next to Katey and scooted his chair just an inch closer to her. I wasn't imagining things; there was a connection between these two people.

"I could use another cup of coffee. Let's talk in the kitchen." Sybil picked up a mug from the desk and headed out the door.

Before I followed her, I glanced back at Adam and Katey. The pair had their heads bent toward each other. I would bet anything they weren't talking about math.

Sybil walked through a swinging door into a kitchen. Like the rest of the apartment I had seen, the room was covered in dark wood paneling and had small windows. I felt as if I was in a cave. In the middle of the kitchen was a giant marble island that was surrounded by metal stools just like the ones we had back in the kitchen at Swissmen Sweets. They were bigger on utility than looks.

Sybil caught me examining my surroundings. "This used to be an attorney's office. That's why there is all the marble and dark wood. It's not really my style; I like things more open and bright, but I can't bring myself to change it and harm the integrity of the building. I believe that all people and all things have an innate character to them." She walked to the coffeemaker on the counter, filled her mug, and then filled a second mug. She held that one out to me.

The coffee smelled like hazelnut.

"Cream or sugar?"

I shook my head. "This is fine. Thank you."

She sat on a stool at the large island and pointed at the one opposite her. "Why did Millie tell you to talk to me?"

"She thought you could help me. . . ." I trailed off.

"In finding out who killed Stephen Raber?" She lifted her coffee mug to her mouth and arched her brow.

Chapter 35

I gaped at the woman across from me. "How do you know that?"

"Don't look so surprised, Bailey King. Do you think I have never heard of you before? Your reputation precedes you."

I wondered if that was a good thing or not.

"Millie is a friend of mine, but I don't know why she would send you here. I have no idea what happened to Stephen. I never even spoke to the man in my life. Most of the Amish I work with and know are ones who want to leave the faith. As far as I know, Stephen was never in that category."

"But Katey is?"

She pressed her lips together. "Yes."

"What is it you do here? Millie said that you help people leave the Amish, but what does that even mean?"

"I know it's hard for someone who grew up English to understand, but the Amish are more secluded from English culture than it may appear. When they are born, they don't have Social Security numbers or birth certificates, making it difficult to leave the faith and live in the English world. I help the Amish who don't have those things so that they can move more easily into their new lives."

"So, you convert them to English life?"

"No." Her voice was firm but not sharp. "The people who come to me have decided to leave before they arrive. If they are unsure, I'm honest with them about what they will need as an English person and tell them to pray about the decision. No Amish person should take leaving the only life he or she has ever known lightly. I don't take it lightly when they come to me and ask for help. Take Katey, for example."

"What about Katey?" I asked.

"She came to me over a year ago because she wanted to leave the Amish. Her family wants her to marry a man she doesn't love. Most Amish districts don't have traditionally arranged marriages any longer, but there can be . . . *pressure* to marry. A woman is still supposed to be a wife and mother in the community. Katey is almost twenty-seven. By her family's estimation she is losing time to have a family and follow the plan God has for her."

I grimaced. I was older than Katey, but not much. If I was Amish I certainly would be in the same position she was in. So, I had been right in thinking that she didn't want to marry Eli. "But Katey is still Amish," I said.

"That's because of what I told you before. I don't talk people out of leaving the Amish. Katey is still undecided, so I let her come here and learn about English life. I think she will leave soon.

She is studying for her GRE and the test is next week. She's a very bright woman, and as nervous as she is about taking the test, I am certain she will pass. When she passes the test, she will have the confidence to leave."

I nodded. "If Katey isn't happy being Amish, she should leave."

Sybil relaxed.

"But why would Millie want me to talk to you? What does this have to do with Stephen Raber's murder?"

Sybil stood up and refilled her mug of coffee. I hadn't even realized that she had finished her first cup. I'd yet to take a sip of mine. "That's unclear to me."

I took a breath. "Does anyone in Katey's family know that she comes here?"

She shook her head. "No."

"Do they know about Adam?" I cocked my head. "Don't tell me that you see them together all the time and haven't noticed how they like each other."

She pressed her lips together, then said, "Adam has worked with me for a couple of years, and he knows I have a policy that we cannot get romantically involved with the Amish who come here for help. It confuses them and may influence their decision for the wrong reasons. Adam may care for Katey, but he would never violate our policy."

I wasn't sure about that but didn't say anything. I stood up. "How long have you been helping the Amish who decide to leave?"

"For the last fifteen years. I left the Amish myself when I was twenty. It was a very difficult transition." She peered into her coffee. "Some unfortunate things happened." She looked up again. "If I can stop what happened to me from happening to anyone else, I will."

I wanted to ask her what had happened, but it seemed to be too personal. Instead, I asked, "Have you ever helped a person named Casey Raber?"

"Raber? Like Eli, the man Katey is supposed to marry?"

I nodded. "He's Eli's older brother."

"When would he have left?" she asked.

"He was only twelve when he ran away. Twenty years ago at least," I said.

She shook her head. "No, I have never heard of him. I'm sorry."

I left my untouched coffee on the island. "Thank you for the coffee."

She nodded. "I hope you find all the answers that you seek, Bailey. I'm in the business of helping people do just that."

I nodded.

"You can go out the back door if you like." She stood up and opened the door.

I stood too, and as I did I noticed a bouquet

of little white flowers on the kitchen counter. They were in bloom and tucked in a mason jar. I swallowed. "Lovely flowers. What are they?" I asked, even though I already knew the answer.

She seemed surprised by my question and looked back at the counter. "Lily of the valley."

"You know they are poisonous," I said.

"I've heard that. Many beautiful things are." She opened the door even wider. "You should go. I have much work to do."

I stepped through the door, and found myself standing in an alleyway with a windowless, two-story, brick building on either side of me.

"Just walk straight ahead," she said. "And turn right when you get to the corner of the building. You'll find yourself back on the main road."

I nodded, and she closed the door. I heard a light click as the bolt on the door slid home. I stood there for a moment chewing on my lower lip. I didn't like the idea of leaving Katey in the building. Millie trusted Sybil, but I wasn't so sure. I thought her mission was sincere, but how could she be blind to how much Adam and Katey cared for each other?

I shook my head. What Katey Beiler did was none of my business unless it was related to the murder. If Eli was the one who had been killed, I would have thought this clue about her leaving the Amish and being in love with an English man was pertinent to the investigation, but Eli was very much alive. His father was dead. His father, who had nothing to do with Sybil Horn or her mission to help runaway Amish.

I followed Sybil's directions and found myself on Route 39 again in the shadow of the forbidding courthouse. Even though the information I'd found out about Katey and Sybil might not be important to the case, I was eager to return to Harvest and talk to Aiden.

I started walking to my car and was in the process of removing my phone from the back pocket of my jeans to see if I had missed any messages from Aiden when a hand clamped on my shoulder. I jumped, and the phone went flying from my hand, landing in the middle of the road. An Amish buggy passed by at that moment, and the horse stomped on my phone before the hard metal wheels ran over it for good measure.

The buggy didn't even slow down. I stood there for a moment in a daze. My phone had been crushed by an Amish buggy. What were the odds? Cass was never going to believe this. Then again, she probably would. The most ridiculous stuff happened to me, including finding dead bodies on an alarmingly regular basis.

Katey covered her mouth. "I'm so, so sorry. Is your phone all right?"

I looked at her out of the corner of my eye. The phone was most certainly not all right. I looked both ways to make sure the path was clear. I didn't want to get hit by a buggy along with my phone. That really would be unbelievable. When I saw the coast was clear, I stepped into the street and picked up my phone. It was in three pieces. There was no coming back from that.

"I really am sorry," Katey said again. This time there were tears in her voice.

I looked at her and gave her a wobbly smile. Mostly because I would have to drive to Canton to get a new phone. There were some cell phone places in Holmes County, but not the carrier that I used. It was going to be a hassle but, looking at Katey's tearstained face, I could see that it was an accident.

"Don't worry about it. I can always get a new phone."

She nodded as if she wasn't so sure about that.

"Did you want to talk to me?" I figured that if I changed the topic from the phone, she would stop looking as if she might burst into tears any second.

"*Ya*, I mean, yes, I would like to talk to you."

I could tell that this conversation was going to be more than a casual chat on the sidewalk, so I suggested that we cross the street and sit on one of the benches next to the courthouse, under the view of the Civil War soldier.

She nodded, and we crossed the street, looking out first for any cell-phone-crushing buggies. Once we were on the other side of the street,

Katey perched on the bench next to me. She sat as far away from me as she could and stared down at her folded hands.

I felt my face soften, and I forgot the broken phone. "Katey, what's wrong? Can I help you?"

She looked at me with tears in her eyes. "Please don't tell my family or Eli what I have been doing. I don't want them to know just yet that I plan to leave the Amish way."

"Why are you waiting to tell them, if I may ask? Eli thinks that the two of you will marry."

She looked back down at her hands. "I know, and I feel terrible about that. I haven't told them because I wanted to wait until I was ready. Adam tells me to wait until I know for sure. Sybil does too," she added quickly. "I'm studying for the GRE, you see." She lifted her chin as if in challenge to me. "I want to go to college and be a nurse." She glanced down at her hands. "If I want to be a nurse, I have to leave the Amish. I'm sorry that it has to be this way because I love the people in my community, but education is not a priority with the Amish and it's always been a priority to me."

"What about Eli? Don't you think you owe it to him to tell him sooner rather than later? You did agree to marry him."

She shook her head. "I never said that I would marry him. My father said so, which is not the same."

This was news. "Then why didn't you tell your father how you felt?"

"It's not that simple. Stephen and my father have wanted Eli and me to marry since we were children."

"Why?"

She sighed. "I have no siblings. My mother died when I was a girl, and my father never remarried. If Eli and I marry, our two smaller farms would combine into one larger farm."

"But Liam Zimmerman is in the middle of your two properties."

She nodded. "That is a problem, but none of us think that Liam will be there very long. It's clear that he's unhappy. Like most English, he won't commit and will move somewhere else."

I wasn't so sure about that. Zimmerman had seemed very committed to his land and his study of the native Ohio plants in the woods. I didn't know much about plants, but I assumed that it would be difficult to move the plants at this point and keep them alive.

She shook her head. "Eli will be fine. It has always been a business deal to him. He doesn't love me. He hasn't done a single thing to prove to me that he loves me. He loves the land. That's all."

"What will happen to the land when you leave?"

She bit the inside of her lip. "As Adam says, that's something I can't worry about. When I

315

walk away from my family, I will be walking away from my family farm too."

"As Adam says . . ." Hmm, that comment wasn't lost on me.

"What do you want me to do, Katey?" I asked.

She looked me in the eye. "Just let me be. Let all of this go. Don't get involved in any of it. That's what I want you to do. For me and for yourself."

She stood up and walked away before I could ask her why that sounded like a warning.

Chapter 36

As I returned to Harvest, my head was spinning. I tried to call Aiden from the shop's landline since my cell was smashed to pieces, but he didn't answer.

Maami handed a waiting candy box to the only customer still in the shop. "What's wrong, Bailey?"

I gave her a wan smile and was relieved that Charlotte wasn't there to overhear our conversation. I told her about my visit with Sybil Horn.

She nodded. "I do know of Sybil. All the Amish in the county do. Many times, she is the first person who is questioned when a child has left the faith. And you say Katey Beiler was there?"

I nodded. "I need to tell Aiden this."

"Do you think you should tell her family?" my grandmother asked.

I shook my head. "No. She made me promise that I wouldn't tell her father or Eli. According to her, it was an arranged marriage that Beiler and Stephen cooked up years ago when Eli and Katey were children as a way to combine the two small farms into a larger, more productive one."

My grandmother thought on this for a moment and then said, "Do you think Stephen changed his mind and was against the wedding? If that's the case, would someone kill him over it?"

"And who?" I asked.

"I can only think of the two people still living who would want this wedding to happen. Eli or Jud Beiler."

I shivered.

"I really have to talk to Aiden. Normally, I would just text him so he would get the message right away. And I have to get a new phone. It's still early afternoon. Care if I run into Canton to do that?"

She patted my cheek. "You go. You've worked very hard today. Charlotte and I can handle the rest of the customers for this last hour or so."

Through the large front window of the shop, I saw children running around the village, enjoying Easter Days. Several Amish families were standing near the toffee rabbit, admiring it, while English families took selfies with it. "If you're sure," I said.

"I'm sure, but just be careful. I will tell Aiden where you went when he calls the shop."

I hugged her. "I'm going to sleep at my own house tonight. I need to go back there. I'll stop by and pick up Puff before going home."

"But aren't you afraid?" *Maami* asked.

"I'm tired of being afraid," I said with more conviction than I felt.

She nodded. "All right."

The drive to Canton was uneventful, and when I walked into the store of my cell phone carrier, I handed the phone to the teenager behind the desk. "Whoa, what happened here?"

"It got run over by an Amish buggy," I said forlornly.

He whistled. "Bummer, but it's not the first time I've heard that one."

I wasn't too surprised.

Two painfully long hours later, I left the store with a new phone all set up with my photos and calendar, which thankfully had been stored in the cloud. I called and texted Aiden that I had a new phone and was heading back to Harvest, but still heard nothing. I tried not to worry about his silence, but I would be lying if I said it didn't concern me a little.

It was dark by the time I reached Main Street, and Easter Days was over for yet another day. It was hard to believe there was just one day left before Easter. I hurried into the shop, collected Puff, and said good-bye to my grandmother and Charlotte before they could talk me into staying another night at the candy shop.

I pulled my car into the little garage and lifted Puff out of the passenger seat. I unlocked the back door to my little house and froze. Overhead, I heard a creak and footsteps. I listened as the footsteps moved across the floor above me. I held Puff to my chest.

I heard the person move to the top of the stairs. I set Puff on the floor and peeked around the side of the wall into the living room. I could see the bottom of the stairs. Whoever was up there was standing at the top of the steps. I glanced at the loveseat where the pillow I'd used to protect myself from Eli's visit had been. This time I needed something more substantial. I hurried into the kitchen and grabbed a cast iron frying pan. Back in the living room, I heard the slow and deliberate footsteps make their way down from the second floor.

When I saw a man's boot appear in my view, I raised my frying pan. "Ahh!" And stopped just short of hitting the man over the head when I saw that it was Aiden.

"What the—?" Aiden appeared in front of me. "Bailey, what are you doing with that pan?"

"Oh." I held the frying pan in my hands as if I had just noticed it was there. "I heard footsteps. I thought it was the man who attacked me."

"Your grandmother told me that you were staying at your house for the night, which I don't think is the best idea. I texted you and said I would meet you here."

"I never got the text," I said. The text must have come through when my phone was incapacitated.

He stared at the frying pan in my hands. "At least now I know that you will defend yourself. That is comforting. Is that cast iron?"

I nodded.

Aiden smiled. "Good. If you are going to hit

someone in self-defense, make it count." Then he asked, "Did you get any of my texts at all?"

"Oh," I said again. "My cell phone was kind of out of commission. Didn't my grandmother tell you that?"

"She said it was broken and you had to go to Canton to get it fixed, but no more than that. How broken was it?"

"It sorta got run over by a buggy."

"How does a buggy run over your phone?"

"Easily if your phone is lying in the middle of Route Thirty-nine. Actually, I really think the horse stomping on it was what did it in."

Aiden looked heavenward and sighed.

Puff peeked around the opening between the kitchen and the living room.

"The coast is clear," I told the rabbit.

Puff hopped into the living room and went straight for Aiden, sitting on his foot.

I grinned. "She missed you."

"Clearly."

"I'm glad you're here. I have a lot to tell you."

Aiden and I sat at the small dining table and I told him about my movements throughout the afternoon. His jaw twitched when I told him about going into Sybil's building. I knew he wouldn't approve of that part.

"What does this have to do with Stephen's death?" he asked.

"I have no idea," I admitted.

"If Eli was the man who was murdered, then you might be on to something, but . . ." He trailed off.

"I thought the same thing." I shook my head and pondered for a moment. "What if it is Zimmerman after all?"

"I don't follow you."

"Zimmerman is all worked up about the Amish walking through his woods and about the fact that Stephen Raber's newest rabbit barn is too close to his property line, right?"

"Right," Aiden said slowly.

"He knew that Eli and Katey were courting, and he must know in the Amish world that is much more serious than dating in the English world. There was a good chance the pair would marry and merge their lands, really messing with his woodland project, and we can't forget that he's a botanist who knows all about plants and their poisonous properties. Not to mention he has lily of the valley growing in his woods. It would be a murder weapon of convenience for him."

"But then why kill Stephen if he wants to stop the wedding?"

I sat back in my chair and sighed. It was a good question. I jumped up in my seat. "Maybe we are going about this all wrong."

"What do you mean?"

"How do we know that Stephen was the person who was meant to be killed? He ate the candy, yes, but maybe he wasn't the intended victim."

"But the notes," Aiden said. "They more than indicate that someone wanted him to be punished for something he did."

"Oh right. But what did he do? Everyone I've spoken to thinks he was the greatest guy ever. Well, except for Zimmerman, but I can't see him being able to convince Amish people to drop notes in the Rabers' phone shed each morning."

"Me either," Aiden agreed.

"Maybe we should look at the notes again?" I suggested.

"You shouldn't have seen them in the first place. I hate it that Eli got you involved in this." He closed his eyes for a moment. "You could have been killed the other night."

I shook my head. "I don't think whoever attacked me wanted to kill me. He had ample opportunity to do it, and he warned me off from the case. He wanted those notes, which is why we should look at them again."

"Or Penny just happened to interrupt him."

I shivered. "I wasn't seriously hurt."

He rubbed his forehead. "Is that supposed to make me feel better? Because it doesn't."

"You can't keep saying you wish I weren't involved. I am involved, and I could be a lot more help if I saw the rest of those notes."

"Okay, I have a printout of them in the car. It will be easier to review than the photos you took with your phone, assuming that you still have them after the buggy incident."

"Don't worry. I didn't lose anything. It was all in the cloud."

"Great. Wait here." He stood up and strode out the front door.

"Where else would I be going? This is my house."

While Aiden was outside, I fed and watered Puff. I filled her dish with bunny food, but she went straight for the carrots.

Aiden walked back inside and spread a number of photocopied pages across my table.

I scanned the notes. Each one made me shiver.

"You will pay for what you did."

"God will exact His revenge."

"Appeal to the Lord for forgiveness."

I looked up at Aiden. "Each one gets creepier."

He nodded. "But we still have no idea who wrote them. I had the handwriting looked at, but without a sample to compare it to, that doesn't help much. The sheriff isn't willing to fork out the money for the full analysis. In this case, I don't blame him. It's expensive for BCI, Ohio's investigation bureau, to look at the handwriting when the effort would most likely go nowhere."

"I think the oddest thing is that Zimmerman said a different Amish person delivered the notes every morning."

"The only witness is Zimmerman, and he's not

a reliable one. He thinks that all the Amish look the same," Aiden said.

"But he said each of these people was different," I insisted.

"I know, but he was unable to describe them. He just said they were Amish. Other than noting whether they were male or female, he couldn't tell us any other detail about them. Trust me when I say that my deputies pressed him for the information. We took Zimmerman down to the station today because he was being a difficult witness."

I grimaced. "I'm sure he loved that."

"It wasn't one of my more pleasant interrogations."

I frowned. "Are you sure you can believe Zimmerman that Amish put those notes in the shed? He's the only witness. I can't believe that Eli or his father wouldn't have seen the notes being delivered too, since they were all left at the same time. I mean, if I were getting threatening notes each morning, I would do a stakeout or something to catch the person in the act of putting the notes in my phone shed."

"I'm sure you would," Aiden said.

I ignored the amusement in Aiden's tone and reread all the notes. I noticed nothing more than I had the first time I read them. Vague threats that alluded to something in the past, but no hints of what that might have been. I sighed.

"It's got you stumped too," Aiden teased.

"I hate to admit it, but yes." I sat back in my chair. "Where do we go from here?"

"I'll check out Sybil Horn. It might be a loose end, but at this point, I'm ready to follow any lead."

I nodded.

He shifted in his seat. "I want you to stay at Swissmen Sweets for a few days until this case is closed."

I shook my head. I wouldn't be scared out of my new home. It had taken me too long to find the perfect place and move here. I refused to be afraid of my own house. "I'm staying here. This is my home. A home that I haven't had much time to enjoy. I don't want to run away from it. I don't want to be afraid to be here."

Aiden pursed his lips. "I can see that you're not going to budge on this."

I shook my head. "I'm not."

He walked over to me. "Well, in that case, I need a pillow and a blanket. I'm spending the night here on the couch."

"That's really not necessary." I stared at the loveseat. "Besides, there is no way you can sleep on that thing. Your legs will hang over the side."

He cocked his head. "Yeah, why didn't you buy a real couch? That baby couch isn't working for me."

"First of all, I didn't buy it. It was a hand-me-down from one of my grandmother's Amish friends. Second of all, I never expected anyone to sleep on it."

"Well, I am."

I made a face.

"Hey, you put your foot down; I can put my foot down too. This is what we call a compromise. It's a staple of all good relationships."

I looked him in the eye. "Is that what we have? A good relationship?"

"It's what I want," he said, not blinking his chocolate brown eyes as he looked at me.

"Me too," I whispered. "And you are in luck. I have an air mattress."

He laughed. "Thank God."

Chapter 37

I had a fitful night's sleep, plagued by nightmares about a giant toffee rabbit that continued to fall on top of me. When I tried to push the giant candy rabbit off me, I realized that it was Stephen Raber's dead body. It didn't help that my cheek, where the attacker had pressed me up against the side of my garage, itched terribly, and every time my cheek grazed my pillow, I woke up. Each time, I would lie silently listening to the house settle. I also listened for any movement from below by Aiden, but I heard nothing. He must have been a sound sleeper. Something I envied.

At five thirty, I gave up trying to go back to sleep. I knew I could go work at Swissmen Sweets at that hour. My grandmother and Charlotte would already be in the kitchen. Before I did that, I needed coffee, preferably by the gallon. I crept downstairs, taking care not to wake Aiden, but it seemed my caution was in vain.

I found him awake and sitting on the loveseat. The air mattress was already deflated and folded up in the corner of the room. The sheets and blankets I had given him the night before were neatly folded on top of the air mattress.

Aiden tied his shoes. "I have to go into the station early this morning. The sheriff is on vacation, so I'm in charge of the department." He clenched his jaw. "I have to do everything right while he's gone. I can't give him any reason to . . ."

I folded my arms over my chest. "To do what?"

He shook his head. "You look cute in the morning with your hair pointed every which way."

I touched the top of my head and felt my cheeks flush. Why hadn't I taken the time to brush my hair before I came downstairs or at least pull it back into a ponytail? My wavy hair was likely resembling a rat's nest.

"What's your plan for the day?" Aiden asked.

"I'm going to the candy shop," I said.

"And?" He arched his brow.

I shook my head. "I don't know yet. This case has me stumped. I think it might help me to step away from it for a bit and sort through what we know, which isn't much."

He grinned. "Music to my ears."

"Don't get used to it."

He laughed. "Oh, I won't. I'm just going to enjoy it while it lasts." He leaned over and kissed me before walking out the door.

As he left, all I could think was how nice it was to see him in the morning, if only for a few minutes.

As I expected, by the time I got to Swissmen Sweets, an hour later, my grandmother and Charlotte were already hard at work in the shop.

They were in the front room, sliding fresh trays of chocolates and candies into the domed glass display case.

"Bailey," *Maami* said. "It is so *gut* to see you. I trust that you rested well at home."

I hadn't rested well, but I wasn't going to tell my grandmother that. "Fine, thanks to Puff." I held up the large white rabbit; I'd brought her with me to the candy shop. "I had this girl for company." I decided it was wise not to mention that Aiden had spent the night at my house. Even though his stay had been completely innocent, my Amish grandmother might still have viewed it as inappropriate.

There was a light thump to my left, and I saw Nutmeg dash out from the short hallway that led to the second floor and slide through the kitchen. He ran straight for Puff and the two creatures touched noses.

My grandmother put her hands on her hips. "That cat and rabbit really love each other. I've never seen anything like it. They should be natural enemies."

Nutmeg rubbed his orange body next to the white rabbit.

"They don't look like enemies to me," Charlotte said.

"At least something is going right," I said.

Maami looked at me. "What's wrong, my dear?"

"It's the murder. I'm not any closer to solving it. Neither is Aiden. I feel like we are just spinning our wheels."

She patted my cheek. "It's not your job to solve this murder. Leave it to Aiden."

"Eli asked for my help."

She nodded. "And you promised. You're a woman of your word, and I am proud of you for that."

"What are you going to do?" Charlotte asked.

"Right now, I'm going to do my job, and that job is to sell candy. I will worry about the murder later."

My grandmother smiled. "*Gut*. We miss having you in the shop."

I hugged her. "I miss being here. It's especially nice to be here and not have to think about how to construct a giant toffee rabbit."

"Amen to that," Charlotte said. "And maybe you can help me decide what to pack for Florida. I'm terribly excited. It's so kind of you to send me with Cousin Clara, Bailey. I've had so many adventures since I met you."

I smiled. "Number one is sunscreen, and don't tell me that Amish don't use sunscreen. You are going to need it with that red hair and fair skin."

Maami, Charlotte, and I worked through the morning. Business was brisk at the candy shop with a lot of Easter Days visitors stopping by. As much as some of the Amish disliked all the activities Margot organized on the square each year, no one could deny that she got results. Swissmen Sweets certainly saw an uptick in business whenever Margot hatched one of her plans, and I was grateful for that. The better Swissmen Sweets did, the less guilty I would feel for filming in New York every six months.

There was a lull in the business close to lunchtime. Most of the crowd was either eating the substantial food offerings on the square or at one of the many Amish restaurants in the county. I removed my apron. "I think I'm going to take a break," I told my grandmother and Charlotte.

"Been away from sleuthing too long?" my grandmother asked with a twinkle in her eye.

I laughed. "I'm just going over to the square to check on the toffee rabbit."

Charlotte started to chuckle, and my grandmother joined in.

I left the shop shaking my head.

On the square, I saw Eli Raber standing alone by the pen of rabbits.

He waved at me as I crossed the street. "I'll be ready to take my father's prized rabbit home tomorrow."

"You want Puff back?" I squeaked. Over the last few days I had become attached to the friendly bunny, and I'd dreaded the thought of Eli wanting me to relinquish her.

"*Ya*, I've decided that I don't want to raise

rabbits. There is a farm in Geauga County that is interested in buying all my rabbits for a good price."

"But," I said, "Puff is a house rabbit. You can't sell her with the others."

He frowned. "Rabbits were my father's business, not mine. I mean to make something out of that farm, and I can't with these animals. I'm going to have horses and cows, real livestock." He sneered at the bunnies in the pen. "Not these rodents."

"Can I buy Puff from you?"

He shook his head. "I gave the farmer the number of rabbits I had to sell and counted Puff among them."

"Maybe just ask him. I promise to pay you a good price."

"I'll see. In any case, I will come and collect Puff from you tomorrow. You will have her at the candy shop?"

I nodded and felt like I might be sick. I hated the idea of Puff going to a farm far away from here and being treated just like any other farm rabbit. Stephen had never treated her that way. She wouldn't do well. She was a spoiled rabbit in a lot of ways and used to a certain lifestyle.

"I need to get back to work." Eli turned away from me and went back to filling the rabbits' water dishes.

I wanted to argue more but stepped away from him. I needed some time to think of a way to convince him not to sell Puff with the other rabbits. Or if he sold her, to sell her to me.

"Bailey." Juliet waved to me from across the square. She had Jethro tucked under her arm, and the little pig's head bobbed up and down as Juliet ran toward me. How she did that in her kitten heels over the grass was a mystery to me. "Bailey, I need your help."

It seemed as if every time I saw Juliet, she needed my help with something.

I went to meet her for fear that she might turn an ankle as she leapt across the green lawn. "How can I help, Juliet?" I asked, waiting for her to say something about my fictitious upcoming wedding to her son.

"Oh, Bailey, Reverend Brook is just beside himself, worried over the break-in at the church. He's worried that the church won't be secure while he goes on his missionary conference next week."

"Have you called Aiden or someone else from the sheriff's department?"

"I have tried, but Aiden is so busy with this murder business. He can't take the time to come over and talk to the reverend."

"Do you want me to talk to him?"

She clasped Jethro to her chest. "Would you? It would be a great comfort to the reverend and to me if you would."

I smiled. "I'm not sure what I can say to make

him feel better since I'm not a police officer, but I can try."

She pressed Jethro and me into a three-way hug. "You are such a good girl. I'm so glad that you will be my daughter just as soon as you and Aiden get around to announcing your wedding. Have you thought about July if June seems too soon? I had Reverend Brook keep a few Saturdays open for you just in case."

I forced a smile. There was no winning this argument with Juliet, so I had given up trying. The truth was I wanted to marry Aiden just as badly as she wanted me to . . . someday. Someday didn't exactly mean in three months though.

Juliet waved to someone else on the square. "Oh, there is Bea. I must talk to her about choir practice for Easter Sunday. You know we have to be spot-on that day because it's the most important service of the year." She rushed off and then called over her shoulder, "Reverend Brook is in his office in the church. You go right in."

I stood in the middle of the square again, debating what to do. In the end, I decided to go to the church, not only because I'd promised Juliet that I would but because it was where the murder had started. Maybe I would learn something about Stephen's death there.

I went to the bright purple front door of the church and opened it easily. I shook my head. If Reverend Brook was worried about security, that would have to be the first change—locking the church when he didn't want people there. I looked around the door and noticed there wasn't an intercom anywhere to be seen. That would be my first suggestion to the reverend, so he could buzz people into the church. I knew he would want to keep the church open throughout the day. Sadly, considering what had happened on the square earlier in the week, that wasn't a good idea.

My footsteps echoed in the empty church. I had never been to the reverend's office, but I knew it was somewhere behind the sanctuary from the many times I had heard Juliet talk about it.

I walked through the white-and-blond wood sanctuary and through the door next to the organ where Charlotte played.

The door opened up into a dark hallway, but at the end of it, I saw light coming out through another door. I inched down the hallway toward the lit room. It was silent inside and I peered through the open door to see Reverend Brook at his desk, bent over something in his hands.

I knocked on the door frame, and the reverend jumped. Whatever he was holding flew into the air before clattering back on his desk. He slapped his hand over it but not before I saw that it was a ring. I held my breath to keep from saying anything even though I had my suspicions as to whom that ring was for.

"Bailey," he half shouted as if to cover his embarrassment. "What are you doing here?"

I stood in the doorway. "Juliet asked me to talk to you. She said you were upset that someone broke in to the church."

His face softened. "Juliet is always so concerned about the church. She is a good parishioner. I don't know how we would do half of the programs here without her."

I knew Juliet was much more than just a parishioner to Reverend Brook, especially considering the engagement ring he had hidden in his hand.

"Juliet is kind, but she didn't need to send you here. I'm fine." His face was still impossibly red.

"Any idea who might have broken in to the church kitchen?" I asked.

"Not a one. Aiden believes that whoever used our kitchen without permission had easy access to the church. There was no forced entry, and Margot did admit she forgot to lock it the night before." He shook his head. "Now, I am going to have to double check every time I let her use the church."

I thought about this. Could a member of Reverend Brook's church be the one to poison Stephen? It seemed to me that was more worrisome than an intruder breaking in.

"Have you thought about locking the church's front door and installing an intercom to buzz people inside?"

"Yes, the church board has been talking about that recently. I do think it's time that we instate some type of security. I hate the idea of the church not being open to all, but these are difficult times we live in." He shook his head. "Just think of the violence that has impacted our little village."

"I'm glad to see that you are all right," I said. "I won't keep you."

He nodded but his hand remained closed.

"Before I go, can I ask one more question?"

He nodded.

"Has everyone who was in the church the day of the murder been asked about the break-in?"

"I've been asked, and so has the church secretary. We were the only ones here that morning other than the cleaning staff."

"The cleaning staff? Did Aiden talk to them too?"

He shook his head. "Not that I know of. It is a crew of very shy Amish women that change constantly, and I didn't want them to be made uncomfortable. I'm sure they didn't know anything, but I believe Aiden insisted on talking to their manager. The manager reported they all said they saw nothing."

I inwardly groaned. The church cleaning staff would be the most likely people to have seen something related to the day Stephen died. Usually people in service positions like that are ignored, treated like wallpaper. I needed to tell

Aiden about the staff and he needed to track them down, no matter what their manager might have said. He needed to ask each young woman about what happened the day Stephen died. I kicked myself for not thinking of this before.

"You don't know who was there that day though?" I asked.

"Juliet usually manages that. It's hard enough for me to shepherd my flock and write my sermons. I need someone else to handle some of the practical business of the church."

"I'll ask her then," I said.

He nodded and looked at me expectantly. I took that as my cue to leave. I turned to do so, but then stopped myself. "Reverend?"

He looked up at me from his desk.

"Yes?" His face was red, and his hand was wrapped tightly around the ring that I knew was there.

"Ask her. She'll say yes."

He turned pale, and I left the room.

Chapter 38

I went back to the square with my head reeling over the idea that the church's Amish cleaning staff hadn't been properly questioned. I knew that Aiden did the best he could while trying to respect the culture, but I hoped Juliet could shed some light on who these women were.

I spotted Juliet standing with Margot next to the giant toffee bunny on the square. I didn't see Jethro with them but knew he had to be close by.

"Bailey," Margot said. "We were just talking about you."

That sounded foreboding, I thought.

"You did such a wonderful job on this sculpture that Juliet was saying she is certain you would want to do others."

"Umm . . . it depends on when you need them. I do have to go to New York from time to time."

Margot waved away this concern. "We will get the logistics all sorted out."

"How was Reverend Brook?" Juliet asked anxiously.

"He was fine. I think he believes you worry about him too much," I said.

"How can I not worry about the man I . . . ." She trailed off and covered her near slipup with a look.

Margot rolled her eyes at me. Like me, she knew what Juliet had almost said. One of the biggest mysteries in Harvest was why Juliet and Reverend Brook didn't admit they cared about each other. It might even be a bigger mystery than the murder.

"He told me that the Amish cleaning staff at the church was never questioned about the break-in—the police only spoke to the manager."

"Oh—" Juliet touched her cheek. "Of course, they weren't because we didn't want to upset the ladies."

"Don't you think they might have seen something?" Margot asked. She shook her head as if she couldn't believe Juliet could be so dense.

"I suppose they might have."

"I think Aiden needs to talk to them."

Juliet shook her head. "They wouldn't like to talk to my son, and the crew changes constantly. I don't even think the company that hired them knows who they all are. They are paid by the job, all cash."

I gaped. "They are paid under the table?"

Juliet frowned. "No, of course not. The church would never hire a company who did that. They are just paid at the end of every shift."

Margot snorted.

"If they won't talk to Aiden, I can talk to them. I just need to know who they are or who the manager is."

Juliet cocked her head and her ponytail dipped to one side. "I suppose that would be all right."

"What are their names?" I asked.

"I just know their first names," Juliet said. "Martha, Louisa, Katey, Mary, and Joan. There might be others, but those are all the ones I can remember."

"Katey?" I asked, feeling my pulse quicken.

She nodded. "Katey Beiler. She's a sweet, bookish Amish girl. Don't you know her? She and Eli Raber are set to marry."

Margot snorted again. "Katey Beiler isn't Amish."

"How can you say that?"

"Because she's not," Margot argued. "I see her in Millersburg all the time dressed like you or me." She stared at Juliet's polka-dotted dress for a moment. "Okay, maybe not dressed like you, but dressed like an English person. She's not Amish."

"Then why is she marrying Eli Raber?" Juliet asked, confused.

"I doubt she is," Margot said. "The last time I was in Millersburg, I saw her on the street kissing an English man."

"What did this man look like?" I asked.

Margot turned to me. "He was about your age and had one of those scruffy, I-don't-care-how-I-look beards that the young men seem to be so fond of nowadays."

It was Adam. It had to be. I had been right about their feelings for each other.

"Did you tell Aiden the names of the women?" I asked.

"The ones I could remember at the time. Joan and Katey just came back to me now." She smiled. "You know I'm not good at that type of detail."

Over Juliet's shoulder, I could see Eli watching us while a family looked at his rabbits. Had he heard Margot's outburst?

I started to walk over to him when I heard Juliet scream. I spun around and watched in horror as the giant toffee rabbit fell to the ground. Its head broke off upon impact.

Everyone on the square stood frozen for a moment as we stared at the wreckage of the giant rabbit. Quietly Jethro came around the side of the rabbit. There were chocolate and toffee pieces sticking to his short snout. It didn't take a detective to guess what just happened.

"Jethro!" Juliet cried. "How could you?"

In all the time I had known Juliet and her little pig, this was the first occasion I had ever heard her admonish him. The pig ducked his face under his front hooves. It must have been the first time he had heard it too.

"Bailey, I'm so sorry," Juliet wailed. "Your masterpiece is ruined."

"It's okay, Juliet. It's just chocolate." I squatted in the grass and scratched Jethro on the top of his bristly head. "It's okay, and Easter Days will be over tomorrow. Don't worry, Jethro. I'm not mad."

He looked up at me.

"She didn't mean to be cross with you," I said. "The falling toffee rabbit just took her by surprise. It would take anyone by surprise."

He pressed his snout into my hand.

"Oh, Jethro!" Juliet cried as she scooped him up. "Bailey is right. It just surprised me. You are the best pig ever. Everyone makes mistakes. I love you." She snuggled Jethro to her chest.

Margot shook her head.

"Do you want me to reconstruct it?" I asked, hoping and praying that the answer was no. Putting that rabbit back together would be no joke.

Margot put her hands on her hips. "I suppose not. Thankfully the press was here earlier today and they took photos of the toffee bunny, so we will see it again. Can you clean up the mess before too many more people see it?"

I got her meaning. A decapitated rabbit wasn't great for tourism.

I nodded. "Charlotte will help me, I'm sure. I just must speak to someone before I go over to Swissmen Sweets and collect her." I turned back to the corral of bunnies.

As I had feared, when I looked back at the bunnies, Eli was gone.

Charlotte and I made short work of clearing up the toffee bunny even though I knew it pained her to throw away all the chocolate and toffee. "Are you sure we can't use the chocolate for our recipes? The chocolate inside is okay."

In general, the Amish were industrious recyclers and upcyclers. Not so much because they were environmentally conscious, but because they saw the value of utilizing something until it was no longer useful. This time I had to put my foot down. I shook my head. "We aren't using recycled chocolate that has been outside for two days."

"I guess when you put it that way, it does sound like a bad idea. At least Margot didn't ask you to make another one of them. If I never look at toffee again, it will be too soon."

I couldn't agree more. It would be a long time before I could eat toffee again, let alone make it.

All the while we cleaned up the mess, I had a knot in my stomach over Katey Beiler. I knew in my gut that Eli must have gone looking for his betrothed. I removed my cell phone from my pocket and called Aiden.

"Brody speaking," he said in his official cop voice.

"Aiden, it's me. I have a feeling that Katey Beiler might be in trouble." I went on and told him what I had learned at the church and Easter Days.

"She was one of the cleaning ladies at the church? Why didn't my mother tell me?"

"She said she just remembered that Katey and another woman named Joan came to clean the church in addition to the women whose names she already gave you."

Aiden groaned. "The company was close-mouthed about the women's names too. I suspect they were being paid under the table, and the company was trying to cover its tracks. I've been trying to get a warrant from a judge to go in there and talk to the manager again."

So they were being paid illegally. I wondered how much trouble the church would be in for its participation even though it was clear that Juliet didn't understand what was happening.

"Where do you think Katey is?" he asked.

"I don't know. My guess would be either at Sybil's place or home."

"I'll head to Sybil's place first. If she is feeling scared, she would most likely go there. That's where she feels like she has real friends. She might be hiding too because she knows who the killer is and is afraid to tell anyone."

"That's what I was thinking too. I wish I'd called you earlier, but I felt like I was being an alarmist."

"It's better to err on the side of caution, Bailey."

"I know, and I will never forgive myself if something happens to Katey." As the words left my mouth, I knew I couldn't just stand around a moment longer. "I'll meet you there," I said.

"Bailey."

"I'll meet you there. Katey could be in trouble and we can't waste any more time."

"All right."

Chapter 39

Aiden beat me to Millersburg. I credited this to the fact that he had sirens on his SUV and could break every traffic law in the book without getting cited. I didn't have that luxury. By the time I parked on the street and ran to Sybil's building, he was already at her front door talking to her.

I skidded to a stop a few feet away from them. Just in time to hear Sybil say, "I don't know where Adam and Katey went. They said they were going to go for a walk to get some fresh air. I haven't seen them for two hours or so. Adam isn't answering any of my texts."

"Did you know that Adam and Katey were romantically involved?" Aiden asked.

She shook her head emphatically. "They can't be. That's one of my rules—can't have that kind of relationship with the Amish young people who come to us."

"They were seen kissing by a reliable witness," I said. I couldn't believe that I was calling Margot a reliable witness.

She pulled her neck back. "Well, that is a shock. It could be that Adam developed a strong feeling of compassion for Katey. She was having a very difficult time deciding whether she was going to leave her old way of life, and he spent a lot of extra time with her."

I bet, I thought.

"Adam has a lot of compassion for these people," she added.

Aiden frowned. "And why does he have so much compassion?"

She pressed her lips together as if she had come to a decision. "Just like me, he used to be Amish, you see. He had a terrible life as an Amish boy and ran away from his family."

Suddenly, my hands felt very cold. "How old was he when he left the Amish?"

She looked at me over her glasses. "Only twelve. Can you even imagine being alone in the world at that age, not knowing a soul? Somehow by his own grit and determination, he made it through. When he came to me and told me his story, I knew he would be a good fit for our mission. He could speak to the young people running away on a very personal level, especially to the young men who leave."

"Oh no," I whispered.

Aiden turned to me. "What?" He pulled me away from a confused-looking Sybil.

"Adam ran away from the Amish when he was twelve."

"Yes," Aiden said. "What does that mean to you?"

I looked up into those chocolate-brown eyes.

"Stephen's first son, Casey Raber, ran away from the Amish when he was twelve."

"What's that have to do with this?"

"What if Adam is Casey?"

Aiden's brow creased and he whispered, "How did you make that leap?"

"I'll show you." I walked back to Sybil. "Sybil, do you know if Adam changed his name when he left the Amish?"

She frowned. "He said that he had to because he didn't want his family to find him."

"Were they abusive?" Aiden asked.

She licked her lips. "He didn't say they were in so many words, but that was my assumption."

"What was his Amish name?" I asked.

She thought for a moment. "He wouldn't tell me. He said he left that old life behind. He left the person he was behind too. He had experienced a terrible trauma as a boy."

"What kind of trauma did he have?" I asked.

She pressed her lips together.

"Sybil," Aiden said. "You can answer the question here or down at the station."

"His mother died in a farming accident when he was very young."

"What kind of accident?" Aiden asked.

At first I didn't think Sybil would answer his question, but then she said, "It was in the grain silo. There was a malfunction with a grain loader and a ton of grain fell on her. By the time they figured out what had happened, it was too late and she was dead."

I shivered as I remembered that empty silo at the Raber rabbit farm. "Just like Ethel Raber," I whispered.

"It gets worse," Sybil said. "Adam said he found a note in his father's Bible that held a confession. His father knew that his wife was in the grain but didn't do anything until she was dead because he was in love with another woman."

I didn't bother to answer and turned to Aiden. "Aiden, we have to find Katey. She could be in real danger. There is no doubt in my mind that Adam is Casey Raber."

Aiden and I left Sybil on her doorstep and dashed for his SUV. I'd worry about getting my car back to Harvest later. It was much more important to find Katey now. I buckled into the passenger seat while he called in the description of Katey and Adam-formerly-known-as-Casey and directed his officers to be on the lookout for them.

When he ended the call, I said, "I keep thinking that Katey was planning to run away from the Amish. If that's true, maybe she and Adam went to her home to gather up her things." I took a deep breath. "Or they could be out of the state by now."

Aiden shifted the car into drive and reached across the console to squeeze my hand. "We will find her."

"If we don't, it's my fault."

"No, Bailey, don't take that on yourself." He squeezed my hand again before letting go. "We will find her. I promise. It's a good idea to try her home first."

I nodded and sat back in the seat with my hands clenched on my lap.

As we drove down the road that led to both the Raber and Beiler farms, my eyes focused on the empty silo. Now I knew why that silo sat empty and why Stephen gave up raising grain for his rabbits. How awful that must have been for young Casey, to grow up without his mother and to know that was the place where she had died. It would be a constant reminder of her death and the loss of a mother's love that he would never have.

I was about to point the silo out to Aiden when Liam Zimmerman came running through his yard, waving his hands. "Hey! Hey!" He waved his arms back and forth and ran into the road.

Aiden hit his brakes and squealed to a stop just before he hit the man. He jumped out of his SUV with his hand on his gun. I jumped out too.

"Put your hands up!" Aiden ordered in a darker voice than I'd ever heard him use.

Zimmerman must have recognized Aiden's tone too and froze. "Don't shoot me. I need your help."

Aiden lowered his gun. "What's going on?"

"There is a crazy Amish kid in my backyard holding two people hostage with a shotgun. I told you the Amish are trouble!"

"Why didn't you call the police?" Aiden shouted. His patience was all but gone.

"My phone is in the house, and I was afraid of getting the Amish kid's attention."

"Who has the gun?" I asked.

He looked at me and didn't seem at all surprised to see me. "It's the bunny farmer's kid."

I was willing to bet Swissmen Sweets that the two people he was holding at gunpoint were Katey and Adam.

Aiden looked at me. "Bailey, stay here with Zimmerman until more officers arrive."

I opened my mouth.

"Bailey, that's an order. I am talking to you as a police officer now, not as your boyfriend."

I bit down hard on my tongue and nodded.

Aiden removed his radio from his duty belt and barked in a list of orders. It wouldn't be long before reinforcements arrived.

I watched as Aiden bent at the waist with his gun drawn and ran around the side of the Rabers' house. My heart caught in my throat to watch him go. Was this what it would always be like being in love with a cop? Worrying about what he would face each day? I placed a hand over my heart. It was the first time I had admitted I was in love with Aiden.

Zimmerman didn't give me time to digest this new revelation. "I told everyone that the Amish were rotten, but no one would listen to me. Everyone thinks they are such peace-loving people. Not in my experience. They are troublemakers."

I heard sirens in the distance. Aiden's backup was almost here. I felt my shoulders droop with relief until I heard a gunshot and a scream. Without thinking, I ran toward the house.

"Where are you going?" Zimmerman called after me. "Do you want to get killed for a bunch of filthy Amish?"

Chapter 40

I raced around the side of the house and saw Aiden holding his hands in the air in front of Eli, who had a shotgun pointed at his chest.

"Eli, you don't want to do this," Aiden said calmly. "You will spend the rest of your life in prison for killing a police office in cold blood. They could even give you the death penalty."

"Maybe I want to die," Eli shot back. "What do I have to live for? Katey doesn't want me. I don't want these awful rabbits. The farm will never live up to its potential if I don't have more land."

I didn't see Katey or Adam. Had they got away?

Then, I spotted them on the side of the phone shed. Adam had his hand clamped over Katey's mouth.

I glanced at Eli, and he seemed to be completely consumed with Aiden. If Katey and Adam ran through Zimmerman's woods, they could get away. They didn't move. Maybe they were frozen in fear. I ducked behind the second bunny barn, which was between Eli and me. When I reached the barn, I pressed my back against it. As I slid along the building on one side, I saw Katey and Adam moving stealthily along the other, headed toward the woods.

I followed them silently into the woods, staying

just out of sight behind a tree as they stopped.

Katey pulled away from Adam.

"Let's go, love," Adam said. "There's nothing for us here."

"What about Eli?" she asked, looking back at the phone shed.

"What do you care? What do we care about any of the Rabers?" He glared in the direction she was looking.

"I don't want Eli to be in trouble for something we did."

He laughed. "We did? You're the one who made the candy and gave it to Eli's father."

She blinked at him. "But you told me to do it. You said—"

"I can't go to prison for convincing you to kill someone. The act of the killing is on you alone."

"I didn't know that he would die from it. You said it would only make him ill!"

Adam shrugged as if that was of little matter.

I stepped forward, giving them both a start as they spotted me. "Casey, did you ask Katey to give your father lily of the valley?"

He glared at me. "That's not my name."

"Maybe it's not now, but it was once upon a time, when you were Amish."

"Why wouldn't I want him to pay? He might not have poured the grain onto her body, but he let my mother die when he could have done something to save her. Everyone said her death in the silo was an accident, but I knew better."

356

"How did you know?" I asked, wanting confirmation of what Sybil had told me.

"I learned the truth when I saw a note in his Bible. After that, I had to run away. I promised myself I would return someday and get my revenge, and I have."

"You sent the notes to your father. You wrote them," I said. "But you had different Amish people deliver them."

He snorted. "People who are running away from the faith like I did." His eyes were bright. "They would do whatever I told them."

"Did you tell them to slash the tires in Jud Beiler's barn or attack me?"

He looked me square in the eye. "Those I took care of myself. It was to warn you both to keep quiet. I can see that it didn't work with you. I should have killed you when I had the chance."

I felt like I might be sick.

He glared at Katey. "If you don't come with me, you will go to jail for the rest of your life. Is that what you want?"

In this case, I thought Katey might be better off in jail than under Adam's manipulation. Heaven knew what he had told her to convince her to give Stephen the lily-of-the-valley-laced toffee.

She looked at me.

"Katey, stay," I said as I heard the sirens arrive. The police would soon have the whole farm surrounded. "It's better to stay and face what you have done than run away."

357

Tears fell from her eyes, and she reached out her hand to Adam. It looked as if she was determined to go. She loved him. He'd tricked her into loving him.

There was a shout and a scuffle behind us. I looked away from Katey and Adam to see Eli running toward us with his shotgun pointed at Adam.

"Eli!" Aiden shouted from behind Eli. "Stop or I'll shoot!"

Eli kept coming and Aiden pulled the trigger. Eli fell to the ground, but not before he got off a shot of his own. Adam/Casey staggered back, holding his shoulder. Blood oozed out from between his fingers while Eli held his right calf, where Aiden's bullet hit him.

Aiden came running and ripped the shotgun from Eli's hand. Eli stared at Adam as if he couldn't believe what he had just done.

Katey fell to her knees beside him. "Adam! Adam! Are you all right? Please tell me you are all right. I love you!"

"Get away from me," he snapped. "I never loved you. You were a means to an end, and you even managed to mess that up when I had it all laid out for you."

She fell back, stricken, and one of Aiden's officers helped her to her feet before cuffing her hands behind her back.

Epilogue

You can train a rabbit to walk on a leash, but don't expect it to go very far or fast. I was learning this lesson as I stood in the middle of the village square, waiting for Puff to move on Easter Sunday. We had made it across Main Street with no trouble, but as soon as the rabbit reached the lawn, she planted herself there and began to eat the grass.

After what had happened on his farm, Eli Raber had given me the rabbit at no cost. He said she would be happier with me than with anyone else. He still planned to sell the other rabbits to a farm up north just as soon as he was through his court date for shooting Adam. I was just happy that I could save Puff from that fate. Nutmeg felt the same way. The rabbit and the little orange cat were inseparable anytime they were together in the candy shop.

As for Katey and Adam-formerly-Casey, they were in custody awaiting their bond hearing. Adam was at the local hospital, and Katey was in the county jail. I wasn't sure who would pay bond for either of them. I was hoping that Katey would get a lesser sentence as she had clearly been manipulated by Adam into believing murder was the only way that the two of them could be together after she left the Amish. She was so blinded by her love of Adam that she would agree to anything to be with him, which I found almost as tragic as Stephen's death. I also hoped that they locked Adam up and threw away the key for what he'd done to her. Although there was still a small part of me that had compassion for the little boy who'd lost his mother so young. Stephen Raber's love for a woman who was not his wife was the root of all of this. I couldn't help but wonder if his second wife, Carmela, knew he had let Ethel die. There was no way to answer that question.

I tried not to dwell on it. It was Easter Sunday, and across the square I could see people stream out of the church's sunrise service. My grandmother and Charlotte were at their district's Easter service, and I stood in the middle of the square in a belted, flowered dress and white-heeled sandals walking the quintessential white Easter bunny as I waited for Aiden to arrive. He and I were to go to the church's ten a.m. service together. Juliet had asked me to bring Puff to join Jethro in the sanctuary. Since she had Reverend Brook wrapped around her little finger, I agreed.

Families poured out of the church and paused to take Easter photos on the square. Children held on to new stuffed animal rabbits and baskets of candy. I felt as if I was walking in a Norman Rockwell painting, and in my dress, for once, I fit right in.

Juliet Brody waved at me as she ran through the pastel-dressed families on the green. "Bailey! Bailey!"

Puff looked up from the grass with a piece of clover hanging from her lip just as Juliet made a beeline for us.

When she reached us, Juliet set Jethro on the ground, and the pig and rabbit rubbed noses. I was learning that Puff was the kind of animal who could get along with anyone. Despite everything that Stephen Raber had done, knowing how much he loved Puff made me like him a little bit more.

"Aren't they the sweetest thing together? They are like two peas in a pod," Juliet cooed.

Her cheeks were pink and she couldn't stand still. I studied her. "Juliet, are you feeling well? You look a little flushed. Are you running a fever?"

"No fever! Look!" Juliet flashed her left hand in my face, revealing a diamond on her ring finger. "Can you believe it? Reverend Brook asked me to marry him! It came out of nowhere."

I had to stifle a smile. I had known this was coming; I was just relieved that Reverend Brook had worked up the nerve to ask.

"I've cared for him for so long, but I never knew he felt the same way." She looked down at her ring. "And then he asked me to marry him. It's a dream come true." There were tears in her eyes. "He's such a good man. I never thought happiness would come for me. I wished and prayed, but never thought I would find love again. I decided instead to be happy in the life I had in Harvest in the church and with my friends."

My heart broke a little for her. On the outside, Juliet was a happy-go-lucky, flighty woman, but I knew she was much more than that. Her first husband, Aiden's father, had been abusive, and she had been brave enough to take Aiden and run away, raising her only son into an amazing man. She deserved all the credit for that, and no one deserved a happily ever after more than she.

"It's a beautiful ring, Juliet," I said with tears in my eyes. "I am happy for you both."

"Thank you," she said. "And I have a favor to ask of you. Would you be willing to make our wedding cake? It would mean so much to us if it came from you."

"I'd be happy to. I've never made a wedding cake before, but I will give it my very best." I smiled. "How hard can it be after making a giant toffee rabbit, right?"

She laughed. "The reverend and I haven't set a date yet. As soon as we do, I will let you know so you can start planning the cake." She scooped up Jethro. "Jethro will be the ring bearer, of course."

I expected that.

"I have another request," she said.

"Oh?" I asked.

"Will you be my maid of honor?"

I blinked at her. "Me? Isn't there someone else you've known longer that you'd like to have in the wedding?"

She shook her head. "No. You're the only one I want to do it. Your family has been so kind to Aiden and me over the years. I would love Clara to be in the wedding, but she is Amish. I know that their customs would not allow it, but you can. You can stand by my side as I marry the man of my dreams."

"Yes, of course, I will do it. I am so happy for you." I felt tears in my eyes.

Aiden's departmental SUV pulled up alongside the square and he got out.

Juliet took in a quick breath. "I haven't told Aiden yet."

I whispered, "Now is your chance."

Aiden grinned at us as he approached. "My two favorite people in one place." He frowned. "What's with the serious faces? Should I have said my two favorite people and my favorite pig and my favorite rabbit? Because that's all true."

"I'll give you two a minute," I said.

Aiden looked from his mom to me and back again. "What's going on?"

"There's something your mom needs to tell you." I picked up Puff and walked with her across the street to Swissmen Sweets. I stood there in front of the candy shop door and watched Juliet tell Aiden her news. She waved her arms and began to cry.

Aiden wrapped his arms around his mother, giving her the biggest hug. Over her shoulder, he had a huge smile on his face that was for me alone.

Charlotte's Toffee Pieces

Ingredients
- Parchment paper
- Candy thermometer
- 1 tablespoon light corn syrup
- 2 sticks of softened butter
- ¼ teaspoon salt
- 2 cups granulated sugar
- 1 cup milk-chocolate chips
- 1 cup chopped pecans or almonds

Directions
1. Using parchment paper, line a 9-x-13-inch pan.
2. Melt the butter, sugar, corn syrup, and salt in a saucepan, stirring continuously over medium heat until a candy thermometer reads 295°F.
3. When mixture is at the desired temperature, pour into pan. Let stand at room temperature until cool, about thirty minutes.
4. Using a saucepan of steaming water and a glass bowl, create a double boiler to melt the chocolate chips until smooth. Stir continuously and don't let the bottom of the bowl touch the water in the pan.
5. Pour melted chocolate over toffee.
6. Sprinkle with pecans or almonds.
7. Let cool completely.
8. Break into pieces and enjoy!

About the Author

Amanda Flower, a *USA Today* bestselling and Agatha Award–winning mystery author, started her writing career in elementary school when she read a story she wrote to her sixth grade class and had the class in stitches with her description of being stuck on the top of a Ferris wheel. She knew at that moment she'd found her calling of making people laugh with her words. She also writes mysteries as *USA Today* bestselling author Isabella Alan. In addition to being an author, Amanda is a former librarian living in Northeast Ohio.

Center Point Large Print
600 Brooks Road / PO Box 1
Thorndike, ME 04986-0001 USA

(207) 568-3717

US & Canada:
1 800 929-9108
www.centerpointlargeprint.com